THE
PERFECT
HOUSEMATE

BOOKS BY LORNA DOUNAEVA

The Wife's Mistake

THE
PERFECT
HOUSEMATE

LORNA DOUNAEVA

bookouture

Published by Bookouture in 2024

An imprint of Storyfire Ltd.
Carmelite House
50 Victoria Embankment
London EC4Y 0DZ

www.bookouture.com

ISBN: 978-1-83790-803-5
eBook ISBN: 978-1-83790-802-8

For Greg and Faye

PROLOGUE

JUNE

June's first thought was that she'd got wound up in her sheets. And that her pillowcase had somehow slipped over her face, enveloping her in darkness. But that didn't account for the stiffness of the material or her inability to shake it off. Her heart pounded in her ears, as she struggled to breathe.

She thrashed about, trying to understand what had happened. Something was preventing her from bringing her hands together, and at the same time her legs felt as though they were stuck together with glue. She fought against the overwhelming fear that threatened to consume her. She kicked her legs and felt a rough, scratchy material. What was that? Rope? She tried to move her arms but they were pinned tight behind her back.

She called out for help, but the coarse material over her face muffled her cries. Even with her eyes wide open, the blackness was so thick that it pressed on her like a hundred hands.

She tried to slow her breathing. In, out. In, out. The only sound she heard was the steady inhale-exhale of her own breath in the oppressive silence.

The fabric against her face was rough like a potato sack.

Experimentally, she rocked back and forth. The sack shifted as she moved, her nose twitching as she breathed in the aroma of dirt and herbs that clung to its fibres. She kept on rocking until she managed to position herself on her knees. Then she leaned forward and pressed her forehead against the ground. Desperately, she shook her head side to side with all her might until she felt the material move. Every muscle in her neck strained as she tried to dislodge it. Finally, with one last powerful thrust, the sack slipped off her head with a cool rush of air.

She inhaled deeply, tasting her dry lips and feeling a tuft of cotton between her teeth. As her eyes adjusted, she saw a faint glimmer of light coming through the thin cracks above her head. She was seated on a rigid wooden floor and the room around her felt like a prison cell – damp, musty and small. Through the wall that separated her from the outside world, she could hear the distant thrum of traffic – it sounded as if she was still in London, or perhaps some other city.

Her head felt heavy, as if she'd come down with the flu. Or as if she'd been doped. But who would want to take her? It wasn't as if she had any money.

The room spun around her. Her heart raced as she desperately searched for any recollection of what had led to this moment. The air felt thick, the sound muffled by the walls pressing against her, holding her tight.

She squinted as a beam of sunlight pierced through the patchy veil of cobwebs. Gradually, more light filtered in and she saw her surroundings clearly. She surveyed the cramped, windowless room. In one corner lay an assortment of flattened cardboard heaped against a small suitcase – in another, tins of paint, brushes and rollers on ancient shelving units. She kept scanning until her eyes came to rest on a canary yellow bike hanging on the wall. She inhaled sharply.

That was her bike. This was her shed.

She heaved herself off the floor, muscles quivering from

the exertion. The coarse rope around her ankles made it difficult to gain momentum, but she gritted her teeth and threw her
weight against the door with a guttural cry. When it held
steady, she used her shoulder to push against the sturdy wood,
hoping to break through, but all her attempts were futile. She
screamed like a wild animal, howling and pounding the door
with her bare feet. Sweat dripped down her forehead and she
felt the strength drain out of her as she strained against the
ropes.

Calm. She had to stay calm.

She focused on her breathing again. In. Out. In. Out.

What time was it? She sensed it was early morning. She
imagined the sun inching higher in the sky above her and tilted
her face towards it, savouring its warmth on her skin. She
listened intently. Heard the sway of the branches in the trees.
She picked out the deep caw of the crows in the distance, the
bright chirps of sparrows on the roof, and the sweet trill of the
robins somewhere in the bushes. After a few minutes, she heard
the trickle of water from the outside drains.

Her eyes flew open. Her housemates must be up. Getting
themselves ready for the holiday. She imagined the scent of
freshly brewed coffee as they congregated in the kitchen. Had
they noticed she wasn't there yet? Surely someone would bang
on her bedroom door?

Except that she was the one who usually woke the rest of
the house. No one would expect June to oversleep.

A chill crept through her body as it all clicked into place.
That was what they wanted, wasn't it? To make her miss the
flight. Scenes from the past few days ran through her mind: the
whispered conversations in the kitchen; the strange looks she
had received at dinner. She could think of only one person who
hated her enough to go to such lengths to make sure she would
miss the holiday, and she was certain now that she knew who
it was.

She pounded against the door with her feet. *Bang! Bang! Bang!*

'Help! I'm locked in the shed. Somebody help me!'

She heard a window slam. Were they deliberately shutting her out? No, they would be locking up the house, preparing to leave. But they had to notice she wasn't there. They had to. It would be obvious when they headed outside. Her housemates would all be there, wheeling their suitcases. Everyone but her.

They would rush back to her room, knock on her door, or simply barge in to find her bag next to her bed, her coat hanging on its hook. If they were really observant, they would even spot her distinctive yellow trainers on the shoe rack. They would work out that she couldn't have gone far. If she was lucky, someone would go out to check the garden. If she made enough noise, they ought to hear her.

Her heart raced as a taxi beeped its horn, the sound echoing down the street. Moments later, a loud knock rattled the door, and excited voices erupted from within the house, followed by shrieks of laughter and off-key singing.

In desperation, she screamed again: 'Help! I'm locked in the shed!'

The only response was the sound of her housemates squabbling over luggage space as they clambered into the cab.

Tears streamed down her face.

'Help!' she yelled at the top of her lungs. 'Somebody! Help me!'

They had to hear her. They had to wonder where she was. Where did they think she'd gone, leaving all her stuff behind?

'Help!' She screamed so loud that the birds squawked in response. But the only reply was the hum of the engine as it roared away.

She'd been abandoned.

The ropes cut into her wrists and ankles as she shifted against her bonds. Her heart beat a rapid staccato in her chest and a thousand dark scenarios swirled in her mind like an ominous fog. This was more serious than a missed holiday. If she couldn't get out of these ropes, she would have to spend an entire week like this, trapped in this shed, with nowhere to relieve herself, and nothing to eat or drink. By the time her housemates came back from Mykonos, she'd be dead.

ONE

JUNE

Five Months Earlier

June frowned and checked the numbers again.

'Sorry. It just doesn't add up. Once we've paid the heating and the council tax, we won't have enough left over for next month's rent.'

Her housemates exchanged worried glances.

The grandfather clock against the far wall seemed to tick faster than usual, its loud chimes punctuating the tense silence.

Kimmy pinched the tip of her nose. 'We could cut back on the food budget again?'

Flick nodded in agreement. 'I don't care if we have to live on spaghetti hoops, so long as we can pay the bills.'

June felt an ache in her stomach; spaghetti hoops were not food. And while she could afford to bring her own snacks into the house, she could hardly enjoy quality meat and vegetables while her housemates subsisted on packet foods and tins. She looked around the table anxiously.

'We can switch off the heating,' she countered. Their large

Victorian house had old bay windows and high ceilings. Pretty to look at but hardly efficient.

This suggestion was met with horrified looks from the other housemates.

'I'm freezing as it is,' Tamsin said.

'We could just wear more jumpers and drink more tea?' June suggested.

Kimmy shook her head. 'There must be something else.'

June thought hard. They had already cancelled their Netflix and Sky subscriptions. There wasn't much else she was willing to give up.

Tamsin chewed on the end of her plait thoughtfully. 'It's a pretty big house,' she said.

Kimmy nodded, an edge of impatience to her expression. 'What are you thinking?'

'Maybe we should get another housemate?'

Everyone froze.

June twisted her hands in her lap.

'But... where would they sleep?'

'The basement? It's a large enough room. We'd just have to heave all the junk out of it.'

Tamsin scrambled to her feet and beckoned to them to follow. With wary glances, the others got up from the table and followed her down the hall, pausing outside June's bedroom door. They peered down the dusty stairs, at the yellowed sign taped to the basement door:

BEWARE OF WHAT LURKS WITHIN

The poster was the work of a previous tenant. It was just a joke, really, but they had inadvertently heeded the warning. The first and last time June had set foot in the basement was the day they'd moved in. That was five years ago and all she could recollect was a heap of old junk.

Flick shuddered. 'There are spiders down there!'

'It's dark and dingy,' Kimmy said.

'We can't rent it out,' June said.

Tamsin met her gaze. 'Why not? There's nothing in our contract to say we can't sublet, and it's not like the landlord ever comes round anyway.'

'No, I mean, we can't let out a room unless it has a window. I'm pretty sure that's a rule. Let me check.'

She headed back to the dining room and picked up her phone, her lips tightly pressed together as she searched. Her housemates returned to their seats. Kimmy let out a loud yawn and stretched her hands above her head. Flick toyed with her navel piercing and Tamsin drummed her tangerine nails against the table.

'Yep, that's a rule.'

'Shame.' Tamsin slumped back in her chair. 'A new house-mate could have been cool.'

'Well, there's no point talking about it,' June said. 'It's not allowed.'

'What are we going to do then?' Flick asked.

June looked over the stack of bills again. 'I really don't know. At this rate, we'll have to cut the food budget *and* the heating.'

An hour later, June was walking out of the kitchen, cup of tea in hand, when she noticed the door to the basement was ajar. A sliver of light shone out from under a crack at the bottom, and strange sounds echoed up into the house.

She headed into her bedroom, set her drink down on the desk, and flopped down on her bed. She'd just started reading a new book and was keen to get back to it. She turned the page, only to hear thudding sounds coming from the floor below. Either the spiders were getting organised, or one of her housemates was doing something down there. She continued reading for a few more minutes, until she heard a clanking sound, followed by a muffled curse.

Curiosity got the better of her. She swallowed the last of her tea and made her way down the creaky wooden steps, clinging to the rail as she descended. She opened the door slowly, shooting a quick glance around before entering. Cobwebs hung from every corner. She shivered as she imagined hundreds of squinting eyes watching her from behind the old furniture.

Tamsin was tugging at a folded bed with springs hanging out.

'What are you doing?'

'Bloody hell, June. You made me jump!'

'Sorry.'

'Here, give me a hand, will you?'

June helped her drag the old bedframe across the room.

'Now the bath,' Tamsin said, passing her a dusty metal tub.

'How old is this thing?' June asked, as she shoved it out of the way.

Tamsin didn't answer. She stood in front of the bookcase.

'We need to clear this.'

She started taking all the junk off it, filling the ancient bathtub. June helped her, grabbing empty jars and handfuls of coat hangers and other rubbish.

'Right, let's pull it out,' Tamsin said, getting into position.

'Don't tell me—we're going to find a hidden room?'

'Something like that.'

June felt a foolish tingle of excitement. She was already picturing rare first edition books, gold coins or perhaps a long-hidden diary. She grasped the sides of the bookcase. The wood felt worn beneath her fingertips. It slid easily across the floor and the room became instantly brighter.

'Look at that!' Tamsin squealed.

June gaped.

Not a hidden room, but a window. A large one. The glass was covered in grime and steel bars were fixed across the cobweb-covered frame.

They both stared at it for a moment.

'How did I never notice this from the street?'

'I've never noticed it either,' Tamsin said. 'But I was looking through our contract to see if there were any penalties for late payments, and I found the plans for the house. I couldn't believe it when I spotted the window, so I just had to come down here and check. I suppose we never noticed it because it's right behind the hedge, but we can cut that back to let in the light.'

'We'd have to remove the bars. Because that's what the requirement is really about. Whether somebody could get out in an emergency.'

'But you think we could make this liveable?'

June considered, surveying the mess. 'We'd have to deal with the spiders, and we'd need to remove all the junk. Give it a lick of paint and add a few lights to give it a more homely feel. We can get some basic furniture from the second-hand shop. It'll take a bit of work, but I can't think of any better ideas. Nice one, Tam.'

Tamsin frowned. 'Do we even have the money for new furniture? We've got that electricity bill coming up.'

June nodded. 'I can borrow a few quid from my savings, but I'll need it back as soon as the new housemate pays their deposit.'

Tamsin smiled. 'Thanks, June. That's really good of you.'

'As for the paint, we've still a few dribs and drabs in the shed. Ought to be enough to do this room. This is going to be quite a job. We'll need everyone to muck in but I think we can manage it between us.'

'Sounds like a plan.'

TWO

JUNE

The warm, earthy aroma of freshly brewed coffee and grilled bacon filled the air as they lounged around the living room after a lazy Saturday morning brunch. June settled into her favourite armchair, adjusting a plaid blanket across her lap as she reached for a steaming mug. Kimmy and Tamsin snuggled under a fuzzy throw on the sofa, their hair still damp from morning showers, while Flick sprawled out, her long body stretching across the floor at their feet. She rubbed her eyes and moved closer to the TV, watching her favourite programme in a daze.

Tamsin grabbed a bright pink bottle of nail polish and unscrewed the cap. She held Kimmy's hand steady, her finger tracing the line of the cuticle as she worked with focused concentration.

The doorbell rang and Flick jumped up to answer it. A moment later, she appeared in the doorway with a man who looked a few years younger than them. June guessed he was a neighbour.

'You all remember Joe?' Flick said.

Everyone nodded and greeted him. He smiled shyly and brushed a hand through his thick black hair. He wore paint-covered jeans and had a weathered leather tool belt slung around his waist. His tools clanged against each other as he and Flick headed down to the basement and soon a rhythmic vibration floated up the stairs.

They emerged twenty minutes later.

'All done!' Joe called.

'Brilliant!' Tamsin yelled. The others echoed their thanks.

'I think you've earned a cup of tea and a slice of cake,' Flick said, leading their guest to the kitchen.

June hauled herself off the sofa and headed down to the basement, curious to see what she was supposed to be thanking him for. Her eyes were immediately drawn to a little pile of dust underneath the window frame. He had done an amazing job. The metal bars lay in a neat pile next to the window. She ran her hand along the filed down edges, impressed at their smoothness. She reached towards the window latch and tugged hard, its hinges groaning loudly as it sprang open. The room seemed to shift as sunlight spilled in, glinting off the dust particles like diamonds and highlighting the cobwebs that draped from every corner.

A little later, Tamsin came down and the two of them sorted through the rest of the junk. Then Kimmy and Flick hauled it all out to Kimmy's car and distributed it to the local second-hand shops and the tip. Afterwards, they took brooms and dusted all the cobwebs off the ceiling, finishing the job with the vacuum cleaner and a mild insect spray.

Once the basement was clear, June went out to the bike shed to look for paint. She found several tins sitting on one of the shelves. She chose the bumblebee yellow she had used in her own room. The cheerful shade would bring life to the dreary space.

Back in the basement, she propped the window open to let the fresh air in, washed down the walls and sanded them. Once prepped, she coated the walls in even strokes. She could already picture how the finished room would look, once they added curtains, a lamp and some warm rugs.

After she'd finished painting, she headed upstairs where Kimmy and Flick sat at the kitchen table. They had been tasked with the job of writing a catchy ad to attract their new housemate. The laptop's screen shone brightly in the dim room. Kimmy scrunched up her nose in concentration and Flick squinted at the screen as her fingers clacked over the keyboard.

'How's this?' Flick asked. 'Housemate wanted. Four young single women seek housemate for Clapham Common basement room in Queen Anne's Crescent. Close to shops and church.'

'For god's sake, take out "single" and "women",' June said. 'We'll get all sorts of creeps. It's not even true, Kimmy's joined at the hip with Ralph.'

Flick shrugged and deleted a few words.

June peered over her shoulder. 'Don't say "basement" either. It'll put people off. And make sure you mention it's no smoking.'

'You need to make us sound fun,' Tamsin said from the doorway. 'Don't mention the church. We don't want people to think we're bible bashers.'

'We don't want people to think this is a party house either,' June objected. 'And let's take out the street name. Just to be on the safe side.'

Flick heaved a sigh. 'I'm losing the will to live.'

'Sorry,' June said. 'But we've got to get this right.'

'Okay. How's this? "Housemate wanted. Four friendly young professionals seek housemate for large Clapham Common house. Close to shops, bars and amenities. Would suit non-smoker."'

She looked up. 'Any objections?'

June shook her head. Tamsin did too.

'Right, I'm hitting send.'

THREE

JUNE

Tuesday evening, June and Flick headed down to Mud and Mingle at Clapham Pottery Studios. They'd been taking pottery classes for six months now and June loved the laid-back sessions that allowed them to work at their own pace. She was glad they'd already paid up front for the term because this was one luxury she could not face giving up.

Entering the cosy studio, they took their usual table at the back and set about gathering their tools. While Flick chatted to the couple in front of them, June collected the supplies she needed and laid them out neatly.

She picked up a lump of clay and began to shape it in her hands before she placed it on the wheel. The clay began to move, dancing beneath her fingertips, as she tried to hold it steady.

Flick's phone buzzed. 'That was Tamsin. She says we've got two more people booked in to see the room.'

June nodded but didn't take her eyes off her wheel. They'd already shown a few people around the house, but so far nobody had been quite right. One young woman had seemed perfect, until she'd revealed she was five months pregnant.

There was no way they wanted to share with a screaming baby.

Still, there was clearly a lot of interest. It was just a matter of finding the right person.

She added more water to her clay and concentrated on holding it steady as it spun round and round. The rhythmic motion was hypnotic, and she felt her shoulders relax as she carefully guided the clay with her hands. Gradually, she increased the speed of the wheel. The clay spun faster and she used her fingertips to add texture to its sides. After several minutes, she stopped and wiped her hands on her apron. She stepped back and eyed her creation with a critical eye.

'That's looking good, June.'

She smiled as their teacher, Nadia, stepped forward to check her work.

Nadia leaned closer and brushed her fingertips against the ridged sides.

'Very nice, but I feel as if you're making the same pot over and over. Maybe you'd like to try something a bit different? Add a handle, or create a different shape? Have a think about it, June. Something to give it a bit of flair.'

Nadia moved on to see how Flick was getting on.

'Keep your hands locked in, elbows firm. That's it. Very nice.'

June sat and looked at her pot. She was pleased with it but it wasn't quite as she had envisioned. She glanced up at the clock. She should have time to make one more before she had to clear everything away. Once she got it right, she would be happy to attempt something else.

Flick's pot came out wonky. Flick laughed as she removed it from the wheel and placed it on the shelf to dry. If June had made one that lopsided, she wouldn't bother. She'd toss it out and start again, but Flick was proud of all her creations, treating each one to a proper finish.

June had to rush her second pot but it wasn't bad considering. Still, as she added it to the shelf with all her others, she couldn't help but feel a little dissatisfied. She knew she could do better.

After class, they trudged across the slushy road to the Tipsy Toad. White smoke rings spiralled from the pub garden, where shivering smokers huddled together.

The heavy oak door creaked open and they were met by a wave of warmth and chatter. Tables were filled with groups of people, drinking frothy pints and laughing uproariously.

'Hey look, there's Kimmy,' Flick said.

June looked and saw Kimmy and Ralph sitting at a table by the window.

Ralph gave them a wave. He had his arm wrapped protectively around Kimmy's shoulders and they sat so close together they might as well have shared a seat.

June and Flick squeezed through to the bar.

'Two pints of beer, please,' June said to the short blonde barmaid.

'What kind?'

'Just whatever you've got on tap,' Flick said.

June leaned against the bar. 'What craft beers have you got?'

The barmaid pointed to the row of taps lined up along the bar.

'Which one's good?'

'They're all good.'

June looked over the selection, her eyes scanning each label. She stopped on one with a blue and white logo. The colours reminded her of a summer sky. 'That one please.'

The barmaid nodded and began to fill their glasses, her large, round eyes remaining on June as she did so. June focused on the beer snacks behind her.

'Did you want anything else?' the barmaid asked in a bored voice.

'No, just the pints please.'

She handed over a twenty-pound note and accepted a handful of coins with a grimace.

'Cheers,' Flick said, reaching for her drink as June stopped to count her change. 'Come on, let's go and join Kimmy.'

'Won't be a minute.'

Satisfied her money was all there, June tucked her wallet back into her handbag. Flick strode ahead with her pint, letting it slosh down her arm as she walked. June followed slowly, taking care not to spill a drop.

'Didn't know you two were out tonight,' Kimmy said, as they dragged chairs over to her table.

'We're not. We've just been to pottery,' June replied.

Flick shuffled in beside Kimmy, leaving June to sit down beside Ralph. He was wearing a little too much cologne. The cloying smell made her nose twitch.

'How was it?' Ralph asked.

'Good, thanks.'

Flick nodded. 'I'm thinking of making a tea set.'

June glanced at her. 'Really? That sounds ambitious.'

A young man wearing a black striped apron arrived at the table carrying two trays of hot, greasy food. He set down a bowl of chips, a plate of chicken nuggets and a large hunk of garlic bread in front of Kimmy and Ralph.

'Dig in,' Ralph said, pushing the food into the middle.

'Thanks.'

Flick snatched up a chip and popped it into her mouth with a satisfied grin before reaching for another. June politely declined. Nuggets and chips were not food as far as she was concerned. She would wait until she got home to cook something fresh.

A little later, the barmaid came over to collect their glasses.

'I'm not finished,' June protested, as she reached for hers.

The barmaid shrugged and moved on to the next table. As June watched, she turned and stared in her direction, her eyes cold and unyielding, like a hawk sizing up its prey. She felt an icy chill down her spine. She was about to say something to her friends when she realised that Ralph was also looking at her. Not directly at her, but at the space behind her. She turned and saw there was a TV mounted to the wall. There was a football game on. That must be what the barmaid had been looking at. She smiled to herself. *Wow, paranoid much?*

Her phone vibrated in her pocket. She pulled it out and grimaced. It was her mum. Usually, she rang like clockwork on the last Sunday of each month just like she had when June had been at uni. That was twelve times a year June was obliged to speak to her. She was five days early, but she would have to take it, otherwise her mother would keep calling until she did.

She excused herself and pushed through the sticky door of the bar, stepping out into the cool evening. The air felt fresh with the promise of spring, and she inhaled deeply as she surveyed her surroundings. Laughter carried through open windows as people enjoyed themselves and the high street throbbed with energy.

She steeled herself and pressed accept. Why did talking to her mother feel so exhausting? She thought of the way Kimmy and Flick spoke to their mothers. She felt puzzled at the way they laughed and joked. They sounded so close, almost confessional as they filled them in on their latest exploits.

'Mum?'

'Hello, June.'

The silence that ensued was smothering, and June felt her palms begin to sweat. Seconds turned into a minute, and still her mother hadn't said another word.

'What's up?'

'I just... wanted to hear your voice.'

'Oh.' She softened. 'Is something wrong? Is Dad...'

'Dad's fine.'

'And you?'

'Just the same as always.' Her mother's voice hitched slightly on the last word and June felt the familiar weight of guilt pressing down on her chest like a boulder, threatening to suffocate her.

'Have you managed to get out this week?'

'Yes, Dad took me out for lunch on Wednesday. We went to that place round the corner from Sainsbury's.'

Did they ever go anywhere else?

'So, how have you been?'

'Me? I'm fine.' She glanced down at her feet and focused on a spot of wet clay on her trainers.

'Any news?'

'Not really...' June fumbled for something interesting to say. It was tricky. She didn't want to share anything too personal, but she didn't want to be difficult, either. The silence stretched out between them like an unbreakable chain.

'We're getting a new housemate,' she finally blurted.

She pictured her mother puffing out her cheeks. 'Where on earth will you put her?'

Of course, she assumed it would be a woman. It wouldn't cross her mind the new housemate might be a man.

'We're making a room out of the basement.'

'Oh. Do you think that's a good idea?'

June felt a weight in her chest. 'Well, yes, I do. Things are getting expensive, what with the cost of living crisis.'

'I hope you've thought this through, June. You've known the others for years. Do you really want to bring some stranger into the house?'

'I don't think we've got much choice. The bills are going up and up.'

'But you're okay, aren't you? You've got a good job. It pays well.'

'Well yes. I have. It's the others...'

June was careful with her money. She put twenty-five per cent of her pay directly into her pension so she could retire early. That meant she didn't have much more disposable income than the rest of her housemates. Fond as she was of them all, she could hardly be expected to subsidise them.

'Make sure they have good references, whoever you get.'

'We will, Mum.'

'Because it can change things, bringing someone new into the house. The other girls, they understand you and your ways. You don't want to rock the boat.'

June clenched her fists. Her mother made her sound like a freak of nature.

'People like me, Mum. Whoever we bring into the house, I'm sure we'll get along just fine.'

And with that, she ended the call.

FOUR

JUNE

Thursday night, June coasted up the driveway and hopped off her bike. The wheels screeched to a stop as she unstrapped her helmet. She hung it on its hook in the shed before locking it up.

As she headed inside, she heard voices in the living room. She walked in and the air seemed to still. Her housemates were gathered around the coffee table, along with a familiar-looking woman with thick blonde hair and large blue eyes. The conversation stopped as all heads turned towards her. Everyone was looking at her with a mixture of hope and apprehension.

'June, this is Poppy,' Kimmy said, a little formally.

'Poppy Kendrick,' Poppy said.

June looked at Flick and Tamsin. They were smiling a little too much for her liking. She had a feeling this was an ambush. She looked at Poppy again.

'I know you,' she said slowly.

Poppy's eyes sparkled with amusement and an easy smile spread across her face.

'Poppy works at the Tipsy Toad,' Tamsin said. 'I went to put our ad up in the pub and she mentioned she's desperate for a new place to live.'

June nodded evenly, recalling how uncomfortable Poppy had made her feel. But that had just been a misunderstanding, hadn't it?

'Perhaps we should give Poppy the tour?' Flick suggested. 'See if she likes the place.'

June set down her bag and let out a long breath. She ran her fingers through her hair before turning to Poppy and forcing her lips into what she hoped was a friendly smile.

'I'll show you around,' she offered. That way she would have the chance to ask her a few questions and suss out if she was really housemate material.

'Let's start at the top.'

As they climbed the rickety wooden stairs up to Tamsin's little attic bedroom, June ran over the house rules.

'There's no smoking in the house. Everyone chips in for food and bills. We like to eat communally as much as is practical. Obviously, some nights people have activities or work. But this is a friendly house. If we have issues, we talk about them.'

They reached the top and stopped outside Tamsin's door, which had a large, swirly dragon painted on it.

'We're allowed to decorate our rooms as long as we don't damage anything. It's fine to put up posters and the landlord doesn't mind if we want to add shelves or extra hooks. We don't see a lot of him and he's pretty easy going.'

She pushed open the door and they peered inside.

There were a hundred different nail polishes lined up on the dresser, along with a couple of ceramic dragons. Tamsin's guitar hung on a hook over her bed, and on the pillow was a large cuddly dragon.

'I guess she really likes dragons?'

June nodded. 'There's just something about them that really appeals to her. She reckons she was a dragon in a former life.'

Poppy tilted her head. 'She knows they're a mythical animal, right?'

'I don't think she means it literally. She just feels a strong affinity to them, being half Chinese, half Welsh. She was even born in the year of the dragon.'

Poppy nodded. 'Right. So what about you? What animal would you be if you had to choose?'

'I don't know. Probably a bee.'

Poppy laughed. 'Seriously?'

'Yeah, why not? They have a good Protestant work ethic.'

'I'll give you that.'

'How about you?'

'Me? I'd be a chameleon. Adaptable, easy to get along with. You won't even know I'm here.'

June smiled and closed Tamsin's door. She led Poppy down to the first floor.

'The main bathroom is on this floor. There's another one downstairs, but this one has a bath.'

She peeked into Flick's room. As usual, it looked like a hurricane had hit; clothes flung all over the floor, posters competing with photographs on the walls. Even the ceiling was covered with bright bohemian tapestries.

Poppy raised a brow. 'Looks like a work in progress.'

'Something like that. Flick might be messy, but she contains it to her bedroom, so I try not to mind.'

'Mess makes you uncomfortable?'

'It actually makes my skin itch,' June said. 'Sounds ridiculous, I know, but Tamsin and I went to a strict boarding school where mess was not allowed—even our bedsheets had to be hospital corners. Tamsin's pretty chilled these days, but I still crave order.'

'I can get on board with that.'

Kimmy's room, by contrast, was pretty and feminine. Pale blue curtains hung across the window, and the wallpaper was patterned with delicate pink roses and purple violets. On one side of the wall was a canvas with a large photo of Kimmy in a long pink evening gown, standing next to Ralph in a tux.

'What a lovely picture!'

'Yes, that was taken the Christmas before last,' June said, looking up at it.

She had helped Kimmy get ready that night. The occasion had been a formal ball at the company Ralph worked at. Kimmy had only been seeing him for a few weeks and she'd been nervous about making a good impression. Tamsin had worked her magic with the curling iron and done Kimmy's make-up for her, but Kimmy had still been nervous about meeting Ralph's colleagues so June had run out and bought a small bottle of schnapps so they could do shots. She hadn't really liked the taste herself, but she drank a couple to keep Kimmy company. It had worked. A couple of drinks and Kimmy had perked up immensely. She wasn't drunk by any means, but by the time Ralph arrived to collect her, her cheeks had glowed and all her nerves had evaporated.

'We danced the night away,' she'd said, when she arrived back home.

'So, you had fun?' June had asked, pleased.

Kimmy had reached out to hug her. 'It was one of the best nights of my life.'

June and Poppy headed back down to the ground floor and June pointed out the bathroom, then her own room. A large bookshelf contained as many books as she could fit on it, though it wasn't nearly big enough for her entire collection, hence there were three more boxes crammed under her bed. Her bedspread was purple to contrast with the bright yellow walls and above the pillow she had a large, framed picture of the Tour de France, the cyclists whizzing by in a blur.

Poppy made a beeline for the blue and yellow pot on her dressing table. She picked it up and held it in her hands.

'I keep seeing these all around the house.'

'I make them,' June said, wishing she'd put it down.

'Wow, you're so talented.'

'Oh no, I'm just a beginner.'

Still holding the pot, Poppy moved to the window to look outside.

'It's quiet here, considering how close you are to the high street.'

'Yes, it's a great location. This is a no-through road, so we don't get much traffic but everything's just on our doorstep. I take it you know the area?'

'Oh yeah, I've lived here about four years.'

'Have you been working at the pub all that time?'

'Yes. I was studying for a degree before but it didn't work out. Then I got into pub management and it turns out I'm good at it. It's more than a job. You're like a therapist, you know? People talk to you, tell you their life story. You learn a lot about human nature, the good, the bad and the downright peculiar.'

June nodded. Tamsin had said something similar about being a nail technician.

'If you don't mind me asking, what happened with your previous flat?'

Poppy pulled a face. 'The landlord happened. He's a bit, you know. Dodgy.'

June nodded, and all at once she felt sympathy. No one should have to put up with a dodgy landlord. Your home was your sanctuary. No one should have to compromise on that.

'Right,' she said, clambering to her feet. 'I've saved the best to last. Let's go and look at your room.'

She watched as Poppy set the pot back down on her dressing table, then she led her down to the basement. It smelt like vanilla down there, thanks to the plug-in air freshener she'd installed. She cast a look around for spiders, but there was no sign of them. The space felt warm and cosy.

'I love it!' Poppy exclaimed, with far more enthusiasm than June had expected.

She admired the newly painted walls, the neat bed, rug and curtains.

'It's quite roomy, isn't it?' she exclaimed, heading straight for the window. The view was nothing to write home about. Flick had cut back the bush, but there was little to be seen but the garden wall and the dustbins. June would have moved them if she'd known they'd be showing someone round.

Poppy didn't seem to mind though. She spun round and admired the wardrobe and side table. 'This is twice the size of my current room. I had to put half my stuff in storage.'

'What a pain,' June said, thinking of all the boxes of books under her bed. She would hate to be separated from them. She gave Poppy a few minutes to examine the radiator and the light fixtures. She half expected her to pull out a tape measure, the way she paced from one end of the room to the other.

'Right. Ready to see the kitchen?'

They made their way up the cumbersome wooden stairs. She hoped Poppy didn't notice the way they groaned under the weight of each step.

The kitchen wasn't nearly as large or impressive as June would have liked but Poppy didn't appear to notice how old the fridge was or how stained the floor. Instead, she admired the vase of brightly coloured daffodils Tamsin had bought earlier that week. The buds had been closed when she brought them home but now the flowers were blooming.

As June told her about the workings of the oven, Poppy poked about, peering into the cupboards, as if she were taking inventory.

'Do you like cooking?' June asked hopefully.

'Absolutely. Mexican is my speciality.'

June beamed. 'Fantastic. I'd love to try some of your dishes.'

'Of course. My tamales are to die for.'

Poppy released the cupboard doors and they closed with a bang.

'Is there anything else you'd like to look at?' June asked.

Poppy shook her head. 'No thanks, I think I've seen enough.'

They returned to the living room where the others were watching TV.

'So, what do you think?' Kimmy asked, turning to look at them.

'It's perfect,' Poppy said.

'Did you show her the garden?' Tamsin said.

June shook her head. It wasn't much of a garden, just a patch of grass and the bike shed.

'I'll show you now,' Tamsin said, slipping into her flip-flops.

June went to follow but Kimmy clasped her arm.

'Sorry, I didn't mean to spring this on you. It's just that Poppy seems ideal. She's got a steady job, good references and we've all spoken to her before at the pub. You know what they say, "better the devil you know".'

June nodded. Not that it really mattered what she thought. They needed a housemate urgently, and it seemed Poppy fitted the bill.

FIVE

JUNE

Poppy moved in the following Friday, just as June was finishing a prosciutto, cranberry and brie sandwich. Wiping her hands on a napkin, she went to greet her new housemate at the door. There was a van parked on the double yellows outside, and the driver was getting impatient to offload. June grabbed a large box and carefully wound her way down the dimly lit stairs to the basement, then returned for another. She must have made the journey up and down at least a dozen times before Flick came out to help with the unloading. In need of a rest, June stayed in the basement, stacking the boxes and rearranging the furniture to fit everything in. Flick and Poppy came down the stairs, carrying a heavy ergonomic mattress between them, and headed back up for more. While they were gone, June shunted it into the corner, out of the way. They returned with three suitcases, a huge teddy bear and then a chest of drawers.

'Bloody hell, where are you going to put it all?' Flick asked, looking around.

'I'll find room,' Poppy assured her, wiping her hands on her jeans. 'Thank you for all your help.'

'No problem.'

Flick drifted back upstairs. June was tempted to leave too. She'd been planning to head to the library but she felt bad about leaving Poppy with so much to do. The sight of all that mess made her skin crawl.

'Do you want me to help unpack?' she asked.

'That would be great,' Poppy said. 'You're so kind!'

June reached for a pair of scissors and slit open one of the boxes. It was full of shoes. The next one was also full of shoes, as was the third. How many pairs of shoes did she need?

Poppy unzipped one of the cases and began putting away her clothes.

'How long did you say you'd lived in this house?' she asked June as she folded a T-shirt.

'About five years,' June said, smoothing out a crumpled piece of packing paper. 'Flick is a Londoner, but the rest of us moved down here after uni.'

'Did you all know each other before?'

'More or less. Tamsin was my roommate at boarding school, and Kimmy and I were neighbours when we were kids. When Kimmy first came down to London, she and Flick worked together on the sightseeing buses—you know, the ones with the open tops? Kimmy drove one and Flick gave the tours. Kimmy is a shop manager now, but Flick still does the tours. She'll give you a free one if you're interested. She knows all kinds of random facts about London.'

'Might be a laugh,' Poppy said, in a tone that suggested it definitely wasn't. 'Seems like you've all been mates a long time. I'm truly honoured you're letting me into your group.'

Were they? This seemed a bit presumptuous.

'So, what did you study at uni?' Poppy asked.

'English lit. I love reading, so it was an obvious choice. Don't ask me how I ended up as an accountant. What about you? How did you end up here?'

'I went travelling for a while, then I moved to London and

bunked with my sister. Her place was okay but her housemates were a bit funny about it so I had to move on.'

June paused, her hand hovering over the next box. 'I thought you said you had trouble with your landlord?'

'Yes, that was my last place. I've had to move seven times in the last year. Can you believe it?'

June felt her throat tightening. Seven times seemed excessive.

'It is hard to find an affordable place in London,' she said to hide her discomfort. 'We've been lucky with this place.'

Poppy nodded, her gaze drifting around the room. 'Yeah, I think I'll be right at home here. Everyone seems really chilled and the location is ideal for work. I already feel right at home.'

June watched as she turned to hang some clothes in the wardrobe, and wondered if she would in fact become one of them, or remain more of an outsider, a stranger who lived with them. As she reached for a hanger, she studied her delicate, small-boned frame that somehow seemed too fragile for the large house. What Poppy didn't know was that her housemates were more like family than any of her actual family ever were. There was an unspoken bond between them, one that had developed over years of living in close quarters and getting to know each other's quirks. It was something Poppy couldn't possibly understand.

She didn't know that Tamsin was more sensitive than she seemed and had never got over being sent off to boarding school before she was ready.

She didn't know that although Flick chattered incessantly, her exaggerated stories and over-the-top humour were a distraction from the emptiness she'd felt since her long-term partner, Dev, left her to explore the world. Flick was great fun to have around but, when the laughter died down and the conversation stilled, the pain was still visible in her soft brown eyes.

As for Kimmy, they had grown up living next door to each

other and barely spent a day apart until the week after June's tenth birthday, when her parents announced they were sending June to boarding school.

After receiving this news, she had gone straight next door, but apparently the rest of the street already knew. She recalled Kimmy opening the door in floods of tears and pulling her up the stairs to the bathroom.

'Lock the door,' she had ordered.

June had slid the bolt across and they had both sat down on the edge of the peach coloured bathtub.

June had watched as Kimmy silently wept, crumpling a tissue onto the cold tiles. Tears had spilled between her fingers, creating a river of anguish that June knew she had caused. Her own chest had ached with guilt. She had searched within herself, her mouth opening and closing as she tried to find the right words to soothe her best friend.

'I need you to do something for me,' she had finally said.

'Anything.'

She had reached for one of Kimmy's mother's disposable razors and removed the protective cover from the end. Kimmy had opened her mouth to object but the words had evaporated in a silent gasp. June had felt her heart pounding in her chest, an equal mix of fear and thrill coursing through her veins as she had pressed the blade gently against the skin of her left arm. The sharp sting had made her wince, but she had managed to make a shallow cut in the shape of a 'K'. They had both watched as tiny droplets of bright red blood appeared on the wound. She had motioned for Kimmy to come closer and handed her the razor. With trembling hands, Kimmy had traced the blade over her own arm, sketching out the letter 'J'. The girls had held their arms side by side, eyes fixed on their wrists as the red lines ran together, blurring until the twin rivers joined into one. A silent unity had settled between them, stronger than words could ever express.

. . .

A loud smash startled June out of her reverie. She turned to find Poppy surrounded by shards of glass.

'What happened?' she exclaimed, taking a step back.

'I don't know. I barely looked at the mirror and it broke.'

June stared at the freestanding mirror she had set up in the corner. It had been a lovely antique piece she'd picked up at the second-hand furniture shop.

'What a shame,' she said, looking at all the fragments. 'Never mind, you wait there and I'll get the dustpan and brush.'

As she headed up the stairs, she thought she heard Poppy snigger. She glanced round, but Poppy had her head down, picking up the largest bits of glass.

No, she couldn't have been laughing. That mirror had been for her to use.

'Get the plasters too,' Poppy called. 'I think I've cut myself.'

'Oh, bad luck,' June called back. That was what they said about broken mirrors, wasn't it? Seven years of bad luck.

SIX

JUNE

June spread a faded blue and white blanket over the damp grass. Her housemates settled on it, then everyone delved into the wicker basket full of picnic goodies. She'd cut raw vegetables into small pieces, perfect for dipping into the creamy hummus. There were salty pitted olives and warm pittas, fresh from the oven. Bunches of red and green grapes, cubes of feta cheese and baby tomatoes.

Tamsin positioned her guitar in her lap and fiddled with the strings, threading her fingers along the fretboard and strumming lightly as the chords of a song began to emerge. She clung on to the instrument like it was a lifeline. It had belonged to her father and whenever she wrapped her arms around it June knew she was thinking of him.

Flick opened a flask and poured them each a cup of cinnamon spiced wine, the steam condensing in the air. The wine slipped down easily, warming her from the inside out. June smiled contentedly. She loved being here, spending time on the common, with its wide expanse of green, dotted with benches and trees.

'Who wants to play frisbee?' Kimmy asked.

Flick jumped up and the two of them tossed a plastic pink disc back and forth.

A gentle breeze blew across the space, carrying the scent of daffodils and damp earth. A rosy glow spread across June's cheeks as she lay back, using her handbag as a pillow. Poppy lay down beside her, the tip of her nose pink from the cold. She lowered her voice conspiratorially.

'So, spill, what do I need to know about my new housemates?'

June considered. 'Fun fact about Flick—she refuses to wear glasses even though her eyesight is terrible.'

'So, she wears contacts?'

'Most of the time. She finds them irritating though, so sometimes she leaves them out. If you find her scrabbling around the house, you'll know why.'

'What about Tamsin?'

June glanced over at Tamsin. She had her eyes closed, completely lost in her music.

'Tamsin's always late. If you want to leave at eight, you have to tell her seven forty-five.'

Poppy nodded. 'I'll bear that in mind. And Kimmy?'

June leaned closer. 'Kimmy's so in love. I heard her singing in the shower this morning.'

'What about you? Are you seeing anyone?'

'Me? No way. I like my life just as it is. I'm happy being single and I love my job.'

Poppy smiled. 'Didn't you say you were an accountant?'

'I love it all the same.'

Poppy propped herself up on her elbows and took a big swig of her wine. 'Sounds like you've got it all sussed.'

Kimmy and Flick flopped down on the blanket, taking a break from their game.

'So, Poppy, are you seeing anyone?' Kimmy asked.

'I only attract crap men,' Poppy said, leaning over Flick to dip her bread in the hummus. 'I mean really sorry, sad specimens.'

Everyone looked at her with interest.

'There was a bloke who used to come into the pub. I was quite fond of him. He was a bit younger, but I didn't mind that. He asked me out for dinner. He said to meet him at this Lebanese place...'

'Oh, was it the one on the corner of George Road?' June asked. 'I went there once. I had lamb shank braised with pomegranate.'

'Yeah, so anyway, I turned up at the restaurant, all dolled up in a nice dress and heels. Well, the guy brought his mum along! He said he really valued her opinion.'

Flick threw her head back and laughed. 'Oh Lord! That would be an instant no.'

'I didn't want to be rude, so I stuck it out, ate the food. I'd already decided I wouldn't be seeing him again, but I was on my best behaviour. Anyway, at the end of the meal, the guy told me that his mum thought I was "too common". I mean, what was she looking for? I'd met him in a pub.'

Everyone laughed. 'That's so harsh,' June said.

'Well anyway, here I am, young, free and single.'

'Most of us are,' Flick said.

Kimmy reached out her arm, her fingertips brushing against the soft green skin of the grapes. She plucked a few off and popped them in her mouth one by one.

'I had my share of bad dates before I met Ralph,' she said, brows furrowed as she chewed.

'How did you meet?' Poppy asked.

Kimmy smiled. 'I was jogging one morning before work, right here on the common, when I saw what I thought was a body sprawled out on the grass. As I got closer, I saw that he was gorgeous. He had perfect blond hair and long eyelashes, like a male sleeping beauty. From the way he was lying, I wasn't sure if he was just taking a nap or if something had happened to him, so I nudged him with my toes but he didn't respond.'

'How come?'

'Turns out he's a very deep sleeper. He'd been out on the razz the night before, and he had his earphones in. He was lucky I didn't call the emergency services. Anyway, I reached out and shook him and he did wake up, thankfully. When I explained that I thought he was dead, he started laughing. He thought it was hilarious. I was a bit cross, because I genuinely was worried. To make up for giving me a fright, he took me out for breakfast. I didn't really have time. I was sweaty from my run and I needed to shower before work, but when life throws a six-foot hunk at you, you don't say no!'

'I wish life would throw a few six-foot hunks at me,' Poppy said, smiling.

'We did think about getting a male housemate for your room,' Flick admitted, 'but we decided things might get complicated.'

'Yeah, I can imagine. Well, lucky for me you didn't.'

'So what happened with your last place?' Tamsin asked. 'You said you had a problem with the landlord?'

'Yes, he was a total nightmare. He was constantly asking me to turn my TV down, even when I wasn't watching anything. He didn't like the sound of me walking about, didn't like me having people over. He told me he was keeping a diary of all my comings and goings. I began to feel like I was trapped in prison, living under his roof. I had to move out for the sake of my sanity.'

She picked a buttercup and peeled the petals off one by one.

'Well, we're pretty normal,' Kimmy said.

'Speak for yourself,' Flick hooted.

Kimmy ignored her. 'We've all lived under the same roof for

five years without killing each other. I think that's pretty good going.'

'Is there any more wine?' Tamsin asked. 'I'm getting cold.'

Flick pulled out the flask and poured the dregs into her cup. Tamsin drank up and they started gathering up all their containers. It was dark now and the moon was bright in the sky.

'It feels really quiet all of a sudden,' June commented. She looked around. 'Are we the only people still here?'

'You're never really alone in London,' Poppy said.

'No, of course not.'

Their voices carried in the cool night air and echoed through the surrounding trees as they made their way out of the common.

June took a quick glance behind her. She could not imagine walking here alone at night. The path was eerily still and the darkness seemed to swallow everything around her. She hurried onwards, passing under street lamps that illuminated their faces in an orange glow. Then she noticed Tamsin veering towards the edge of the pavement. She reached out and took her by the arm, pulling her away from the road.

'You're such a lightweight,' she said fondly.

'No, I'm not, I'm fine.'

'Then why were you walking so close to the road?'

'Seriously, I was fine.'

'Some of those cars were getting a bit close. Better safe than sorry.'

Tamsin shrugged and held her guitar case a little closer. They walked on in silence.

Later that night, June tiptoed down the hallway, trying not to step on any creaky floorboards. She glanced up at Tamsin's attic room where a warm light glowed from beneath the door frame. She heard the gentle murmur of her music in the air. The rest of the house was in darkness as she let herself into the bathroom. She used the toilet quickly, then washed her hands with a thin layer of foamy soap. She sighed with exhaustion as she looked at her reflection in the mirror. Her light brown hair hung limp and straight and her eyelashes were so pale they were almost invisible.

She opened the bathroom door, prepared to step out into the hallway and instead came face to face with Poppy. She stumbled backwards.

'Oh! Sorry, I didn't see you there.'

Poppy averted her gaze. 'That's okay.'

'Well goodnight,' June said, stepping out of her way.

She walked back to her bedroom, but as she opened the door an unsettling sensation crept over her. She glanced back to find Poppy still rooted in place, watching until she disappeared inside her room.

SEVEN

JUNE

The sun seeped through June's blinds on Saturday morning, and she scrambled out of bed, keen to make the most of the day. She yanked on a pair of jeans and a T-shirt, pulled her hair into a neat ponytail, and crept out the bedroom door without making a sound.

When she reached the living room, she paused in surprise. Poppy was curled up on the sofa with her knees to her chest, cradling a large mug filled with steaming coffee. Dark circles smudged the skin beneath her eyes.

'You're up early,' June said.

The rest of the housemates were sleeping. None of them ever got up early unless they had to.

'Oh, no.' Poppy let out a low laugh. 'I haven't gone to bed yet.'

'Haven't you?' June found this peculiar. She couldn't fathom why someone would choose to stay awake all night.

'What are you doing up?' Poppy asked.

'I'm heading down to the market. They sell deli meats and cheeses, artisan loaves, that kind of thing.'

'That sounds fun. Mind if I tag along?'

'Course not,' June said with a smile.

Usually, she cycled to the market but since Poppy didn't have a bike, she decided to walk. As they headed down the road, she slowed her pace to match Poppy's shorter stride. She loved going to the market. It was one of her little rituals.

'You know, it's been really heart-warming, how you've all taken me in,' Poppy said. 'I feel so lucky. Some houseshares are utter nightmares, you know? In my sister's house, they all fight over toilet paper. She has to keep hers in her room because if she puts it in the bathroom, someone will steal it.'

'How ridiculous!'

'I know, right? It's nice to find a house where people actually like each other. You're not just strangers sharing a house. You're actual friends.'

'Oh, we do have our moments,' June said truthfully. 'One week last year, we lost the remote. Everyone was at each other's throats for a couple of weeks. We had to order a new one, then it turned up randomly in the bread bin. No one ever owned up to it. I reckon someone put it there after a night out.'

'How random!' Poppy said, amused.

They reached the corner and paused before crossing the street, taking it all in; the smell of warm coffee wafting from the cafés, the hum of conversations between strangers, and the soft pastel shades of Kimmy's stationery shop, The Paper Pantry. June pointed it out to Poppy.

'Oh, nice! Does she own it?'

'No, she runs it for someone else. She was really happy to get the job. She's on her own most of the time so no one cares if she closes early or takes a long lunch break.'

Poppy raised an eyebrow. 'Alright for some! And she's the one with the hot boyfriend too?'

'Yeah, things are going well for her right now.'

'Let's hope it rubs off. I'm overdue for a bit of good luck.'

Poppy checked her phone. 'Looks like I'm working tonight.

What about you? Any plans for the weekend?'

'I have a book to read,' June said with a smile. 'But I also want to see the new *Mission: Impossible* film. The trailer looked really good. Maybe we could all go?'

'Sounds good.'

They walked up to the marketplace, where the air was filled with mouth-watering aromas of freshly cooked food. They drifted between stalls, marvelling at the sheer variety of products available. The first stall was the spice stall where June splurged on a jar of saffron.

'This is the good stuff,' she told Poppy. 'It's expensive, but pop a bit of this in with your rice and it tastes amazing.'

Poppy stopped in front of a stall selling home-made biscuits and sampled some of the offerings, while June tested different types of cheese.

'This is why you shouldn't shop on an empty stomach,' Poppy said, as they continued to wander around.

Given that she was the one responsible for the food budget, June was generally quite restrained, but she hoped she had found a kindred spirit in Poppy, who seemed as interested in the fresh produce as she was. June bought two different loaves of bread, a tub of olives, some fresh peaches and a selection of her favourite pastries. Poppy chose some smoked sausage and two bottles of red wine. They walked a little further, checking out a few more stalls.

Poppy's eyes lit up as she watched a stallholder pull a lump of dough into thin, glossy ribbons. 'Can we get some of that fresh pasta?' she asked.

June smiled. 'Better get two packs to make sure there's enough to go around the five of us.'

They grabbed two jars of sauce too; it was expensive but June didn't mind just this once.

The smell of freshly made hot waffles was too enticing to walk past and they stopped and bought one each. They dawdled home, chewing as they went. The sweet smell of maple syrup lingered in the air.

'You know, you're not at all what I expected,' Poppy said, stopping to toss her wrapper in the bin.

'Why, what did you expect?'

'I don't know. The others said you were...'

'What?'

'They said you were great.'

They started walking again, and June scrunched up her face in confusion. 'What did they actually say?'

Poppy stopped and tilted her head. 'They said you march to the beat of your own drum, or something like that.'

'Who said that?'

Poppy rubbed her palms together and looked at the ground. 'It doesn't matter, does it? Pretend I never said anything. I don't want to start any trouble.'

They walked on home in silence. June felt a little perturbed. She wondered who had said that about her, and why.

When they reached the house, they walked down the hall and dumped all the bags on the kitchen table.

Poppy yawned widely. 'My bed's calling. Are you okay to put this stuff away?'

'Yeah, no problem.'

June didn't mind at all. She enjoyed looking at all the food they'd bought and arranging it in the cupboards. She put the wine in the rack and filled the refrigerator with the cold meats and cheeses. Then she arranged the fruit in a glass bowl and put out the bread and pastries for her housemates to find when they woke up.

Once everything was squirrelled away, she stepped into her bedroom and kicked off her slippers, settling onto her bed to read. She pulled an old quilt around her shoulders and grabbed her book from the nightstand. An hour passed in a blur as she lost herself in the story. She let out a contented sigh as she reached the last page.

'That was so good!'

She gazed at the book in wonder. It was a shame none of her housemates were avid readers. She had no one to share the joy with. She turned to the back and looked at the other titles in the series. Perhaps they'd have the next one at the library.

As she walked through the house, the others were stirring. Kimmy sat at the kitchen table, rubbing her eyes as she spooned cereal into her mouth, while Flick was slumped on the sofa with a mug of milky coffee clutched in both hands. June waved to them before heading off on her bike.

To her delight, the library had three more books in the series. She hugged them to her chest and went over to browse the new arrivals. Somehow, she ended up with a big pile of books. She hoped she was going to be able to fit them all in her saddle bags.

As she stepped out of the library, the sun warmed her skin and a gentle breeze tickled her cheeks. She spotted Ralph jogging towards her. His trainers were scuffed and worn at the edges but his socks were white and pristine, like something out of a detergent ad. He gave her a little wave and continued to pound the pavement. She hopped on her bike and enjoyed the ride. The weekend traffic seemed calmer than her workday commute, less impatient. There were no cars around as she turned into her road but she gave an arm signal anyway as she slowed and dismounted.

She found the house quiet.

'Hello!' she called. 'Anybody home?'

There was no reply.

The air smelt of Kimmy's perfume. There were coffee cups left out on the table, and dirty plates in the sink. But no housemates.

Then she saw the pink Post-it note on the fridge: *Gone to*

see the new Mission: Impossible movie, back soon, Kimmy, Flick,
Tamsin and Poppy x

She squeezed her fists together so tightly that her knuckles
turned white. Going to see *Mission: Impossible* had been her
idea. She distinctly recalled mentioning it to Poppy. She
couldn't believe they'd gone without her.

Why hadn't they called her, or arranged to see a later view-
ing? She checked her phone but there were no missed calls, no
messages, nothing. She balled the note up and threw it into the
bin before stomping out of the kitchen.

Settling on the sofa, she flipped through the pages of one of
her new books, but she couldn't focus. The last time she'd been
to the cinema, the adverts had lasted ages, and then there had
been the trailers. Perhaps she could still make it?

She picked up her phone and checked the show times. Her
heart sank. The film had already started, and even if she left
now she'd miss the first twenty minutes.

It was so infuriating. Why had no one texted her? She'd
been in town anyway. She could have met them there.

Eventually, her housemates arrived home, laughing and
talking noisily. Flick and Poppy were carrying polystyrene
containers. They must have gone for burgers afterwards.

June rose to her feet, wanting them to see how upset she
was. To her annoyance, Kimmy sailed right past her, phone
pressed to her ear as she headed up the stairs. The others
headed straight to the kitchen. June followed them and planted
herself in the doorway, scowling until Flick finally noticed her.

'What's got your goat?'

'You went to the cinema without me!' she said. 'I wanted to
see that film too.'

'Sorry, I didn't think it would be your cup of tea.'

'I told Poppy I wanted to see it just this morning.'

Poppy shook her head. 'Did you? I don't remember that.'

June placed a hand on her hip. 'I told you on the way to the market. How can you not remember?'

Poppy gave her a half smile. 'I've slept since then. My mind is always a bit fuzzy when I wake up. Then Kimmy said something about seeing the film and everyone was up for it. We'd have asked you but you weren't home.'

'You could have called me.'

'I didn't think it was a big deal, besides, we were in a rush. Once we'd looked up the film times, we had to leg it down to the cinema to catch the showing.'

Tamsin slid an arm around her, but June turned away. She didn't like being treated like a petulant child.

'Just forget it.'

She flicked on the kettle, and its coils glowed red. But as she searched the cupboard for her favourite mug, Poppy wouldn't stop talking about the film. She tried to tune her out, but it was impossible. As the steam rose from the spout, something inside her snapped.

'For goodness' sake, I haven't actually seen it yet!'

'Oh sorry, spoiler alert!' Poppy said.

June studied her face, but she didn't know her well enough to be able to tell if she was being deliberately provocative.

She turned and poured her tea. Poppy stood and watched as she plucked the teabag from her cup before flicking it into the bin with a jerk of her hand.

'There's another showing at seven,' she said. 'You could go and see it then?'

The tone of her voice sent a chill down June's spine.

Was she imagining it, or was Poppy gloating?

June headed to her room and read for a while until her anger dissipated. She was being silly. Of course, Poppy hadn't purposely left her out. Why would she? They barely knew each other. People were so inclined to believe in conspiracies. She had read that somewhere. They were wired to look for patterns everywhere. That was what made outlandish theories so appealing. Poppy wasn't out to get her. These things just happened, and she needed to get over it.

She raised her head. The house was quiet now, and she sensed they were all hiding in their rooms. They had a tendency to do that after an argument. Retreat to their own corners to lick their wounds. Not that this had been that big a spat. She was just annoyed, that was all. Her housemates weren't usually so thoughtless.

Her stomach rumbled and she decided to go and get a pastry from the kitchen. Stepping outside her room, she almost tripped over Poppy who was sitting in the hallway, her short legs propped up against the wall while she played games on her phone.

'Why are you sitting there?' June asked.

'The internet isn't very good in my room.'

'You could sit in the living room.'

'I'm fine here thanks.'

June's anger reignited like a hot flame. She stepped past, avoiding eye contact as she made her way to the kitchen. Tamsin was there, buttering a slice of toast. She took one look at June and glanced at the clock.

'Oh shite, I was supposed to ring my aunt.'

June watched as she scurried back to her room like a frightened mouse. She drew in a breath, feeling even more annoyed, especially when she opened the bread bin only to find that her housemates had eaten all the pastries. They hadn't even left her one. She grabbed a banana and returned to her room. She thought of the cinema again, and a flicker of heat rose from her neck to her cheeks. She snatched up her phone and selected some violin music. It was supposed to be relaxing, but the high, screeching notes only made her more tense, so she switched to a gentler classical piano piece. There, that was better. Settling onto her bed, a wave of calm slowly spread through her body. She picked up her book and drifted back into the story.

She had been reading for a couple of hours before she heard a knock at the door.

'Come in,' she called, not bothering to get up.

Tamsin and Poppy burst in, holding plates of freshly baked biscuits.

'We thought you might be hungry,' Poppy said brightly.

Tamsin smiled apologetically. 'We really are sorry about earlier.'

June swallowed her pride. 'It's okay, I'm over it,' she said, accepting a shortbread. It melted on her tongue in a mixture of sweetness and warmth.

'Do you want to come and play Monopoly?' Tamsin asked.

'Not really.'

'What about a programme? We could binge watch that new comedy you like?'

'Okay.'

June set her book aside and followed them out to the living room. Flick and Kimmy were already there. Instead of the comedy she'd been promised, they were watching a reality TV show she cared little about but she decided to join them anyway. Poppy plumped herself down in June's favourite armchair so she squeezed in beside Tamsin and Kimmy on the sofa. It was uncomfortable, being wedged in like that, so she got up and grabbed a chair from the dining room. Its wooden legs screeched against the floor as she dragged it into the living room, earning her a frown from Flick.

She positioned the chair next to the sofa, but Poppy kept leaning forward, obscuring her view. Every time she thought she had found a good vantage point, Poppy shifted in her seat, cutting her off once again. With a sigh, June pulled out her phone in defeat and absent-mindedly scrolled through her news feed. At one point, she caught Poppy glancing round at her, and when their eyes met Poppy smiled a little too brightly, as if she knew she'd won.

EIGHT

JUNE

As June unwrapped her ham sandwich, the tangy scent of mustard went right up her nose. She reached for a tissue and sneezed loudly before resuming her lunch. The best thing about working in finance was that she got to have a private office, away from the hubbub of the big open-plan room next door.

Her desk was organised with military precision. Her pens were all lined up in the holder, like perfect little soldiers, and the coaster to her right contained the big yellow mug that her friend Grace had given her, but her favourite item was the plush leather chair she was sitting in. Whenever she needed to clear her head, she'd close the door and spin around in circles, clearing the cobwebs from her mind.

She had sat through three hours of meetings that morning, and felt entitled to a proper lunch break. She pulled out her library book and read as she ate, careful not to drop any crumbs on the pages. She started a new chapter and felt her phone buzz in her pocket. Pulling it out, she saw she had three unread messages in her Facebook Messenger, all from people she didn't know. She viewed the first one, from someone called Nigel:

Hi Sexy,

Has anyone ever told you how beautiful you are? Would you even believe me if I told you that you are just my type?

She rolled her eyes and looked at the next one, from someone called Shaun:

Hi there,

From the moment I saw your face I knew you were the one.

She trashed that one too, annoyed that her spam filter was letting so much junk through. But the third one made her pause:

Dear June,

I hope you don't mind the direct approach but I couldn't help but notice your love for books and cycling. Perhaps we could share those interests over dinner…

She swallowed. How did this bot know so much about her? Assuming it was a bot.

She put down her phone, feeling like a hunted animal.

A little later, her phone beeped with a new message.

Hi June,

My name is Colin, and I'm an accountant like you. I'm thirty-one and live in Clapham. If you fancy going for a drink some time, give me a call.

She stared at the message for a moment, her breath a little shaky.

She clicked on his profile. He looked like a real person, with a job and a life.

She sent him a message.

Hi Colin, where did you get my info?

She took a bite of her sandwich. Her boss Marilyn was in the conference room, yelling down the phone at someone. She sank a little lower in her seat.

Her phone pinged, but the new message wasn't from Colin but another wannabe suitor. She drummed her fingers against the table impatiently. This was getting ridiculous.

She turned back to her computer, her keen eyes spotting a mistake in the spreadsheet she'd been working on. She corrected it and sent a copy to Marilyn for the staff meeting in the morning.

Then she checked her phone again. Colin had replied.

I can't remember. It was either DatingLocal or YoungHotSingles. Sorry about contacting you on Facebook, but it wasn't hard to find you. Just wanted to get ahead of the competition.

Her eyes widened, horrified. She shoved her lunch to one side and opened a new browser. Strictly speaking, her work computer wasn't for personal use but everybody else did it.

She typed in 'DatingLocal.com.' As she explored the site, her worst fears were confirmed. There she was, smiling out from a headshot with her age, occupation and interests listed along with her name and a contact button. She couldn't believe what she was seeing. The picture looked recent but she didn't recognise it, and she was being 'promoted' as a 'New Single in Your Area'.

Her blood boiled. How bloody dare they?

She tried to send a message to the page admin, but the site wouldn't allow her to do that without first signing in. She couldn't even get to the delete page. She swallowed her pride and called her colleague Gulnara from the IT department.

'I'll be right up,' Gulnara said.

'Thank you,' June said tightly. She didn't want to call attention to the page, but she could hardly leave it up there.

Gulnara was with her in ten minutes, still swallowing the last of her coffee. Her thick glasses sat on the bridge of her nose and framed her oval face. She went straight to the computer and grabbed June's mouse, moving it briskly around the profile, clicking here and there.

'Is it a phishing scam?' June asked.

'Maybe. Where's the picture from? Did you post it on your social media?'

June shook her head. 'Maybe one of my friends uploaded it? I don't recognise it, but I wear that shirt a lot.'

Gulnara raised an eyebrow. 'In that case, I think it's more likely someone set this up. An ex looking to get revenge, maybe? Or a friend trying to help with your love life.'

June sat back in her chair. 'I haven't been out with anyone in ages and my friends all know I hate dating sites.'

Gulnara shrugged. 'All the same, someone did this.'

'So how do I get it down?'

'I've notified the site admin that it was put up fraudulently. If they're a legitimate site, it should be taken down in the next couple of days.'

'And if they're not?'

Gulnara shook her head. 'You could try the police. They could track the IP address if they wanted but I wouldn't hold my breath.'

A flush crept up June's neck. 'Well that's not very reassuring!'

Gulnara gave her an apologetic smile. 'No, well. Hopefully they'll take it down. Try not to worry about it. Sorry, I've got a meeting to get to.'

'Okay, thanks anyway.'

She watched as Gulnara headed out the door, then felt her

shoulders droop. She pushed through the workday feeling disorientated by the freaky messages. She didn't like the thought of her details being out there for anyone to find, and she felt powerless to do anything about it. That dating site was specifically intended for people to meet up with other singles in their area, which meant that all the freaks who were messaging her lived in or around Clapham. It was an unsettling thought; she could run into any of them in the street and she wouldn't even know.

'My, you're on fire today,' Marilyn said, pleased when June sent the accounts through early.

June smiled grimly. She had channelled all her adrenaline into her work, but now she just wanted to get home and curl up with her book and a big glass of wine.

The ride home was therapeutic, the wind whipping past her face and tangling her hair. She inhaled the familiar smell of damp grass and rain-washed roads as she glided up to her house, her wheels squeaking to a stop. She locked her bike in the shed and stepped inside to find Poppy in the kitchen. There were pans piled high in the sink. Dirty chopping boards, bowls and knives on every surface.

'What's all this, then?' she asked, struggling to keep the judgement out of her voice.

'Taco night,' Poppy said, flashing her first genuine smile in days. 'I spent a year in Mexico. So tonight I'm going to cook up some of the dishes I learnt while I was there. I hope you like spice?'

June did.

'Can I do anything to help?' she asked.

'Oh, no. It's all under control.'

Poppy took June's potato ricer and began mashing the beans

with it. June gritted her teeth. Probably best not to watch but all that mess was her getting to her.

She rolled up her sleeves and began to wash up.

'You don't have to do that. I'll stick them in the dishwasher after,' Poppy said.

'That's okay. It's easier to do them by hand,' June said, wondering how she had managed to use every single pan they had.

The pans must have been in the sink a while because the grime was caked on and it took a while for June to scrub it all off.

Poppy continued to cook as she scrubbed, chopping so many onions that June's eyes watered. When the backlog was cleared, June hung up her tea towel.

'How long do you think it will be till dinner?' she asked.

'Not too long.'

'Okay, well give me a yell if you need a hand setting the table.'

She headed to her room and flopped down on the bed. She might as well catch up on her reading while she waited.

She immersed herself in her book, reading for what seemed like hours, but still Poppy did not call her. She glanced at the time. Was it really eight already? The smells from the kitchen were enticing. It must be almost time. But then eight o'clock became nine and June started to lose it. She went out to see what was happening and found Poppy watching TV.

'What's happening with dinner?' she asked.

'Don't worry, it's all under control,' Poppy said, without taking her eyes off the screen.

June grabbed a peach and disappeared back to her room, trying not to show her agitation.

Poppy finally served dinner at ten. She didn't seem the least bit bothered about the time, but why would she, considering how late she stayed up at night? June was tired by now, but the rest of the housemates didn't complain, so she did her best to enjoy the meal.

Poppy had gone to a lot of effort to make everything look authentic. She'd set the table with thick, woven placemats in bright colours that matched the chilli and lime patterned napkins. Candles flickered in red and yellow holders at each end of the table, casting a warm glow. She'd also laid out sombreros for them to wear.

'Isn't this cultural appropriation?' June asked, picking up one of the colourful straw hats.

'Cultural appreciation, more like,' Poppy said. 'Imitation is the greatest form of flattery, don't you think?'

June shrugged. She didn't want to get into an argument.

'Well, everything looks delicious,' Kimmy said.

June nodded, her mouth already watering at the thought of tasting the guacamole. But before they could all dig in, Poppy produced five shot glasses and filled them with a clear liquid from an ornate bottle of tequila.

'Not for me,' June said, waving it away. She didn't do tequila.

'Don't be a spoilsport,' Flick murmured, and Tamsin shot her a pleading look.

'Oh alright, just the one.'

She took a small sip and grimaced at the bitter taste that filled her mouth. The smell evoked memories of retching into the rose bushes back at uni. She tilted her head back and forced the contents of the glass down, swallowing quickly. Everyone around her cheered as if she'd just accomplished some impressive feat. She felt like she was back in freshers' week, being forced to take part in drinking games and watch never-ending rugby matches, while fellow students belted out tuneless songs with sexist lyrics.

To rid herself of the taste, she ate a large spoonful of salsa, straight from the bowl. It was spicier than she'd expected, and her eyes watered. Poppy looked over at her and grinned.

'That's the hot salsa, June. If it's too much for you, the mild one is down this end.'

June drew a deep breath as beads of sweat collected on her forehead. 'No thanks, I'm fine with this one.'

She drained her water glass, then concentrated on piling her plate with a bit of every dish on the table. Poppy poured more shots and entertained them all with anecdotes of her adventures in Mexico with her then boyfriend, Miguel.

She shook her head and laughed. 'He was like a firework—you never knew when he was going to go off. He had this wild attitude like nothing mattered except the moment we were in. I remember one time he said, "Let's spend the weekend in the mountains!" Without even stopping to pack a bag, off we went. We had hardly any money or food but we just winged it, taking whatever opportunity came our way. A weekend became two months. We slept in our campervan and got work at a local bar. The pay was a pittance, but they fed us. We had to save up until we could afford the petrol back to Miguel's flat in the city.'

'I couldn't live like that,' June said, reaching for the refried beans.

'He sounds like your complete opposite,' Flick said, pointing a fork at her. 'It'd drive you crazy.'

June shrugged. 'I like to plan,' she said. 'What's wrong with that?'

'Nothing,' Tamsin said loyally. 'Without you, nothing would get done around here. We can't all be crazy and spontaneous.'

'So, what happened to Miguel?' Flick asked.

Poppy shrugged. 'The last time I saw him, he fell down a well.'

'Was he alright?'

'Who knows? He's probably still there for all I know. He

was a bit of a prat.'

The table was silent for a moment, before Flick started to laugh. Then Kimmy, and then everyone joined in.

'You know, I used to go out with this loser who refused to pay for dinner,' Kimmy said.

As she spoke, the group's heads turned towards her. Kimmy ran her finger along the rim of her glass, smearing away the condensation.

'It was a fancy place,' she went on, 'with starched table-cloths and waiters wearing tuxedos. We had a three-course meal —steak, potatoes au gratin—and some expensive French wine. He asked me if I wanted anything else, and when I said no, he told me to go to the ladies and climb out the window.'

June was horrified. 'I would have refused.'

'I thought he was joking but then he went outside for a cigarette and I watched him disappear down the road.'

'So, what did you do?'

Kimmy shrugged. 'I didn't have much choice. I couldn't afford those prices.'

Poppy leaned forward. 'Did you see him again?'

'To my shame, I did. He snuck us into a wedding we weren't invited to. It was VIP all the way. We drank champagne and danced like we belonged. No one twigged, not even when we took a picture with the bride and groom. He was a lot of fun, but a bit too edgy for me.'

'Ralph's a much better match for you,' June said, wiping her mouth with a napkin.

'In what way?' Poppy asked.

June hesitated, biting her lip and looking away briefly before meeting Poppy's gaze again. 'Well, he's a good person. Reliable, dependable.'

'Yawn! You're putting me right off,' Poppy said.

'No, I mean, if he says he's going to do something for you, he will. He follows through. So many men promise you the earth and then don't deliver.' She looked around the table. 'Do you remember when Kimmy mentioned she loved that old TV programme and he tracked down a bootleg copy for her?'

'So he can google,' Poppy said.

'No, he's also very sexy,' Tamsin said, wiggling her eyebrows.

Flick nodded.

'Is he seeing Kimmy or all of you?' Poppy asked.

Tamsin smiled. 'Put it this way, if we could clone him, we would.'

'Well. Let's drink to that.'

Poppy refilled their glasses and, against her better judgement, June drank another shot. The spicy salsa was the perfect antidote for the bitter flavour. Before they knew it, the bottle was empty.

'Not a problem,' Poppy said, leaping up and fetching another from the fridge.

Everybody cheered as she topped them all up again.

June rose from her seat. The food had been delicious and she felt a little tiddly, but she was anxious not to repeat the humiliation of the rose bush incident, so she collected up the plates. As she carried them out to the kitchen, her stomach dropped at the sight that greeted her; every surface was covered with grease-stained pans, utensils and vegetable peelings. There was tomato sauce all over the stove and splotches of sour cream on the floor. Poppy couldn't have made more mess if she'd tried.

Really, June ought to leave the dishes for someone else, but she doubted any of her housemates would bother with it at this time of night and she couldn't bear to face all this chaos in the morning. So she filled the dishwasher with as much as she could, then scrubbed everything else while the others remained at the table, drinking and talking, their voices carrying through the house. It was gone midnight by the time any of them made it to bed.

NINE

JUNE

June cycled down the street, her head pounding in time with the rhythm of her unsteady pedals. She was thankful that she hadn't been stopped by the police. She hadn't thought she'd overdone it the night before, but the tequila curse had struck again and it felt like there was a bird pecking at her skull.

She arrived at her office building, swiped her ID card to get into the lift, and travelled up to the fourth floor. As she shuffled along the corridor, she kept her eyes on the ground, hoping to slip by undetected – but no such luck. Marilyn, her boss, stood in the middle of the open-plan office surrounded by a group of employees.

'Morning, June!' she called out.

She narrowed her gaze.

'Hold it right there! Don't tell me you had a hot date last night?'

Embarrassment crept up June's neck as everyone turned to look at her. She tried to smooth down her dishevelled hair and hoped her boss couldn't smell the alcohol that lingered on her breath.

'Just a rough night,' she muttered, looking down at her feet.

Marilyn scrunched up her face. 'Well, you look like you haven't slept for a week.'

June wanted to disappear into the floor.

'I'm fine, really. I'm going to get stuck in.'

She scurried off to her office, glad that she could shut the door on the world. She collapsed into her chair and flicked on her monitor, breathing a sigh of relief when she saw that the day's schedule was free of meetings. Hallelujah!

She switched on her coffee machine and brewed a dark roast. Soon, the nutty aroma filled her office. She checked the dating sites. Thanks to Gulnara, her profile was already down on one of them, but the other was proving trickier. The annoying messages continued to drip into her Facebook Messenger. Most of them were pure cheese.

'I want to cover my body in golden syrup and dance naked for you,' one man had written. Another was keen to share his passion for 'tantric outdoor sex'.

June shuddered. Why did people have to be so weird?

She opened a spreadsheet and squinted at it, trying to make sense of the numbers. It was slow going; each tired keystroke felt like wading through Marmite. But she stuck with it until her eyes burned and her muscles ached. As soon as the clock struck three, she closed the file, shut down her computer and headed out the door early.

She arrived home to find the hallway littered with shoes. Since Poppy had moved in there were too many pairs for the shoe cupboard, so people had taken to lining them up neatly along the wall. June had been fine with that, but now they were all over the place, and it looked as if they had multiplied overnight. She straightened them up before walking through to the living room.

The coffee table sported an empty drink can, along with an

upturned handbag and a tube of lipstick. Two mismatched slippers lay in separate corners of the room and a bright scarf had been casually draped on the back of the sofa.

She straightened it all up and stepped through to the dining room. There she found the cutlery drawer from the kitchen, with all its contents spilled across the table – napkins crumpled up here, candles scattered there, along with various other detritus. It seemed like someone had started a clear-out and then abandoned it midway.

Frowning, she walked into the kitchen. The light-blue countertop was covered with flour. Cupcakes, just out of the oven, perfumed the air, but she couldn't appreciate their sweetness. Her gaze quickly shifted to the wall, where streaks of butter ran down the backsplash. The ground below her felt gritty. She looked down and found that a film of sugar had crystallised on the floor, glistening in golden whorls beneath her feet.

'Hello?' she yelled, trying to gauge who had done this, but nobody answered.

She already knew who it was anyway. Her housemates could be messy, but never this bad. And Poppy was the only other person who liked to cook. She marched down the stairs and hammered on Poppy's bedroom door. When there was no response, she pushed it open and a wave of pungent, acrid vapour rolled out, making her eyes sting.

She blinked. The basement seemed impossibly dark, as if someone had boarded up the window. She stumbled forward, tripping over a chest of drawers.

'Poppy?'

She backed into the wall and her fingers brushed the surface, feeling for the light switch. With a click, the fluorescent bulb flickered to life, casting eerie shadows across the room.

Her mouth dropped open. All the furniture had been dragged away from the walls and draped with faded sheets. The warm yellow walls she had worked so hard on were now a dismal shade of aubergine, transforming the look of the room from cosy haven to creepy dungeon.

TEN

JUNE

'What the hell?'

She thought of all the effort she had put into this room, prepping the walls and laboriously rolling on two coats of paint. She had given up a whole weekend to make it nice. Her fists clenched involuntarily as a wave of frustration coursed through her veins. Poppy had said how nice it looked when she'd shown her round. Was she just being polite, saying what June wanted to hear so she could have the room? What other lies had she told?

She stumbled back out the door, unable to look at it a moment longer. She headed upstairs and spent the next hour cleaning. She wiped down the tables and countertops with disinfectant, then mopped the floor with a soapy solution until it sparkled. She returned the cutlery and candles back to the kitchen drawer and even rearranged the shoes so they were tidy. Then she collapsed onto the sofa, just in time for her house-mates to return.

'Oh June, you cleaned!' Kimmy said, as she walked through the door. She sounded pleased, as if June had done it for the fun of it. Tamsin and Poppy were right behind her. Poppy had a tub of ready-made chocolate icing in her hand. She smiled at June. She was very convincing. It felt like a real, genuine smile.

'Thank you for dealing with the mess, you didn't have to do that. I just nipped out to get the icing for my chocolate orange cakes. We can have them for pudding.'

June drew in a deep breath, ready to unleash her fury, but instead released it in a long, steady breath. Just because she hated mess, didn't mean everybody else did. Just because she liked sunny yellow walls, didn't mean Poppy did. She looked at Poppy and forced herself to step away. Years of communal living had taught her to not let her need for order and cleanliness infringe on other people. It had also taught her to bide her time.

Just at that moment, Flick breezed through the door and shrugged her shoulders out of her bright green jacket.

'Alright, June? I'm just going to grab some spaghetti hoops, then I'm ready to go.'

June looked at her blankly. Then realisation dawned. It was Tuesday night, which meant time for Mud and Mingle. A warm feeling spread through her chest and she smiled broadly. An evening of pottery was just what she needed.

'Where are you two off to?' Poppy asked fifteen minutes later, as June and Flick put their coats on.

'Pottery class,' Flick said, sliding into her pumps.

'That sounds fun. Maybe I'll join you?'

June shook her head. 'I don't think you can join in the middle of term.'

Poppy shrugged. 'I'll just pop along with you and ask. If it's not cool, I'll go to the pub. You can come and meet me after.'

June bit her lip, her gaze darting between Flick and Poppy. Flick seemed unconcerned by the suggestion.

'Okay then, we'd better get going.'

June set off at her usual pace, eager to get to class, but Poppy plodded along behind them. After a while, they were so far ahead that they had to stop and wait for her. June found it exasperating, how slow Poppy was. She understood that Poppy had a shorter stride but she seemed incapable of walking any faster, almost as if she wanted to make them late.

When they arrived at the studio, June watched as Poppy approached their teacher. She couldn't hear what she was saying but Nadia smiled and laughed, nodding her head vigorously as Poppy talked. Then Poppy turned and gave June a sly thumbs up before taking a seat between Flick and June in the middle of the bank of desks. Her presence seemed to fill the space almost immediately, leaving little room.

Nadia came over and gave Poppy a quick lesson in pottery, demonstrating how to knead and shape the wet material until it was soft and malleable.

As soon as she walked away, Poppy flicked the switch on her pottery wheel and watched it whirr to life. Her fingers pressed into the clay, coaxing it gently. The clay rose up with each movement of her hands. Poppy made instinctive changes here and there, and hummed to herself as the pot took shape. For a first timer, June had to admit she was pretty good. She looked over at Flick who was also impressed.

She tried to concentrate on her own work but she couldn't help staring at the beautiful pot forming in Poppy's hand.

Flick shook her head.

'Wow, Poppy, you're a natural. You should have seen my first effort!'

Proudly, Poppy removed her pot from the wheel and everyone came to look at it.

'That really is very good,' Nadia said. 'Are you sure you've never done pottery before?'

'Never,' Poppy said. Her cheeks were warm and she looked thrilled with herself.

June tried to keep her eyes on her own pot. She wanted to get it just right, then next week she would start on something else. She took her time, crafting it as gently and carefully as she knew how. She was almost ready to take it off the wheel when Poppy burst out laughing at something Flick had said and toppled towards her.

'Watch out!'

June grabbed Poppy's arm, her yell echoing through the room as she tried to push her away from the spinning wheel. But it was too late. The clay pot crumpled on impact. June blinked away tears as she flipped off the switch and stared in disbelief at the remains of her work.

'For god's sake, Poppy! Look what you've done.'

'Oh my god, I'm so sorry. I don't know what happened. I just slipped...'

Poppy babbled her apologies and wrung her hands, causing several people to turn around and stare. Frankly, it was embarrassing the way she went on like that, as if taunting June to overreact.

Flick looked over at her.

'Don't beat yourself up. Accidents happen,' she consoled Poppy. For some reason, that made June even more furious, but she bit back her resentment and looked up at the clock. It was too late to begin another pot now, she might as well start clearing up. She carried her things over to the sink and turned on the tap. Her gaze shifted to the shelf where Poppy had placed her pot. She ran her fingertips along the edge of it, imagining what it would feel like to knock it off. One little nudge and they would be even.

'It's good, isn't it?' said Nadia, from behind her.

June stiffened. She slowly turned around, feeling guilty and exposed at being caught touching Poppy's work.

'It's er... I...' she stammered.

Nadia smiled. 'Your work is good too, June. I look forward to seeing a mug from you, or maybe a teapot?'

June nodded, unable to look away from Nadia's kind eyes as she fought to compose herself.

After class, they headed to the Tipsy Toad. Kimmy and Ralph were there again, wearing matching football shirts.

'Do they do that on purpose?' Poppy asked in a low voice.

'I don't know. I think they're just really in sync,' June said.

Poppy rolled her eyes but didn't say anything. She was probably jealous, June decided, since her own love life was such a disaster area. They bought beers at the bar and headed for Kimmy and Ralph's table.

'Not working tonight?' Ralph said to Poppy.

'No, I'm working tomorrow night instead.'

He nodded and turned his attention back to Kimmy, who proceeded to tell them about some amusing customers she'd had in the shop that day. Flick spotted some friends and went over to talk to them. Meanwhile, Poppy turned her attention to a group of men at the next table. She butted into their conversation, and flashed an alluring smile, then sat down at their table. She kept glancing over at June, signalling her to join them, but there was no way June was going to do that. She kept her head down, feigning immense interest in her packet of salt and vinegar crisps.

Then Poppy raised her voice, and June realised she was arranging a date.

'Perhaps you could bring a friend for my friend?' she suggested, pointing over at June.

June was mortified and shook her head firmly, not wanting any part of it.

Poppy pursed her lips. 'You're no fun,' she said, a little too loudly. June felt her cheeks go red as heads swivelled in her direction. She wasn't sure if it was with anger, or humiliation. Then she thought about the dating sites she had been signed up to and her mouth set in a thin line. None of her friends would have set her up without asking, but all bets were off when it came to Poppy.

Saturday morning, June awoke to the unfamiliar warmth of the sun shining through her bedroom window. She squinted at her phone and realised it was almost ten o'clock. She sprang out of bed and scrambled to get dressed, pushing her feet into her favourite yellow trainers, eager to get down to the market.

As she was buttoning her coat, a loud pounding reverberated through the hallway. She hurried towards the front door, thinking it must be the postman, but when she opened it, she found Poppy standing on the doorstep with armfuls of bags.

'What...'

Poppy blew past her into the house. 'Guess who's been shopping?' she said in a sing-song voice.

June gaped. 'You went to the market without me?'

'Yeah. I popped my head round your door but you were sleeping like a baby.'

June was speechless as she followed her through to the kitchen. Poppy set down her bags and laid out all the groceries on the counter; packets of cheese, sundried tomatoes, croissants, baguettes and sparkling cider.

'I expect there's still some good stuff left if you want to go,' Poppy said generously.

June shook her head. There was no point in her going to the market now.

'You're welcome!' Poppy said. She smiled brightly, then grabbed a can of Coke from the fridge and skipped down to the basement, her blonde hair bouncing behind her. A wave of heat surged through June. She had done this on purpose. She was certain of it.

ELEVEN

JUNE

'What's cooking?' Poppy asked as June snipped some fresh coriander from the plant she had growing on the window sill.

June eyed her housemate warily. 'I'm making coconut curry with rice.'

Poppy tilted her head. 'Is it spicy?'

'It's supposed to be but I make it mild because Kimmy doesn't like spice. I'll slice up some chillies for the rest of us to add.'

Poppy seemed to consider this. 'Sounds yummy. What's in it?'

June indicated the array of ingredients on the table.

'Oh, I don't like mushrooms,' Poppy said. 'Can you put those on the side too?'

June swallowed her annoyance.

'They need to soak up the flavour of the curry. I can keep them big though, so you can pick them out.'

'I suppose so.'

Poppy kept looking at her. She couldn't help having such large eyes, but June found her intense stare unnerving. She moved to the cupboard to get the rice. She was going to cook it with a little saffron. She looked in the spice drawer, but there was no sign of the saffron. She checked all the other drawers and the fridge, but it was nowhere to be found. How frustrating. They couldn't have finished it already. She was pretty sure she was the only one who cooked with it.

Everyone enjoyed the curry, in fact almost everyone had a second helping. June tried not to look at Poppy, who made a big show of picking all the mushrooms out, screwing up her face with distaste each time she found one. She hadn't even used that many. She was sure Poppy was doing it intentionally.

When she had finished, Poppy hopped to her feet.

'My turn to wash up,' she said, and started gathering up plates while the rest of them were still eating. She walked off to the kitchen and made a loud clattering sound.

'She's making that racket on purpose,' June murmured to the others.

Tamsin laughed. 'She's just doing the washing up.'

'At least she's doing her bit,' Kimmy said.

June looked at Flick, but she continued eating, refusing to be drawn into it.

After dinner, June finally caught up on her comedy series with Tamsin. They made hot chocolate, with cream and marsh-mallows, and huddled on the sofa to watch. When the programme ended, June wiped her eyes. 'I don't think I've laughed like that in ages.'

'Me either,' Tamsin agreed.

They headed back to their rooms. June was planning an early night. She picked up her book, telling herself she would just read for half an hour but, before she knew it, it was eleven. She yawned and placed the book on her nightstand, stepped into her slippers and padded down the hallway to the bathroom.

She used the loo, then reached for the toilet roll holder. Her hand stopped short. It was empty. She glanced up at the windowsill. There had been a spare roll up there earlier, but now it was gone. She gritted her teeth. Poppy must have taken it all.

Poppy's light was still on when she came out of the bath-room, and she could hear her music playing. It wasn't especially loud, but when June returned to her room, the volume went up a notch. She climbed into bed and closed her eyes, but every so often, the music would take an unexpected turn and she would be jostled out of her sleep. She threw back her covers and padded out of her room.

She stood at the top of the stairs, one hand on the banister. She hesitated for a moment, then walked down and knocked on Poppy's door.

'Come in,' Poppy called, as if she'd been expecting her.

Poppy looked pleased to see her. Too pleased. June's eyes wandered around the room. The dark walls made sense now. Poppy had lit the place up with twinkling fairy lights. The effect was in fact quite charming. Like entering a secret lair.

'What can I do for you?' Poppy asked with a crocodile's smile.

'The music,' June said. 'It's keeping me awake.'

'Why don't you join me?' Poppy said. 'I've got a nice bottle of wine here.'

'No thanks, I've got work tomorrow.'

'Oh, that's a shame.'

'So, can you turn it down?'

'Yeah, no problem.'

Poppy leaned over and nudged the switch.

'Thank you.'

June returned to her room and got back into bed. She could still hear the music, but it wasn't loud enough to be a problem now. She closed her eyes and drifted off to sleep, only to be awoken by an unexpected drum beat. The music stopped again and she rolled over, too tired to even get annoyed, but once again, she was jolted awake by a sudden burst that stopped as soon as it started.

Fury burning in her chest, she ripped off her covers and stormed out to the hallway. She looked up the stairs to see if anyone else had been disturbed by Poppy's antics, but all the other doors were closed and no lights shone through the cracks. Of course, she was the only one who had to sleep directly above Poppy, and it seemed as though she was set on making her life as difficult as possible. She considered going back down there and demanding Poppy turn it off, but she suspected it wouldn't do much good.

As she crawled back into bed, the pulsating bass rumbled up through her mattress. The notes were sharp and distorted, like an old-fashioned transistor radio. She felt the vibrations in her body, tickling her toes and making her quiver as if tiny electric shocks were running through her bed. And through the noise, she heard the infuriating sound of Poppy's laughter.

She fumbled in her nightstand drawer for her earbuds, threw them into her ears, and hit play on her whale music playlist. But still, the walls rumbled with an incessant vibration that she felt through her whole body. It was as if she were stuck inside a giant engine, and the bass line shook every piece of furniture in the room.

TWELVE

JUNE

June stopped at Sainsbury's on her way home from work. She needed to buy a few ingredients for dinner, including some saffron to replace the jar that had gone missing. She parked her bike beside another cyclist, who was fumbling with his pockets as if he had forgotten something.

'D'you have a lock?' he asked.

She nodded and pulled out the chain from her bag.

'Can I ask you a favour? Would you mind locking your bike to mine? I don't want to leave it out here to get nicked.'

'Okay.'

She knelt down to latch both bikes together.

'What if you come out before me?' she asked.

'Then I'll wait for you.'

She stepped through the automatic doors, her mind on the list of ingredients she had to find.

When she emerged, there he was, leaning against his bike. The corners of his lips curved upwards in a small smile.

'Thanks for letting me use your lock. I owe you one,' he said as she unclasped the chain that bound their bikes together.

'No problem.'

She wiped her palms on her trousers and stowed away her shopping in her saddle bags.

He lingered, fiddling with his helmet strap.

'How about I take you for a coffee to thank you?' he finally asked.

For a moment, all she could think about was getting her groceries home and into the fridge before they spoiled. But when she looked at him, an unexpected warmth flooded her body. She hadn't got a good look at him before but now she saw that he was tall with broad shoulders. He wore a navy-blue T-shirt that hugged his lean frame and his deep brown eyes sparkled.

'Go on, then.'

His grin deepened. 'I didn't get your name.'

'It's June.' She felt the heat on her cheeks.

'Hi June, I'm Dan.'

She followed Dan to a small café, tucked away from the bustle of the common. When they opened the door, she was hit with a wave of warm air that carried the scent of freshly brewed coffee. Dan pulled out a chair for her at one of the small, wobbly tables in the corner.

'What would you like?' he asked.

'Cappuccino, thanks.'

He stood up and made his way to the counter, leaning against it while he waited for their order. The barista placed two white porcelain cups on a tray. Dan paid and carried it over to their table. June thanked him as he set the cups down. Dan inhaled the steam wafting from his drink before taking a sip and resting his elbows on the edge of the table.

Kimmy's voice was in June's head, nagging her to say something and break the awkward silence.

'So, what do you do for a living?' she asked, wondering why that was the only conversation starter she could think of.

'I'm a wildlife photographer.'

'Are you?'

She looked at him, delighted. 'How much wildlife do you find to photograph in London?' She was genuinely curious.

'You'd be surprised. I'm especially fond of urban foxes—they're clever and almost magical the way they manage to thrive in a city like this. But there are also hedgehogs scurrying about the gardens, mice foraging in the rubbish bins, and my personal favourites, pigeons.'

June smiled, trying to figure out if he was serious or if he was pulling her leg.

'I like to get out on the bike,' he said with his next breath. 'I combine the cycling with the photography. It's really just a hobby that grew into a job.'

'How lovely,' she said, impressed.

'Well, I say hobby, but really it's more like an obsession at this point. I spend late nights in my darkroom printing and developing the photos by hand.'

She brought her cup to her lips, feeling the warmth of the creamy liquid as it slipped down her throat. It was a good blend, earthy and sweet. Dan seemed to have words enough for both of them, talking easily about his work. On occasion, she would offer an opinion or chuckle at a funny anecdote.

'You never said what you do,' he said.

He leaned forward, waiting for her reply. She fidgeted with the edge of her shirt as she searched for something, anything, to tell him that was more interesting than being an accountant.

She loved her job, but she knew it wasn't the response he was hoping for.

'What do you think I do?' she asked.

'You're an astronaut?'

She couldn't help but laugh at his enthusiasm.

'Acrobat?'

'Guess again.'

He continued, undeterred by her reaction. 'Cricketer?'

His face was so hopeful she wished it was true.

'I'm sorry, but we'll be closing soon,' the barista said.

Dan smiled apologetically. 'I suppose we'd better get going.'

June nodded, rising from her seat. 'Thank you for the coffee.'

She strode towards the door and reached for the handle when he called her back.

'Wait, June!'

She slowly spun around to face him.

'My bike's locked to yours, remember?' he reminded her.

'Oh, yeah...'

They walked out of the shop, and headed for the lamppost where they had left the bikes. Her fingers closed around the cold metal chain and she undid the lock that connected them together. They disentangled their bikes, and she fiddled with her helmet, pushing a strand of hair out of her eyes as she prepared to leave.

'Bye then,' he said softly.

'Thanks for the coffee.' Her fingers lingered on her strap.

'I didn't get your number.'

She hesitated. Kimmy had drilled it into her that you never gave a man your number. You took his. But then she took in his soft brown eyes. She liked this man. Against her better judgement, she rattled off her number and he programmed it into his phone.

He pocketed his phone and smiled a slow, intimate smile. He stood close enough for her to feel the heat of his body, and his eyes met hers with an intensity that seemed to draw something out of her, but he made no move to kiss her. Finally, he swung one leg over his bike and straddled it, the harsh glare of the streetlights glinting off its metallic frame. He cycled away in the opposite direction, leaving only a hint of his cologne lingering in the cool night air.

June smiled to herself as she watched him disappear. The

sun was low on the horizon and a chill breeze blew through her hair. She quickly mounted her bike and pedalled away, watching the sky change to a deep orange as dusk set in.

As she cycled up her street, a deep bassline thundered out from her house. She quickly locked her bike in the shed and headed up the garden path, praying that the music wasn't coming from inside.

As soon as she walked through the door, she was hit by a wave of laughter, chatter and music. She could barely squeeze into the hallway. People filled every corner; drinking, dancing and talking together in small groups. On the dining room table were paper cups with different coloured drinks. An assortment of crisps and dips had been arranged in small bowls along with plates of pizza.

She shouldered her way through the throng of people. Everyone was having fun, while June felt nothing but rage. People were resting their hands on the walls, leaving sticky marks, traipsing through the house in their shoes. Laughing and shouting to be heard over the music.

She peered into the living room. Kimmy and Ralph sat with a group of strangers, Kimmy's arms gesturing wildly as she told a story. Poppy was perched on the arm of her chair, laughing heartily. Who were all these people? June didn't know any of them. She wanted to tell them all to leave, but she could see she was outnumbered.

She turned and spotted Flick on the stairs. Flick gave her an absent wave. She was in deep conversation with an older man with grey hair. He looked vaguely familiar. She thought he might be a neighbour. She shifted her gaze to the top of the stairs. Tamsin's door was open and she had someone up there. They were kissing passionately in the doorway.

June shook her head in dismay. She had never been much of a party person. But this, a spontaneous gathering without any warning, was unbearable. Why hadn't anyone checked with her that it was okay? Her housemates had never done anything so thoughtless in the past and it didn't take a genius to guess who was behind it.

She turned and found herself looking at a man with soft grey eyes.

'Just arrived, have you?'

June searched her mind for the correct response, which he seemed to take as an invitation to continue talking. 'Can I get you a drink?'

'No.'

It seemed preposterous, the idea that a stranger was offering her a drink in her own home. She felt as though the whole world had gone mad.

Except he wasn't a stranger exactly. There was something familiar about that nose, and the slant of his chin. Had he attended her old French conversation group? Or perhaps he worked at the off licence on the corner. Whatever it was, she couldn't remember.

'I've just started a new job at Stavros, you know the Greek restaurant? The food is delicious. They do tzatziki and gyros and all that.'

June nodded vaguely, her eyes scanning the place, trying to work out what was going on.

'Maybe you'd like to try some of it?' he asked. 'I hear you're a foodie like me?'

She glanced at him with bewilderment. Was this man child asking her out? A giggle bubbled up inside her chest and she burst out laughing. Her house was under siege from a hoard of strangers and this guy wanted to take her out on a date?

His eyebrows knitted together and she realised that wasn't the reaction he'd been expecting.

'Sorry, it's not you. It's... well it's not me either. You caught me off guard. What are you doing here anyway?' She gestured around her. 'What is everyone doing here?'

She pushed her way through the throng of revellers. She could barely even get into the kitchen for all the people in there and she needed to put her lamb chops in the fridge.

'Excuse me!' She shoved her way through, much to the surprise of the couple snogging each other's faces off. She fought her way to the fridge and opened the door. It was crammed full of drinks. She removed a six pack of beers to make room for her groceries. She didn't arrange everything neatly the way she normally did, just shoved it all in and then stormed off, desperate for the sanctity of her bedroom.

A group of girls sat in the hallway, giggling and drinking cups of what looked like punch. They were wearing a lot of make-up, and dressed in achingly fashionable clothes, but June couldn't say for sure if they were grown-ups or schoolgirls. She just hoped they weren't going to be sick all over the landlord's one-of-a-kind Afghan rug.

When she reached her room, she flicked on the light switch, and an ominous yellow glow filled the room, illuminating two strangers intertwined in the centre of her bed. The sheets had been twisted around them like a cocoon, their skin slick with sweat. She stared for a moment, frozen in shock, until the sound of skin slapping against skin cut through the air like a knife. She let out a scream, causing the couple to curse and jump apart.

'Get out!' she shouted, her voice shaking with rage.

The two forms scrambled out of her bed, arms and legs still tangled in the sheets. They grabbed their clothes and stumbled out into the hallway. There were shrieks of laughter and then Poppy's voice echoed off the walls, 'Whose bum was in the air?'

The laughter kept coming until June could no longer stand it. She ripped the sheets off her bed and threw them into the corner of the room. Then she gritted her teeth and grunted as she shoved her heavy chest of drawers in front of the door, creating an obstacle that no one could pass through. Sweat dripping down her forehead, she sank to the ground, exhausted.

Her heart felt like it was pounding out of her chest, and she gasped for air. All the rage she'd ever felt towards Poppy suddenly seemed to swell within her until it threatened to explode from her pores. She had had enough. Poppy had to go.

THIRTEEN

JUNE

June was awake half the night but she didn't venture out of her room until dawn. And then she found it an effort to pull the chest of drawers back from the door, revealing a large scuff mark on the skirting board. The house was finally silent, apart from a faint hum coming from the basement. She walked down the hallway, deliberately stepping on the creaky floorboards. Her housemates had shown her no consideration, so she didn't care if she woke them. In fact, she hoped she did.

Her breath caught in her throat as she saw the state of the living room. There was overturned furniture and broken glass, and cigarette butts littered the floor. She noticed scorch marks on the carpet. There were even smoke marks on the ceiling.

She got out the hoover and dealt with the glass, just to make sure no one hurt themselves. She had no intention of clearing up after them, but she took pleasure in the noise the hoover made. She hoped it woke them all up. They deserved it.

Her eyelids drooped as she sat in her morning meeting. Marilyn droned on while everyone else stared off into space. The only sound in the room was the soft scratching of pens on paper. She felt a jolt of surprise and realised that her pen had moved across the page, leaving an ink trail.

A colleague nudged her, snapping her out of her trance. She sat up straight, legs crossed at the ankles, hands clasped together on her lap. Thankfully, at that moment, an assistant wheeled in a trolley filled with mugs of coffee. June reached for one eagerly, hoping the rich aroma would wake her senses.

Marilyn gestured towards an open spreadsheet on the projector screen and asked June for an explanation of the figures. June's heart sank as foggy thoughts clouded her mind; it was like all the knowledge had been drained from her brain. She could feel every pair of eyes boring into her, and her face burned with shame. She had spent years honing her craft, but today she was unfit for the job.

She cleared her throat, fidgeting with her pen as she scanned her notes. 'Er... these are the figures for this month.' She tapped a column of numbers on the spreadsheet with her finger. 'As you can see, this is what we've spent so far.'

Marilyn frowned. 'And what does the second row indicate? Are those projected figures?'

June stared at the numbers, desperately trying to make sense of them in her head. Her heart sank as she realised her mistake.

'No... I mean, that would be... that's last year's, actually.'

Her face reddened as Marilyn sighed and shook her head. 'Well thank you, June, for making that as clear as mud.'

June stumbled to correct herself, but embarrassment grew like a balloon inside her. She dared a glance up, only to meet the eyes of her colleagues. Some seemed surprised to see her having an off day, while others looked sympathetic. June did not want their sympathy. She wanted to go back to being her super-efficient self.

Later, Gulnara swung by her office.

'How's it going?' she asked.

'Fine,' June said, forcing a smile. Her shoulders tensed as she shifted in the chair. It creaked like an old man getting out of bed. Nothing was going right today. Earlier she had jammed the printer. Now it looked like she'd printed out the wrong version of the documents she needed. She took a deep breath and sifted through the stack of papers on her desk.

'Looks like your profile has been removed from all the dating sites now,' Gulnara said. 'Did you ever get to the bottom of who did it?'

'I have a good idea.' She told Gulnara about Poppy.

Gulnara listened and frowned. 'You need to talk to your housemates.'

'How do I do that? Poppy's always there.'

'You need to make it happen. Seriously. You need to give them an ultimatum. Either Poppy goes or you go. You can't live like that.'

'Do you think?'

Gulnara nodded. 'Stop being so nice. You've given her enough chances. Now you need to get her out.'

Dan rang, just as she was walking out the office door. She paused, looking around to make sure none of her colleagues were eavesdropping.

'You called,' she said, trying to sound casual.

'I wasn't sure how long I was supposed to leave it. I didn't want to crowd you. I'm not very good at these things,' he said, nervousness tingeing his voice.

'Me neither,' she replied, smiling despite herself. It felt good to talk to him – the one bright spot in her otherwise crappy day.

'Look, if you're not doing anything on Friday, do you want to go for dinner?' he asked hesitantly.

'That would be great.'

'How about I come and pick you up, say about eight?'

She paused. 'Actually, I'm having a few issues with my housemates at the moment. Would it be okay if I meet you at the restaurant?'

'Whatever works for you. I'll book somewhere and send you the details.'

'That sounds lovely. I'm looking forward to it.'

The ride home was invigorating. She pedalled hard as the rain poured down, her bike kicking up small sprays of water as she rolled through the puddles. She was so happy Dan had asked her out to dinner and not to watch him play rugby, as one previous boyfriend had suggested, or to go to an escape room as another had done. Half an hour locked up with that bozo had been more than enough.

Buildings blurred as she raced past them. Then she got stuck at a red light and her joy dissipated as she remembered the chaos that awaited her at home.

Queen Anne's Crescent was quiet, in stark contrast to the day before. She wheeled her bike through the alleyway and lingered in the garden, patching up a small puncture and pumping both tyres with air before she locked her bike away for the night.

As she let herself into the house, faint snores echoed through the hallway and she realised most of her housemates were still in their beds. Her stomach dropped as she saw the empty beer cans strewn across the floor.

She stormed down the stairs to the basement, her breath shallow and quick. Her fists pounded against Poppy's door, the sound sharp and angry. The door creaked open, revealing a sickly looking Poppy. Her voice was laboured.

'I'm not feeling too good.'

'I don't care,' June said, her face twisted with anger. 'You kept me awake all night and the house looks like a warzone.'

Poppy recoiled at June's words. 'I'm sorry,' she said, barely able to get the words out. 'I'll clean it up. It's just that I'm feeling so shi—'

'Too right, you will clean up. And replace the bloody loo roll.' June snapped as she spun around and barged out of the room, slamming the door behind her with a bang that reverberated through the walls of the house.

In the kitchen, she looked around in dismay at all the empty bottles and cans. It was supposed to be her turn to cook tonight, but instead she made herself a cheese and ham toastie and slunk off to her room.

Around five o'clock, she heard voices outside her door. There was a knock.

'Can we come in?' Tamsin asked.

June wanted to say no, but her housemates all crowded in, looking incredibly sheepish. Including Poppy.

'Sorry the party got out of hand,' Flick said.

'Why were you even having a party?' June asked. 'It was a weeknight, for goodness' sake, and no one even asked me.' Her gaze landed on Poppy. 'I'm betting it was your idea, right?'

'No, we all got carried away,' Kimmy said. 'Poppy had a couple of friends round, and then Ralph turned up with his mates, and Flick got talking to a neighbour on the steps. It all started spontaneously.'

'We've cleaned up all the mess now,' Tamsin said, as if this was something to be proud of.

'Oh good, you've cleaned up your mess.' June didn't mean to be petty, but she couldn't keep the sarcasm out of her voice.

No one dared speak; they just exchanged awkward glances.

Finally, Kimmy stepped forward, brushing June lightly on the arm.

'We're going to watch *A Nightmare on Elm Street*. Do you want to come and join us?'

June glanced at the window. The thin lace curtains fluttered in the breeze. She didn't feel like spending another night cooped up in her room.

'Alright,' she agreed.

She followed them into the living room. Tamsin brought a spare chair from the dining room and June took back her armchair. She noticed that Poppy waited for her to sit down, then sat on the other side of the room. It was as if she was avoiding any chance of physical contact with her. As if she had some kind of contagious disease.

Her phone buzzed in her pocket. She pulled it out expectantly, hoping it was Dan, and was annoyed to see it was Colin, the guy from DatingLocal. She put it away and watched Poppy out of the corner of her eye, an idea formulating in her mind.

FOURTEEN

JUNE

June's hand pushed against the carved wooden door of The Paper Pantry. As she walked inside, a light tinkling sound resonated through the room. She walked further into the store, feeling small under the soaring shelves reaching up to the high ceiling. The walls were lined with drawers and cabinets filled with all manner of stationery – notebooks in various sizes, pens in every colour, glue sticks, pencil sharpeners and even a few printers. She felt her heart swell at the sight of it all; she could spend hours browsing this shop. There was always so much to look at.

She carefully placed her box of refreshments on the counter – plastic cups of coffee and an array of colourful macarons she had picked up from her favourite bakery. The sweet smell of sugar-coated delicacies wafted through the air.

Kimmy had her back turned, as she rearranged items on the display shelf behind the counter.

'I take it I'm the first to arrive?' June asked softly, not wanting to startle her.

Kimmy turned around. Her brows were furrowed and her eyes seemed a little distant.

'How's business?' June asked.

'A bit slow, to be honest,' Kimmy said, letting out a sigh. 'I sold a few bits with that Valentine's promo but it's been slow again ever since.'

'Why don't you advertise in the local paper or something?'

'Haven't got any budget for that.' She eyed the refreshments June had brought. 'What's all this in aid of anyway?'

June pressed her lips together. 'I'll get into that when the others arrive.'

'Flick's already here. She just went to the loo.'

'Ah, good. Just Tamsin then.'

'You said not to tell Poppy?'

June looked down at her hands. 'That's right.'

'So, I presume this is about her?'

'Let's wait till Tamsin gets here, shall we?'

She took a look around while she waited, tracing her fingers along the shelves, running them over packages of watercolours, oils and acrylics.

'Do you want to go to the cinema on Saturday?' she asked.

'Maybe. I'm not sure what we're doing yet.'

It irritated June that Kimmy always had to consult with Ralph these days. If she wanted to go to the cinema, why didn't she just go? She couldn't imagine deferring to a boyfriend in that way. She bet Dan wouldn't stomach that kind of behaviour. He was way too laid back.

She hid a smile as she thought about him. She was looking forward to their dinner date. She hadn't mentioned him to any of her friends. It was fun to have a little secret. Besides, she didn't know where this was going yet. She didn't want to jinx things.

Tamsin walked in at that moment, wearing a dress over a T-shirt and knee-high socks. On Tamsin, the effect was girlish and cute. If June attempted to wear anything like that, she would look ridiculous.

Flick emerged from the loo and June battled with the airtight seal of the macaron box. Kimmy passed out the coffees then turned to June, her eyes expectant.

'All right, June. Let's hear it.'

June's throat constricted. 'The fact is, I want Poppy out of the house.'

Her friends exchanged uneasy glances.

'Look, I'm not comfortable around her,' she elaborated. 'I don't like her and I don't trust her.'

Kimmy raised an eyebrow.

'It was just one party.'

June shook her head. 'No, this isn't about the party. Or not just about that.'

'Is it because she makes a mess in the kitchen? She's a good cook.'

Tamsin nodded. 'Didn't you enjoy taco night?'

June folded her arms. 'It's not about any of that, although I do find her noise and mess intolerable. It's about the way she is with me. There's an atmosphere. I don't like the way she looks at me. I don't feel safe in my own home. She gives me the creeps.'

Nobody blinked.

'I haven't noticed anything,' Flick said.

'Me neither,' said Tamsin.

June tried to keep her voice level. 'That's because she's fine with all of you. It's me she's got it in for.'

'I have to say, June, you're sounding a bit paranoid.' Tamsin didn't look at her as she made this accusation.

June threw up her hands. 'I know how it sounds but you've got to trust me on this. How long have you known me?'

There was silence. Kimmy took a macaron and popped it in her mouth.

'I mean, she is paying her share of the rent,' Flick said. 'Even if we wanted her out, we'd still have to give her notice.'

'Let's do that then,' June said.

'It would be really awkward,' Tamsin said. 'We'd have to live with her for another month or two while she found a new place. You can't just chuck her out on the street.'

'I'll deal with it.' June was getting desperate by this stage. 'I'll help her find a new house, pack, move, whatever it takes. I'm sorry, but I can't live with her any longer.'

Flick scratched her head. 'This all seems a bit over the top, June. Are you sure you and Poppy can't work things out? Maybe spend a bit of time together. You might find you have stuff in common.'

June folded her arms across her chest. 'I'm telling you, I'm getting a bad vibe off her.'

'How about we give it a couple more weeks?' Flick said. 'Maybe till the end of the month. See if things improve?'

The others were nodding.

'They're not going to improve,' June said, jaw clenched. 'I swear, she hates me.'

None of them looked convinced. It was infuriating. They were supposed to be her friends, not Poppy's.

'Kimmy?'

She looked at her oldest friend. If she couldn't make Kimmy understand, then she really was doomed.

'Alright.' Kimmy steepled her hands in front of her face. 'If we agree to this, then you've got to be the one to tell her, June. And you've got to find us a new housemate, do you understand?'

'Yes!' June said, trying not to sound too eager.

The others looked at each other unhappily and June pushed the macarons towards them, sealing the deal.

They headed home together. Poppy was not there.

'She just texted to say she's working late tonight,' Flick said, looking at her phone.

'Oh,' June said, feeling deflated. She didn't know how she

was going to get through the evening. She wanted to give Poppy her marching orders. The sooner the better.

She couldn't relax all evening. Now that she'd got the go-ahead, she just wanted to get it over and done with. It was infuriating the way Poppy worked such odd hours. She never knew when she was going to be in or out.

She considered biking over to the Tipsy Toad, but then she thought better of it. What if Poppy took the news badly? She could hardly have her burst into tears at work. If she knew anything about Poppy, it was that she wasn't going to take this lightly. There was going to be drama, and June would be right at the centre of it. She just didn't know if she would shout or cry.

To her great annoyance, Poppy was still not home by half eleven so June ended up going to bed and even then she lay under the duvet, waiting for the sounds of her noisy housemate. But for once, Poppy didn't make a sound.

All day at work the next day she practised what she would say in her head.

'Poppy. I'm sorry but it's not working out.' She imagined Poppy's disgruntled face. She would probably lose her temper. She might even throw something, but if she did, that would just prove her point.

She cycled home faster than usual. She felt a little nauseous as she arrived home. She set her bag down on the coffee table and walked through the house, noting that Poppy's coat was on its hook. Good.

Taking a deep breath to steel herself, she marched down the stairs to Poppy's room and knocked on the door.

There was no answer. June was infuriated. Was Poppy deliberately ignoring her? Had she somehow discovered this was about to happen? It wouldn't surprise her if she'd overheard the other housemates talking about it. Subtlety wasn't exactly their strong point.

She knocked again, more aggressively, but Poppy still did not answer. June pushed open the door and looked inside. The aubergine walls had changed once again and were now a deep shade of blue. It was an improvement, even if Poppy had dripped blue paint over the desk and wardrobe. She'd have to sand that off before the new housemate moved in.

The room was otherwise untidy. There were clothes strewn all over the floor but she supposed it was no worse than Flick's room. There was no sign of Poppy. Annoyed, June left the room and stomped back up the steps, almost colliding with Poppy as she came out of the bathroom.

'Poppy!' she said.

Her carefully rehearsed phrasing went straight out of her head.

'I'm sorry but it's not working out. I'm going to have to ask you to leave the house. Of course, you can stay while you find a new place and I will be happy to help you—'

Before June could finish her spiel, Poppy let out a piercing scream that echoed through the house. To June's amazement, she lunged backwards, teetering on the edge of the steps. Her eyes were wide with panic as she searched for something to grab onto. With a loud crack, her body hit each step until finally she crashed to the bottom with a heavy thud.

FIFTEEN

JUNE

'Poppy!' June hadn't realised Flick was standing behind her. She must have just come out of the bathroom. She took a step forward and they both peered down the stairs.

Poppy's screams grew louder and more anguished. She lay on her back, her eyes wide and dramatic.

'Oh, for goodness' sake, can't you see she's faking?' June started down the stairs. 'Alright, Poppy, you can get up now. Stop pretending.'

But the closer she got, the worse Poppy looked. Her face was deathly pale, and her right arm stuck out at a sickening angle.

Kimmy ran into the room. 'What's going on?'

Flick's forehead creased in confusion. She looked down the stairs at Poppy, who stared up at them in a daze.

'She and June were arguing. The next thing I knew, Poppy went flying down the stairs.'

Kimmy stepped closer to June, her voice low yet accusing. 'What did you do?'

A single bead of sweat trickled down June's neck. For a moment, she was too shocked to speak. Flick seemed to come to her senses. She hurried down the steps, with Kimmy right behind. June sank down onto the top step, too shocked to speak.

She ran over and over the accident in her head. She had been concentrating so hard on what she was going to say that she had barely looked at Poppy. Barely noticed that she was standing at the top of the stairs. She could kick herself now, because it had been a foolish, ill-conceived place to have a serious conversation. All the same, she was certain she hadn't touched Poppy. She hadn't even got that close.

She had no reason to do it. Everything was going her way. Her housemates had agreed she could boot her out. She had got what she wanted.

She watched as Flick knelt on the ground, speaking softly while Kimmy shuffled round beside her. They talked in low, soothing voices as they checked the damage. June saw Poppy flinch when Kimmy got too close to her injured arm.

'We need to get you to A&E,' Kimmy told Poppy. She looked back at June. 'Don't just sit there, get her some painkillers to take the edge off.'

June staggered to her feet and grabbed the first aid box from the kitchen, pulling out a pack of ibuprofen. When she returned, Kimmy and Flick were helping Poppy to her feet. She looked terrible; pale and trembling.

June started down the stairs and handed over the pills.

'Can you get her some water?' Flick asked.

'Please,' Poppy said faintly.

June stared at her for a moment. It was as if this weak, pathetic specimen was a completely different person from the one she'd been talking to just a few minutes ago. She returned to the kitchen and found a glass, filling it from the tap while she listened to what was happening. Poppy cried out as they tried to get her up the stairs. If she was acting, she was incredibly good at it. June could only assume she had actually hurt herself.

She returned with the water and handed it to Flick. She

didn't want to go anywhere near Poppy. She didn't know whether to be angry or scared. They all waited while Poppy swallowed down the pills, which she did without a word. Then she slowly climbed the stairs with Flick and Kimmy hovering close by in case she fell again.

June watched as she made it to the top and shuffled past her, towards the door.

'I really didn't do anything,' she called after them.

No one answered. Either they were too intent on getting Poppy to the hospital or they simply didn't believe her.

After they left, June sat alone in the living room, her fingers tightly gripping the armrests of her chair, her mind a storm of worry. She jumped at the sound of the door handle turning, and snapped her head up to see Tamsin in the doorway, guitar swinging from a strap on her shoulder. Her dark eyes shifted across the room with uncertainty.

June opened her mouth to tell her what had happened, but then she realised that someone must have already told her, because she fixed her with a long, stern look.

'What the hell happened?' she asked.

'One minute we were talking, the next she was falling down the stairs. I don't know if she did it on purpose or if she tripped.'

'Of course she didn't do it on purpose!' Tamsin said. 'That would be crazy.'

'Well, I didn't push her,' June said firmly.

Tamsin said nothing.

'I didn't!' June called after her, as she trudged up to her room.

After a few minutes, a sombre melody echoed down the stairs. June slumped back in her chair, burying her face in her hands. She clamped her teeth shut and exhaled through her nose. She was so frustrated, she wanted to scream. Instead, she stood up abruptly. She couldn't just sit around waiting. She needed to do something. She was hardly in the mood to cook but someone had to.

She stalked into the kitchen, pulled out a baking dish, and tossed in some chicken breasts. She sprinkled them with rosemary and oil. She slid the tray into the oven and grabbed a pot so she could prepare the rice.

'Hey, where's the saffron?'

She rummaged through the spice drawer but it was nowhere to be found. Not in the baking drawer either. Or the fridge. For goodness' sake. This was getting ridiculous.

She made the rice without saffron. When it was ready, she called up the stairs to Tamsin, 'Dinner's ready!'

Silence followed, and it was a relief when she finally heard a door open and footsteps on the stairs.

The two of them ate at the kitchen table, since they had no idea how long the others were going to be.

Tamsin took a bite of chicken and chewed it slowly. 'This is really good, June.'

June smiled tersely, but things still felt weird between them. Tamsin kept looking at her with big mournful eyes.

'I didn't do anything! Poppy should have been more careful.'

Tamsin threw her hands up. 'I wasn't there.'

'But you believe me, don't you?'

Tamsin hesitated for a fraction of a second. 'Of course I do.'

June slowly chewed her food, pushing it around with her fork. She didn't feel like eating any more so she pushed away her plate and stood up. She left Tamsin to wash up and trudged into the living room. She switched on the TV and the set lit up, displaying an image of a colony of ants swarming over a dirt mound. She'd been meaning to watch this documentary, but her entire being was consumed with a seething anger that burned like fire in her veins. All she could think about was what Poppy had done. Of all the crazy, manipulative tricks. How could her friends believe her, even for a minute? It was like they didn't know her at all.

Her housemates arrived back just after nine. Poppy looked a lot brighter. The colour had returned to her cheeks and her arm was now in plaster.

'It's broken in two places,' she announced, as Tamsin examined it.

June dished up dinner for the three of them and they ate hungrily, but no one would make eye contact with her. Kimmy kept darting looks at her and Flick kept the conversation going all by herself, talking about some hot guy she'd got talking to in the waiting room.

Once the plates were cleared away, everyone gathered around to sign their names in bright colours on Poppy's cast. Kimmy handed her the pen and June looked at Poppy awkwardly.

'Just sign your name if you can't think of anything,' Poppy said.

'You should do one of your little doodles,' Tamsin suggested.

So June drew a bright yellow sunflower and a watering can, pouring water over it. 'Get well soon,' she wrote underneath.

They headed into the living room and Poppy took the armchair. June squished onto the sofa beside Kimmy but her friend's body felt rigid beside her. She kept darting looks at her and she got the sense they were all waiting for her to say or do something. Then Poppy went to the toilet and everyone inched closer.

'I think you should apologise to Poppy,' Kimmy said.

June felt her cheeks go red. 'But I didn't do anything!' She looked at Flick. 'Tell her.'

'I wasn't wearing my contacts,' Flick admitted. 'It was all a bit of a blur.'

June shook her head in disbelief and stormed off to her room. She took to her bed, the scene playing over and over. She saw Poppy inch backwards, grasp the air and tumble down the stairs. It had all happened so fast. She hadn't done it. She hadn't meant to do it. They were the same thing, weren't they?

There was a knock at her door and Kimmy came in. She sat down on the end of her bed.

'You've got to believe me,' June said.

Kimmy was silent for a moment. Then she looked June right in the eye.

'You didn't push Poppy, and you didn't push your mum either.'

June's bottom lip trembled.

'This is completely different.'

Kimmy's brown eyes darkened. 'Is it?'

SIXTEEN

JUNE

Sixteen Years Ago

'It's my birthday. I should get to do what I want,' June ranted.

What she wanted was to catch the bus into town with Kimmy to spend her birthday money and get a milkshake at their favourite café.

'I don't understand why you can't,' Kimmy said.

'Because Mum's making me go out for lunch with Gran and she takes ages trying to find something on the menu she can stomach. I swear she reads it at least five times before ordering, and then she takes an eternity to eat. By the time we get home all the shops will be closed.'

Kimmy reached her arm into the depths of her bag, shuffling textbooks and a coloured pencil case aside. She smiled triumphantly as she brought out a brightly wrapped parcel.

'Here, I got you this.'

'For me?'

The wrapping paper was bubble-gum pink but June didn't hold that against her. She unwrapped it, flattening it out so it could be reused. She picked up the sleek new black backpack, then lifted her gaze to Kimmy, who was watching her eagerly.

'Why did you get me this?' she asked, examining the backpack as if it were some kind of alien artefact.

'Because it's your birthday.'

'But why a backpack?'

'Because you can't go round with that *Power Rangers* one any longer,' Kimmy said, wearily.

June felt her cheeks grow hot. 'What's wrong with *Power Rangers*?'

'There's nothing wrong with them, but kids are going to laugh at you if you're still using that in Year Six.'

'I like it.'

'I know you do and it's fine at home, but you need to grow up a bit. It's important to fit in.'

June shrugged. She didn't understand fashion. Why was everyone so obsessed with being the same as everyone else? *Power Rangers* was her favourite programme. She watched it every day when she got home from school, often the exact same episode. She bet she wasn't the only one who still liked it. It was just the other kids lied and pretended they all liked the same things. Like Kimmy pretending she was into Girls Aloud when June knew for a fact she preferred Coldplay.

'Well thanks,' June said, remembering her manners. 'I guess I'd better go and get changed. Mum's bought me a hideous new outfit.'

'Come and knock for me when you get home,' Kimmy said. 'You never know. There might still be time to go out.'

'I doubt it.'

June picked up her backpack and stomped indoors to get ready.

She headed into the kitchen, hoping to find a biscuit or something to keep her going.

She looked in the cupboard but, of course, there were no biscuits. She reached for a handful of peanuts.

'What are you doing?'

She whirled around to find her mum watching her, hands on her hips.

June blinked. Wasn't it obvious? 'Getting a snack?'

'We are going out for lunch in ten minutes. You're supposed to be getting ready, not filling up on junk.'

'It's just a handful of nuts.'

'Doesn't matter, go and get ready. Your new dress is on your bed.'

June shut the cupboard door. There was no point arguing. There was never any justice in their house. It was her mother's way or the highway.

She stomped up the stairs with tears welling in her eyes. There was no use appealing to her father, either. He always backed up everything her mother said. Sometimes, June wondered if her mum had complete control of his mind.

She went into her bedroom and stared at her new dress with dismay. It was revolting. She'd asked for something yellow, but this wasn't yellow. It was a hideous mustard colour. She guessed her mother had bought it because it was fashionable, never mind that it would make June look like a walking hotdog.

She unzipped the back of the dress and stepped into it. The ugly fabric clung to her body like a second skin, drawing her in at the waist before cascading down her legs in a puffy A-line. She grimaced at her reflection in the mirror and wished she could just wear her jeans.

Taking one last look, she resigned herself to a tedious lunch, knowing full well that if she didn't show up, both her mother and grandmother would give her an earful.

She clomped down the stairs and planted her feet into the plush living room carpet. Her mother was dressed in a distinguished cream dress with intricate pleats and delicate buttons.

She had on towering beige stilettos that made her seem even taller than usual. June couldn't comprehend how anyone could walk around in heels like that – it must feel like she was walking on stilts.

'You look lovely, darling. So mature!'

June knew her mum was attempting to sweeten her up after their last uncomfortable conversation but she wasn't interested in reconciliation. All she wanted was to get lunch over with so that she could enjoy the rest of her birthday.

They stepped outside. Her mother locked the door and gave June an expectant glance before setting off. She trailed behind, feeling bitter and resentful. She looked down at her dress. In the harsh glare of the sunlight, it seemed to clash with every blade of grass as they walked across the lawn. Her mother had a spring in her step as she led the way, while June dragged her feet, feeling like she was being led to her execution.

She waved to Kimmy, who was perched on the swing in the centre of next-door's garden. She made a face, indicating how much she hated her dress. Kimmy smiled sympathetically, but knowing her, she probably liked it. Kimmy cared about things like fashion and even read some of the same magazines as June's mother. It was amazing they were such good friends.

'Have a nice lunch,' Kimmy called. 'I'll see you later.'

June nodded and scurried after her mother. How she walked so fast in those heels was a mystery. A bus rounded the corner and June quickened her step.

'Mum, wait!'

She dashed down the path, trying to keep pace with her mother, annoyed that she wouldn't wait. It took a moment or so to catch up with her, but by then June was sticky and panting. Deliberately, she collided with her, shoving her from behind. Her mum stumbled forward clumsily, her six-inch heels slipping out from under her body. June's gaze followed the path of a bus as it lumbered down the road toward them. Shrieks of terror rose around her but, for June, it felt as though what happened next was taking place in a film. She felt completely detached as her mother bounced off the windscreen like a ragdoll. It was only when she landed with a thud on the tarmac that June snapped back to reality. She gaped at the sight of her mother's sturdy frame, lying like litter in the street.

There was a moment of hush. Her mother lay still in the road, her eyes glazed over. June watched helplessly as people gathered around them. It all happened so fast, she couldn't take it in. She did not utter a word until she felt Kimmy embrace her.

'What did you do?' she whispered in her ear.

Hours later, June's father sat with her in the hospital waiting room, his eyes trained on the clock as if willing time to move faster. He barely acknowledged June when she tried to explain what had happened, shooting her a cold look that chilled her to the bone.

'You're ten years old,' he said gruffly. 'That's the age of criminal responsibility. You'll be lucky if they don't lock you up and throw away the key.'

June buried her head in her hands and prayed that her mother would be okay. She replayed the accident over and over in her head, unable to get it right. She had only meant to give her mum a bit of a jolt. It had never occurred to her that there would be such severe consequences for her childish action.

Her father was pacing up and down when the doctor emerged from the other room. He offered June a sympathetic smile before turning to her father and delivering the bad news. Her father sank into a chair, sobbing, as the doctor explained that her mother had severely damaged her spine and it would be highly unlikely she would be able to walk again.

. . .

For the next few weeks, June and her father floated about the house like ghosts. If they happened to pass in the hallway, he barely seemed to notice she was there. They lived on casseroles supplied by the neighbours because her father wasn't much of a cook, and everything centred around visiting her mother in hospital. She dreaded those visits. Seeing her mother covered in tubes and wires, and her father left to do all the talking. Every time she entered the hospital, she felt as though everyone was looking at her. Everyone knew what she'd done.

Then, one day, they arrived to find they had unhooked her from the monitoring machines, and propped her up in her bed. The colour had returned to her cheeks and she looked more like herself than she had in weeks.

'You look much better,' June said.

Her mother smiled, her eyes glistening with tears.

'You have to understand that the damage is permanent,' her father said gravely. 'Your mother can't come home until we get the house adapted for the wheelchair.'

Her parents exchanged a meaningful glance.

'We've talked it over and we think it would be best if you went off to St Winifred's for a while,' her father said.

'St... where's that?'

'St Winifred's. It's an all-girl boarding school down in Devon.'

June swallowed, her brain struggling to take this in.

'I know it's a big change but your mother won't be able to look after you. She's going to need to focus all her energy on her recovery.'

June stared at her father in shock, but once his words sank in, they lit a fire in her chest. She would finally have some distance between herself and her parents, and unlimited time to focus on her studies. She didn't know if her parents were bluffing, or if they genuinely wanted to send her away, but when she showed enthusiasm for the idea, her father's face turned red in disbelief. He went ahead and made the arrangements.

People felt sorry for her when they heard she was being sent off to boarding school. Some judged her parents for sending her away. But whilst June was deeply ashamed of the accident she'd caused, she felt as though her life was just beginning.

SEVENTEEN

JUNE

When June arrived at the Lagos restaurant on Friday night, Dan was already waiting outside. He wore a crisp white shirt that highlighted his muscular arms and broad shoulders, and his hair was freshly combed. She stopped short, a wave of nervous energy washing over her. When he saw her, his face broke into a smile.

'You came!'

She allowed herself a smile. 'You too.'

'I guess we should go inside then?'

A gentle breeze caressed her skin as he held open the door for her and they stepped inside. The waiter led them to a table near the window overlooking the street. He pulled out a chair for her and she sat down, taking in the spicy aroma.

'What kind of cuisine is this?' she asked.

'Nigerian. Have you tried it before?'

She shook her head, her hair bouncing around her shoulders. 'Can't say I have but I'm excited to try it.'

The waiter returned and they ordered wine, then studied the menu intently.

'Have you ever tried goat stew?' Dan asked. 'They do it really well here. I'll order some and you can try it if you like.'

'Okay. I think I'll go for the beef skewers.'

He nodded approvingly. 'Oh yes, those are good.'

Once their orders had been placed, he leaned back in his chair and looked into her eyes.

'It's so nice to meet someone who likes to try new foods. My friends have very plain tastes.'

'Yeah, I have the same problem. Most of my friends think scallops are exotic.'

He shook his head. 'Don't get me started on seafood. It boils my blood how we send most of our British fish abroad. I mean, what is the point of living on an island if we don't reap the bounty?'

'I couldn't agree more.'

The waiter arrived with two tall glasses of ogogoro. They each took one and their eyes locked as they toasted each other. The smell of honey and spice drifted up to June's nose as she took her first sip. She blinked in surprise at the unexpected sharpness on her tongue. The taste reminded her of gin.

'What do you think?' Dan asked.

'I think this stuff could get me very drunk.'

'Just as well you've got me to carry you home.'

She hid a smile. He was trying too hard, but it was endearing.

'So how have you been?' he asked.

She let out a sigh and told him about Poppy throwing herself down the stairs.

His eyebrows shot up and his mouth gaped slightly. 'My god, the woman sounds a bit unhinged.'

'You're not wrong. The worst part is, I was giving her her notice when she fell. Now my housemates say it would be bad to throw her out when she's injured. I'm sure some of them think I really did push her. I can feel their eyes on me whenever we're in the same room. She's got them all wrapped around her little finger.'

Dan shook his head. 'You need to be careful,' he said. 'If I were you, I'd stay out of her way as much as possible.'

'Believe me, I'm trying. It isn't easy when we live under the same roof. And now she's off work for a bit, so she's constantly at home. I can't make a cup of tea without her suddenly appearing in the kitchen, watching me. It gives me the creeps.'

'I'm so lucky that I've only got the one housemate. Kelvin's really easy going.'

'Yeah, you'd better hope he never moves out.'

The waiter brought over two large plates of food and June waited impatiently as he explained what was in each dish. As soon as he left, she reached for one of her tender beef skewers and sampled it, delighted at the burst of flavour on her tongue.

'You have to try this,' Dan said with enthusiasm.

She reached across and took a spoonful of his stew. The smell of smoky onions and herbs tickled her nose as she tasted it – the flavour was complex with a hint of sweetness from the tomatoes.

'Have a bit more,' he said, seeing that she liked it.

'You have to try my skewers.'

They indulged in each other's dishes until they were so full that neither of them had room for dessert.

Dan waved to the waiter to bring the bill. She let him pay, just this once. If there was a second date, she would insist on paying.

They stepped out of the restaurant and the night air was cool against their skin as they walked down the high street. The moon was half-hidden behind a blanket of clouds, casting shadows across the road.

'You don't have to walk all the way with me,' she said, but he just smiled and took her hand.

They passed the tube and took the turning towards Queen Anne's Crescent.

'This is me,' she said, when they reached her house.

They paused for a moment on the doorstep; then he leaned in and brushed his lips against hers. June felt a cascade of tingly warmth bubbling up inside her chest and she wondered if she should ask him in, but then he took a step back.

'I've had a lovely evening,' he said. 'If it's alright with you, I'll call you and we can talk about where we want to go next time.'

'I'd like that.'

She watched him walk away, and she stood there for a moment, smiling as he headed up the street.

But when she opened her front door, the warmth that normally filled the house felt absent. She peered into the living room and found all her housemates relaxing in front of the TV. They were completely absorbed in the programme they were watching and she couldn't help but notice that Poppy was once again sitting in her favourite armchair.

'Evening,' she called from the doorway, but no one seemed to hear her.

She had the weirdest feeling, like she had been replaced.

There was one upside to Poppy's injury. When Tuesday rolled around, Poppy stayed home while Flick and June got ready to go to pottery. June couldn't help but feel triumphant as they walked out the door but Flick didn't share her glee.

'Poor Poppy. She was just getting into the pottery. It sucks that she can't take part.'

'Yeah, but she can hardly spin a pot with one hand.'

They walked on in silence. June had been looking forward to having this time together but Flick seemed unable to move on from Poppy's accident. It was all anyone would talk about.

'You know, she's not going to be able to work for a few weeks, and if she can't work, she can't pay the rent,' Flick said.

'True,' June said. 'Perhaps she should have thought of that.'

Flick grew silent for a while but June understood what she was hinting at. She thought June was at least partly to blame for Poppy's accident and, therefore, she should help Poppy pay her rent. If she really had been responsible, she would agree, but Poppy had done it to herself. She hadn't had anything to do with it. She was almost certain.

They arrived at Mud and Mingle and Nadia called her over before she could get out her wheel.

'June, what are you going to make this week?'

She considered. 'I was thinking of trying a mug.'

'Very good. For a moment, I thought you were going to make another pot.'

They both laughed, but June had indeed intended to make another pot. Now she would have to rethink things. She didn't want Nadia to think she was nuts.

As she headed towards her table, she saw that another student was already occupying Flick's usual workspace. She wanted to say something, but Flick was talking to someone so she would have to wait.

The other student smiled politely and June nodded back at her. Anxiety churned in her stomach. That was Flick's seat. She glanced back at Flick and saw that she was now talking to someone else. For goodness' sake, when was she going to come over?

She went and found all her supplies and laid them out on her desk. She kept looking over at Flick, trying to signal to her to come over but she couldn't catch her eye. Beside her, the person in Flick's seat was already preparing her clay. She was going to start spinning her pot any minute, and then it would be too late for her to switch places.

Flick finally glanced over and June sent her a pointed look

but Flick merely shrugged and indicated that she would stay where she was. June's eyes stung with disappointment as she watched her friend across the room. She didn't just come to this class to make pottery. She also valued the time she got to spend with Flick. It seemed as though even when Poppy wasn't around, she still somehow managed to drive a wedge between them.

With a sigh, June rolled out a lump of clay, quickly moulding it into an oval shape before beginning to taper it in. Her concentration was intense as she worked her thumbs over the curved surface. The scent of wet clay filled her nostrils and she looked at it thoughtfully. A mug was basically a pot with a handle wasn't it? She would start by making her usual pot, and maybe this time she would get it just right.

'Are you going to the pub?' she asked at the end of the class, as she and Flick placed their creations on the shelf for safe-keeping.

'No, I'm meeting my brother tonight.'

June's eyes narrowed. 'Okay,' she said softly.

The two women stepped out onto the street. June watched sadly as Flick trudged off towards the tube station. She knew things weren't right between them but had no idea how to make it better.

EIGHTEEN

JUNE

Eight Weeks Later

June kicked her bike into gear and pedalled down the road after Dan. The neighbourhood was alive with energy as they whizzed past buildings and shop fronts. After a while, the horizon opened up to reveal rolling hills, dotted with sheep and trees that branched out against the bright blue sky.

'Pub alert!' Dan bellowed, as he caught sight of a white building nestled in the valley below.

They coasted down the winding country lane, the sun warming their skin as they pulled into the car park. They hopped off their bikes and locked them in front of the pub.

Dan tugged June's hand, pulling her close. The warmth of his body seeped into hers as their lips met and she wound her arms around his neck.

Dan was the first to back off. 'Ahem. I think we'd better sit down before we get carried away.'

June laughed and shook her head in amusement. They reluctantly pulled away from each other and wandered over to one of the picnic tables scattered around the pub garden. There was a menu tucked into a metal holder. She looked at it briefly.

'I'll have the chicken,' she decided.

'Sounds good,' he said.

He went inside to place their order. He returned with a cold pint in each hand and set them on the table before taking her hands in his own. They sat in contented silence. She couldn't remember ever being so comfortable in a relationship.

With Dan, there was no need to make excuses if she wanted to stay inside all day instead of going out. He understood completely and didn't demand anything from her. He also had his own hobbies and passions that kept him busy. For the first time in her life, she could have a relationship without having to compromise who she was.

Their food came, and she had a moment of regret as she saw how delicious his lamb looked.

'Here, try some,' he said, cutting a sizeable chunk off for her.

June grinned at how well he understood her.

Once they'd finished their meal, they rode further into the countryside. They came across a lush expanse of trees, and Dan stopped his bike to take out his camera. June pedalled a little further until she spotted a patch of mushrooms. She hopped off her bike and crouched down to investigate. She carefully lifted a slender, funnel-shaped cap and inspected its underside. Tiny pores dotted its surface, telling her that these were edible fungi. A wry smile crept across her face as she recalled how she had first got into foraging – as a sullen child who would rather find her own food than eat lunch at home.

They rode on a little further until the trees became too dense. Then they hopped off their bikes and leant them either side of a sturdy oak tree. Holding hands, they pushed through dense foliage onto a path that seemed to stretch on into infinity. Finally, they arrived at a lush green clearing full of tall grasses that waved gently against the wind, and wildflowers in pink and yellow. In the distance, June spotted movement and held her breath. There was a fawn grazing in the meadow. Dan dropped her hand and slowly reached into his jacket for his camera. He took four or five shots before the fawn lifted its head and bounded away out of sight.

He turned and looked at her, excitement shining in his eyes.

'Did you plan that?' she asked.

'Oh yes. I rang the deer earlier and asked if it could make an appearance.'

June grinned. 'Well, consider me impressed.'

He leaned forward and pressed his lips to hers. The clearing seemed like a pretty good place to kiss, too.

When they arrived back in Clapham, a funfair was being set up on the common. Flagpoles with banners that blew in the breeze, and red, blue and yellow tents had been erected.

'Do you fancy going to that later?' she asked Dan.

'Sure, why not?'

'My housemates will want to go.'

His brow furrowed. 'Don't you think it's about time I met them? You can't keep me a secret forever.'

'I know.' She forced a smile.

The atmosphere at home was still a little strained. With her arm in plaster, Poppy hadn't been able to do much cooking these past few weeks, and she'd calmed down on the partying too. Since they still couldn't agree on what had happened that day, the other housemates avoided the topic like the plague. No one had mentioned Poppy moving out again and June had given up on the idea for now. In the meantime, she avoided her as much as she could, preferring to spend her time in her room when she wasn't out with Dan or at work. But there had been no major incidents. Poppy had not played her music especially loud and she had stopped hanging around outside June's bedroom. If June didn't know better, she'd have said Poppy was scared of her.

It was dark when June walked down to the common with Flick, Tamsin and Poppy. It felt like old times. They were all in high spirits, making silly jokes and talking about what rides they wanted to go on. As they reached the fair, they could hear the sounds of laughter and screaming as people flew in all directions on the rides.

They paid the entrance fee and stepped inside, breathing in the delicious smells of popcorn and candy floss. Poppy skipped ahead, spinning around with joy now that her arm was finally free of its cast. She quickly set about making up for lost time, chucking balls at the coconut shy before moving onto the shooting range where she took aim at the plastic ducks.

Squeals of delight escaped from the whirling teacups as riders were spun around in circles. A carousel of hand-painted horses galloped along to the sound of cheerful music. Inflatable slides swayed in the wind, while a towering Ferris wheel spun around slowly, its multicoloured bulbs glistening against the night sky.

June spotted Kimmy and Ralph on the rollercoaster. Kimmy waved and shrieked as they rounded a sharp corner.

'We should do that!' Poppy squealed.

'You go ahead,' June said quickly. She felt sick just watching.

'I'll go on with you,' Flick said. 'But first I need food.'

They stopped at a van and everyone bought hot dogs and candy floss.

Kimmy walked over to join them. She looked lovely with her new green scarf, her cheeks pink from exertion.

'You okay?' Tamsin said.

'Yeah. That rollercoaster was amazing!' Kimmy said.

'Where did Ralph get to?'

'He just spotted some friends. Does anybody want to hook a duck?'

Before June could reply, Dan arrived. He was wearing a brown leather jacket and he smelt clean and fresh as he pulled her towards him.

'Found you!'

'Hey, who's this?' Kimmy asked, her eyes almost popping out of her head.

'This is Dan,' June said.

Dan smiled politely whilst her friends looked him up and down, assessing him like a show pony.

'Hi, I'm Poppy,' Poppy chirped.

'Where have you been hiding him?' Tamsin wanted to know.

June shifted her weight. 'Dan's into cycling,' she said.

She was sort of enjoying the attention. She could see her friends were truly shocked to see she had scored such a catch. Dan wasn't classically handsome in the way Ralph was, but he had an easy smile and a gentle nature that was very attractive.

'Right, shall we go and take a look around?' she said to Dan.

He nodded.

'It was nice to meet you all,' he said to her friends. He took her hand and they weaved their way through the crowded pathways, taking in the sights and sounds. The air was filled with laughter and music from various rides. Everywhere they looked there were stalls of novelty toys, brightly lit games like ring toss and the sight of people enjoying themselves.

He led her to the spinning ride. 'If you're going to try one ride, please try this one,' he said. 'It's my favourite.'

June swallowed. It was one of the rides Poppy had tried to get her to go on. 'Oh, go on then.'

They fumbled with the straps of the seat before they were securely in place. The ride lurched forward, spinning them at increasing speed. June's stomach felt like it was doing somer-saults as she clung on for dear life. Then she spotted Tamsin and Poppy on the opposite side. They were both shrieking in delight and throwing their arms up in exhilaration. When the ride came to a halt, June wobbled unsteadily, her head reeling as she climbed down.

'I'm not doing that one again,' she declared, clutching her stomach.

'What would you like to do then?'

'How about the bumper cars?'

'I think they're dodgems,' Dan said.

'What's the difference?'

'You're supposed to avoid crashing into each other.'

'Well, that's no fun.'

They stood in the queue and watched.

'Do you want to share a car?' Dan asked.

'No way!'

He chuckled. 'Okay then.'

She blushed. 'No, I mean I've already chosen which one I want.'

She tapped her foot impatiently. He pulled her towards him, providing the perfect distraction. When she turned back to the bumper cars, people were clambering out and walking in wobbly lines towards the exit.

When everyone had got off, a fairground worker waved them in. Dan climbed into a red car, while June swung open the door of a bright yellow one and settled into the driver's seat. They listened to loud thumping music for a while as they waited for more people to get in. At the very last minute, Flick, Tamsin and Poppy ran onto the ride and climbed into the last three cars. There was a moment's pause, while they grappled with their seat belts, then the attendant raised his hand and the cars started to move.

June felt the wind in her hair as she whipped her car around the track. She spotted Poppy zooming towards her, the crazy cow. Quickly, she ducked out of the way, feeling a zing of satisfaction as Poppy crashed into the barrier. She turned and saw Flick coming her way with a determined expression on her face. She accelerated and they crashed into each other with fits of laughter. Then she spotted Poppy up ahead and drove towards her. Poppy braced herself for impact as June slammed into her side. June drove off again, careering around the circuit once more, this time almost colliding with Tamsin before making a sharp turn away. Dan remained on the other side of the track—he seemed intent on driving his car properly. Poor guy. June set off towards Poppy, ready for another collision. To her disappointment, the lights came up and the cars slowed to a halt.

'What now?' Dan said, as they climbed out, damp with sweat. 'Do you want to go in the haunted house?'

June looked up at the eerie wooden structure, its yellow-tinged façade illuminated by ghastly beams of neon green. The windows were boarded up and plastic thorns grew along the walls.

She nodded. She'd always liked haunted houses. Even though she didn't find them particularly scary these days. When she was a little girl, it had been different. She had believed that the spooks that jumped out at her were real. She had really feared what lurked behind each corner.

They paid the bored attendant, who was slouching in a metal chair. He took their money and waved them through without a word. A thick curtain hung in the doorway, blocking out any hint of what lay in store. Dan pulled back the fabric and they stepped through. The darkness inside was disorienting. June stumbled blindly with her hands outstretched until she bumped into a hard object that groaned in response. She yelped and jumped back before realising it was a skeleton dangling from a chain attached to the ceiling, swaying with its bony arms outstretched.

Dan walked a few feet ahead, entranced by the glowing pumpkin on a stick. June looked up and noticed neon green ooze dripping from the ceiling. She hastily took a step back, not wanting to get it on her favourite T-shirt. A high-pitched scream filled the air, coming from around the corner. She quickened her pace. Two teenage girls stood quivering in front of an old cupboard, and before June could blink, its doors burst open and an illuminated skeleton jumped out, causing them to squeal with delight before running off down the hallway.

June ventured further into the darkness, her eyes adjusting to the shadows. She followed a long, narrow tunnel, the walls damp and slimy to the touch. She didn't see anyone for a few minutes and she began to wonder if she was going the right way. The tunnel was completely still, and yet she thought she could hear something. It sounded like someone breathing.

'Dan?'

Someone grabbed her from behind and an icy pair of hands encircled her throat.

NINETEEN

CREEP

I move silently behind her, my black hoodie blending into the darkness. Adrenaline surges through my body as I follow her down a dark tunnel. My heart pounds with anticipation as I snake my arms around her neck and hold it for a moment, in a vice-like grip.

I feel a rush of power, knowing that her life is in my hands. I could snap her like a twig if I chose. But then it would all be over too quickly. Not enough pain. Not enough suffering. Nothing like she deserves.

I hold on for a few seconds then I release her. It's enough to give her the fright of her life. As soon as I let go, she goes sprinting off down the passageway while I remain in the shadows. It's an incredible feeling.

Finally, I'm in control.

TWENTY

JUNE

June's mouth opened in a silent scream as her eyes bulged wide. She struggled for breath as the hands tightened around her neck, cutting off air. Through the ringing in her ears she heard the muffled thump of her assailant's heart and the heavy intakes and exhales of their breath.

Then, a moment later she could breathe again. The hands were gone. She fell back against the wall, startled and shocked. She didn't understand what had happened. Was that someone's twisted idea of a joke or were they really out to hurt her? Her mind flashed to Poppy. Could it have been her? She had seemed almost friendly tonight, the sparring on the dodgems had just been a bit of fun, hadn't it?

Tears welled in her eyes as she panted hard for breath in the dark night air. Her throat felt raw, and although she wanted to call out for Dan, she could barely manage a whisper. Most of all, she was terrified it might happen again. She had to get out of here. Now.

Her feet pounded against the packed earth as she sprinted down the dark, dank corridor, desperate for an escape. She felt along the wall with outstretched arms until her fingers brushed against a new, lighter tunnel and she abruptly veered into it. A mechanical skeleton jumped out of the darkness and she shrieked, her voice pathetically weak. She kept on running, stumbling along until she made out the faint glimmer of light at the end of the tunnel. With renewed energy, she blundered outside, shielding her eyes from the brightness.

She saw the two teenage girls again by the exit, their faces illuminated by the bluish glow of their phone screens.

'Someone grabbed me!' she gasped, clamping a hand to her chest.

The girls' eyes widened as they looked up from their phones. They squealed in delight.

'No, I mean it,' she said, desperation lacing her voice. 'There was someone in there.'

She staggered over to the attendant, the words spilling out quickly as she tried to explain what had happened. But it was clear he wasn't listening; his gaze was fixed on something far away.

'It's a haunted house,' he said, eyes shining in the moonlight. 'It's supposed to be creepy.'

'Not like that. Someone put their hands round my neck.'

'Yeah, well it's dark in there.'

June couldn't deal with this level of stupid. She retraced her steps and found Dan, ducking his head as he emerged from the tunnel. His lips were stretched into a happy grin.

'That was a laugh,' he said. 'Some of those skeletons were quite believable.'

Taking a deep breath, she told him what had happened.

His eyes widened. 'Do you think it was a member of staff? They had people in there to scare us.'

'No,' she said firmly. 'Someone grabbed me like they wanted to strangle me.'

His face turned grim and a vein in his cheek twitched. 'Do you want to call the police?'

'No,' she said with a sigh. 'What are they going to do?'

He thought about it for a moment, eyes scanning the common.

'There are some really messed up people around.'

She sank against him. 'Tell me about it.'

'You know, your neck looks a bit red still. Does it hurt?'

'I'm okay. It just gave me a fright.'

'Come on,' he said gruffly. 'Let's get out of here.'

'I want you to stay over tonight,' she told him. 'I don't want to be alone.'

'Are you sure?'

She nodded and reached for his hand. They walked through the fairground, waving to her housemates when she spotted them standing next to the drinks tent. Tamsin gave her a wink and a thumbs up. June smiled weakly, then glanced over at Flick who was chatting to the young guy who'd been at their party. The one who had asked her out. She stared at him for a moment and he stared back at her, then pointedly turned his back.

The walk home helped calm her down. She felt safer knowing Dan was beside her. She fought to suppress the memories of the haunted house as she unlocked the front door. She led him into the kitchen and grabbed a bottle of pinot noir from the rack, pouring out two generous glasses. She handed one to Dan and picked up the other. They clinked glasses and she took a large gulp of the dry refreshing wine, hoping her nerves would settle.

He stepped closer with a soft sigh, and his arms encircled her in a warm embrace. His lips were gentle and inviting and he explored her mouth with his tongue. The kiss deepened until she could no longer think straight. Every touch sent electric sparks down her spine, and she felt her heart beat faster as he ran his hands over her shoulders and down her back.

His eyes smouldered as she took his hand and pulled him

towards her bedroom. Their bodies melded together perfectly on the bed as they settled into its softness. He touched every inch of her skin and she responded, trembling with desire.

In the darkness, their breathing synchronised as if they had done this hundreds of times before; their passion merging into something deeper – something beyond sex. June couldn't help but hope that this was more than fleeting. This might be love.

June stood in the kitchen, flipping pancakes on a cast-iron griddle. Golden and fluffy, they sizzled softly as she served them onto two plates. Kimmy walked in, biting her lip to suppress a smile as she grabbed a yoghurt from the fridge.

'Do you want one?' June asked, gesturing to the pancakes.

'Oh no, don't mind me,' Kimmy said, with a knowing smile.

June sliced up some strawberries and added them to each plate before setting them down on the table.

Dan smiled as he picked up his fork. 'You know my expectations are sky high now.'

'That's good,' June said, meeting his eyes. 'So are mine.'

They lingered over breakfast, with Dan insisting on stacking the dishwasher before he left.

He grabbed his jacket and gave June one last kiss before he headed out the door. As soon as he was gone, June released a deep contented sigh and retreated to her bedroom. She flopped onto her bed and smiled up at the ceiling. Her night with Dan had almost made her forget the horror of the haunted house, but it came back to her now, in a sudden flash of memory, those cold hands around her neck. It made her shiver.

She curled up on her bed, reading her latest mystery novel, but when she heard her housemates' laughter, she set the book aside. She made her way down the hallway and into the living room where Flick, Tamsin and Poppy were gathered, watching a new comedy. She perched on the edge of the sofa and tried to catch up.

Then she heard the front door open and Kimmy walked in, back from lunch with Ralph. She was grinning from ear to ear. Flick immediately grabbed her arm, eyes wide with excitement.

'Let me see!'

Kimmy slowly raised her left hand and revealed a glistening solitaire diamond ring set in white gold. Everyone in the room gasped in awe and June's eyes grew wide with shock.

'You're kidding?! You're engaged?'

Kimmy's cheeks were pink. She'd never looked prettier.

'So, when's the wedding?'

'We haven't set a date yet, but we want to get married soon, probably in the autumn. I think the falling leaves will look really romantic in the pictures.'

'Never mind the wedding, when's the hen night?' Poppy said. 'I take it you are going to have one?'

'Maybe you could organise that for me,' Kimmy said. 'I want you all to be my bridesmaids.'

'Ooh! I've got loads of ideas,' Poppy said, rubbing her hands together.

June waited for Kimmy to say something, to tell Poppy she wasn't included in her plans, but Kimmy just smiled.

How could she be so blasé? It made sense that Kimmy was asking the rest of them. They had been friends for years. But who the hell was Poppy to be given such a privilege? She shouldn't even be invited to Kimmy's wedding. She shouldn't be part of their lives at all.

'So how did he ask you?' Tamsin asked.

Kimmy sighed. 'It was so romantic. He organised a flash mob outside Marble Arch station.'

'You're kidding!'

'God, how embarrassing!' June said.

Everyone looked at her. 'I mean, for me it would be.'

'I would love it!' Poppy said. 'I've always wanted to see a flash mob.'

'Me too,' Kimmy agreed. 'It was totally amazing. There was singing and dancing and everything, and at the end there was this trio of violins, all playing our song.'

Poppy's eyes shone. 'That's so romantic.'

The wedding was all anyone could talk about all day. June was pleased for Kimmy, but she had little to contribute as her housemates debated dresses, styles and colour schemes. Then it struck her. Kimmy would be moving out. Once she had that thought, she couldn't think about anything else. Logically, she knew they couldn't all stay in this house forever. But now she knew it for sure. Even if she managed to turf Poppy out, Kimmy would be leaving, and someone else would have to take her place, and then she'd have another new housemate to deal with. A hollow feeling grew at the pit of her stomach. Happy as she was for Kimmy, a part of her felt like she was in mourning.

TWENTY-ONE

CREEP

When I was little, I used to have an imaginary friend. At first, Creep only came out when no one else was around. We would play ball together, or cards or whatever. But bit by bit, Creep started to visit more and more often. Dad would be lecturing me about something and Creep would pop up next to him and pull faces. It was a struggle not to laugh.

Then Creep started to follow me to school. I did alright back then, I found the work fairly easy, but my teacher worried that I didn't interact much with the rest of the class. She told my parents I seemed lonely.

How wrong she was because when you had an imaginary friend, you really don't need anybody else. The more time we spent together, the bigger and stronger Creep became. If someone put me down, Creep would always think up the perfect comeback. Only I was never quite brave enough to repeat it.

Sometimes, when it's very quiet, I still hear Creep whispering in my ear.

TWENTY-TWO

JUNE

Monday morning, June cracked two eggs into a hot pan, stirring them with a rubber spatula until they were fluffy. She spread two slices of seeded brown toast with ripe avocado and spooned on a dollop of spicy salsa, before taking her first bite. She browsed the online news while she ate. She liked to be up on current events, especially as it gave her something to talk about if she got trapped at the water cooler at work. She had never been much good at small talk, had never seen the point in it, but working in an office meant that sometimes it was unavoidable.

After rinsing her plate in the sink, she stacked it carefully in the dishwasher and grabbed her bag, ready for the morning commute.

Flick appeared in her dressing gown.

'Aren't you a bit late?' June asked.

'I'm doing a late shift today, not that it's any of your business.'

June stared at her housemate. It wasn't like Flick to be so tetchy.

'Have I done something to upset you?' she asked.

Flick bit her lip. 'You don't know?'

'No.'

She leaned back against the counter. 'It wasn't very nice, the way you treated my brother.'

June shook her head. 'I honestly don't know what you're talking about. I've never even met your brother. Have I?'

Flick looked at her, and it finally clicked.

'Wait, the young guy who came to the party. That's your brother?'

She recalled now, how there had been something familiar about him. Something she couldn't place.

'He really liked you, June. You could have let him down gently.'

'Oh, god. I'm so sorry, Flick. I would have if I'd known. I really am terrible with faces. I thought he was just some random.'

Flick sighed. 'Okay, I get it.'

'Look, will you tell him I'm sorry? I never meant to hurt him. I wasn't even sure he was serious when he asked me out. I thought he might have been pulling my leg.'

Flick cracked a smile. 'Man, you've got a low opinion of yourself, haven't you?'

'Well, so would you, if you were me.'

June left it at that and shoved her feet into her shoes. She felt better, now that she'd cleared the air with Flick. Now she understood why she'd been so standoffish with her lately. She'd thought it was Poppy's doing, but no. June had messed that one up all by herself.

It was sunny outside as she walked out to the shed and fiddled with the lock. She found the right combination and the door flew open. She looked all around. Flick's scooter was in its usual place and there was a pile of boxes and other assorted junk. But her beloved bike was gone.

TWENTY-THREE

JUNE

She blinked. How was that possible? The shed had been locked.

She walked all the way around it. It didn't take long to figure it out. The window was smashed, all the glass knocked out. It wasn't a large window but it was just big enough for someone to climb in and out.

She stood in disbelief, gazing at the empty spot where her bike had been just the day before. It wasn't a valuable bike. She'd bought it second-hand but she'd gone to a lot of trouble, replacing the brakes and repainting the frame. Someone had gone to great lengths to take it away from her. They must have really wanted it. Or really wanted her not to have it.

Thoughts swirled through her head. She should call the police to report it. Her bike was registered, so that might make it easier to get it back. She searched through her phone, looking for a picture of it, but she didn't appear to have any. It hadn't occurred to her she would need one.

She glanced at the time. It was already eight fifteen. She had better go and catch the bus. Work was the last thing she felt like, but she had a meeting at nine and she knew better than to keep Marilyn waiting.

. . .

Her meeting went on for what felt like hours, with complex arguments and back and forths that seemed to lead nowhere. June had almost dozed off in the process; she had filled the margins of her notebook with a labyrinth of intricate patterns and shapes in an effort to stay awake.

'Right then, we'll take it from here next time,' Marilyn said, glancing at the clock on the wall. 'June, you were taking notes—would you mind typing them up and sending them out to everyone?'

June forced a smile, her heart sinking. She quickly gathered up her papers from the table and stood, eager to get away.

Once she escaped to her desk, she scoured the local community pages on Facebook. Stolen property often ended up on there because the thieves were usually not very bright. If they had any sense, they would spray the bike a different colour. She had painted it that bright canary yellow colour in order to make it more visible to traffic. It would definitely stand out.

There was a knock at her door. She sat up straight, but it was just Gulnara.

'What's all this then?' she asked, looking over June's shoulder.

June told her about the stolen bike.

Gulnara's eyebrows shot up.

'Where was that housemate of yours when the bike went missing?'

June shook her head. 'It might have been Poppy, but it could also have been some random. It's hard to say.'

'But what do your instincts tell you?'

'I think it was Poppy. She's been behaving herself lately, but she often stays up late, and her arm's healed now, so she might have decided to go for a joyride.'

'There you are then.'

June nodded unhappily. 'What I don't understand is why.'

Gulnara brushed a piece of lint off her jumper.

'I don't know. Some people are just sick. If it were me, I'd be looking for another house by now. Better safe than sorry.'

'But it's my home, and they're my friends,' June argued. 'She's the one who came crashing into my life. Why should I be the one to move?'

June groaned inwardly as she walked into The Blushing Bride boutique. Kimmy was already bouncing on her heels in anticipation, while June tried to wrap her head around the task of finding a bridesmaid outfit that flattered everyone; from small blonde Poppy, to tall punkish Flick – who had never once expressed an interest in wearing a dress.

As they weaved their way through the shop, she couldn't help but marvel at all the gorgeous floor-length gowns that hung from the racks. The dresses were incredibly detailed, covered with ornate lace, glittering beading and delicate embroidery.

'June!'

She swung round and collided with a mannequin in a long ivory veil.

'Sorry,' she muttered, then immediately felt foolish for talking to a mannequin.

Kimmy waved her over. She was standing in front of a shelf full of wedding shoes. Her face lit up as she pointed to a pair of pale pink stilettos with small diamanté buckles on them.

'These are perfect!' she exclaimed, her voice filled with excitement. 'I want everything to be pink!'

June gaped in horror at the towering heels. She'd never worn such shoes before, not even for special occasions. Her poor feet were doomed.

'Hey, they look expensive,' she said, catching sight of the price tag.

'Don't worry too much about the cost,' Kimmy said. 'Ralph's folks are paying. We can get anything we like within reason.'

'Wow, that's great.' She was glad Kimmy was getting the wedding she wanted, but it was a shame that meant she had money for the awful shoes.

She drifted a little further, till her eye caught a beautiful dress on one of the racks. It was a pale pink colour and had intricate beading along the bodice with a mermaid silhouette. She held it against her body and twisted in front of the mirror, feeling like she'd stepped into a fairy tale.

'What do you think?' she asked.

'It's nice,' Kimmy said, but she kept looking.

Poppy held up a bright pink dress with a plunging neckline. Made from a shiny, slippery satin, the fabric shimmered in the light of the store as she swirled it around. June's eyes widened in horror at the thought of wearing such an eye-catching item.

'That's gorgeous,' Kimmy said, stepping forward to admire it more closely.

'There's only one,' June pointed out. 'We need four matching dresses.'

Kimmy took the dress to the counter. The shop assistant gave them an indulgent smile as she checked the inventory on the computer. 'We have several of that particular dress,' she said triumphantly. 'You can choose from three different sizes.'

They each picked their size and waited while the assistant fetched them from the storeroom. Then they headed to the dressing room to try them on. There were only three cubicles, so June waited her turn in the outer room, which boasted a large mirror.

Poppy changed quickly and emerged from her cubicle, looking a little too pleased with herself.

'What do you think?'

She spun around and around, admiring the way it twirled around her legs.

June mumbled something unintelligible and headed into the cubicle. She shed her work clothes and stepped into her dress, zipping it up the side. The fit was good but when she looked at her reflection, she shuddered. The neckline plunged too low for her liking and it didn't feel appropriate for a wedding. She tugged at the sleeves to cover more of her skin, but this only made her feel even more on display. Surely Kimmy wouldn't think this was a good look?

She drew back the curtain and found Tamsin in front of the mirror.

'Is it supposed to look like this?' Tamsin asked. She tried pulling her dress this way and that but there was no avoiding the fact that it was too revealing.

June shook her head. 'If my grandmother could see me now, she'd be spitting. Kimmy can't possibly want us to wear this in church.'

'She's not having a church wedding though, is she?' Flick said, emerging from the other cubicle. 'They're getting married at the town hall.'

'All the same.'

'Well, I like it,' Poppy said.

'You're the only one who does,' June said, glaring.

'Kimmy likes it,' Poppy pointed out.

'Maybe she won't go for it when she sees how it looks on,' Tamsin suggested. 'Let's go and show her.'

They walked out into the shop and Kimmy's face lit up.

'Oh, you all look so beautiful! Even you, Flick!'

Flick burst out laughing. 'Even me?'

'Oh god, sorry, that came out wrong! You never wear anything this dressy! I just meant...'

Flick reached out and touched her arm. 'It's okay. I know what you meant. Look, if this is really the look you want then I'll wear it, but I have to say it really isn't me.'

Kimmy smiled. 'Believe me, you're going to look so beautiful.'

June forced out an uncomfortable laugh. She had hoped Flick would be the one to object, but it seemed she was going along with it, and June didn't want to be the one to rock the boat. She had thought about asking Dan to be her plus one at the wedding, but now it was out of the question. There was no way she was going to let him see her in this awful dress.

'I don't want anyone posting pictures on Instagram,' Kimmy warned. 'No spoilers! In fact, I think I'll take a break from Insta, just to be sure.' June exchanged a look with Flick. 'I couldn't agree more.'

They all changed back into their regular clothes and, when they came out, the shop assistant took all the dresses and placed them in a zip-up bag with hangers.

'I've got the car if anyone wants a lift,' Kimmy said, as they walked outside. Tamsin, Flick and Poppy all piled in.

'I'll see you back at the house,' June said, turning to go into the library. She needed a few minutes in her happy place.

She headed straight for the self-service checkout, scanning the books she had just read and dropping them into the return bin, all but the one she wanted to renew. She pulled out her wallet and looked for her library card. It wasn't there. She searched her bag, her pocket and her wallet again but it wasn't anywhere.

With an agonised look at the books on the new release shelf, she trudged out and headed home.

'You alright?' Poppy asked, as she stomped through the front door.

Since June was in no mood to confide, she nodded. She searched her room, then checked down the sides of the sofa, between cushions, even scouring the kitchen drawers. But it was nowhere to be found.

. . .

The following morning, June pressed her face against the bus window, her eyes following the slow progress of the houses and trees as they trundled by. As they passed the common, something in the greenery caught her eye. There was a wheel, poking out from one of the bushes. Her heart raced as she leaned forward in her seat to get a better view. Yes, it looked like a bike wheel. Could it be?

She leapt up out of her seat, grabbed the handrail and rang the bell, signalling frantically for the bus to stop. Passengers stared, some tutted in annoyance, but she paid them no heed. As soon as the doors opened, she burst out and ran across the street, dodging cars blaring their horns in protest.

She tugged, pulled and strained at the bicycle, which was wedged deep in the bushes. A passer-by saw her struggling and came over to help. Together they yanked it free from the branches, sending leaves and dirt flying in all directions, before finally setting it on the ground.

June took a good look at it. It was definitely her bike, that distinctive canary yellow paint was unmistakable, but her lucky bell had been removed and the handlebars were bent in opposite directions, the spokes clogged with mud and twigs. She turned it over and looked at the other side of the frame. There was a message spelled out in splotchy black ink.

'There's a special place in hell for you.'

TWENTY-FOUR

JUNE

June stuck her hand in her pocket and brought out her phone. She dialled Marilyn and told her she was ill. Truth be told, she really did feel sick. The crumpets she had enjoyed for breakfast that morning threatened to work their way back up and spill all over the street. She wheeled the broken bike home. The wheels wobbled and thumped with each rotation, as if they were trying to escape.

She dragged it through the alleyway and into the garden where she showered it down to wash away all the dirt. She applied nail varnish remover to the graffiti but no matter how hard she scrubbed, she couldn't erase it all.

She spent half the day working on the bike. She tightened screws and replaced tyres, determined to fix every ragged edge. She painted over the nasty words, leaving the bike to dry in the sun, but there was not much she could do about the handlebars. Later, she wheeled it inside, unwilling to put it back in the shed until the window was fixed. She felt strangely protective of it. She couldn't bear the thought that someone had treated something she loved so badly.

She was supposed to be meeting Dan for a drink that evening but she wasn't in the mood so she texted him to explain what had happened. He arrived on her doorstep forty minutes later with a new bell, tied with a red ribbon. She flung her arms around him, hugging him tight. He patted her on the back.

'It's alright,' he said. 'I'll help you fix it.'

He took a look at the handlebars, turning them this way and that.

'I think we'll need to get them replaced,' he said.

She liked the way he said 'we' as if this were his problem as well as hers.

He examined the bike properly, checking her repairs.

'Bloody joyriders,' he muttered.

'I don't think it was joyriders,' June said, glancing at her bedroom door.

He lowered his voice. 'You think it was Poppy?'

'Who else would do this?'

'I thought you said she'd been leaving you alone.'

June squeezed her eyes shut. 'I've really let my guard down, haven't I?'

'Hey, there's no way you could have predicted this.'

'What I don't understand is why she would go to the effort of breaking the window? She knows the code for the shed. We all do.'

He shook his head. 'I don't know. If it was Poppy, then she was probably covering her tracks.'

He stepped forward and enveloped her in a cocoon of warmth. She sank into his embrace. The bed springs squeaked beneath them as their bodies intertwined. She closed her eyes and surrendered, lost in the heat and energy that sparked between them.

Afterwards, she leaned forward on one elbow, her skin glistening with sweat.

'You can stay over if you want?'

He looked at her with a bittersweet smile. 'I'd better not. I've got an early start tomorrow—I'm photographing birds on the common for a new wildlife calendar. I'm going to be up ridiculously early and I'd only disturb you.'

'Okay then, but you're missing out on the world's best bacon and eggs.'

'Another time.'

'There had better be.'

That weekend, she asked Kimmy to drive her to the hardware store, where she chose nails and sheets of iron from the racks. Back out in the garden, she worked tirelessly, hammering thick plywood over the window cracks on both sides of the shed for extra security. She attached a new lock to the shed door and added bolts to the handle.

As she set down her hammer, she heard a sound behind her and saw Poppy leaning against the house with her arms crossed. She met her eye but Poppy didn't back off. She sank into one of the garden chairs and looked down at her phone, flicking a glance at June every so often, as if to show that she was watching her.

June reached for the hammer again, feeling its weight in her hand.

'You did this, didn't you? You wrecked my bike.'

Poppy's eyes grew wide with mock fear. 'Are you threatening me, June? Are you going to attack me with that hammer?'

June worked her jaw and her knuckles tightened around the handle. She was so angry she did want to swing it at Poppy. But that was exactly what Poppy wanted. For June to come at her so she could play the victim again.

'What the hell have I ever done to you?' June demanded.

Poppy smirked in response, sending fresh rage shuddering

through her body. As she felt her boiling temper reach its limit, she carefully set down the hammer and headed indoors.

A couple of hours later, she heard Poppy out in the hallway. She opened her door a crack and saw she was putting her shoes on. Great. It looked like she was going out, probably to work at the pub. It really didn't matter where she was heading, as long as she would be gone for a while. She waited for the door to slam, because Poppy was incapable of closing it quietly, before she ventured out of her bedroom.

Flick had made a simple dinner of jacket potatoes with cheese and baked beans and they all sat around the table, enjoying easy conversation like they used to.

Tamsin's phone beeped and she looked down at the message, then shot a look at June.

Then Flick's beeped in her pocket.

June narrowed her eyes. 'Is that Poppy? Is she texting you?'

'It's nothing,' Tamsin said. She pocketed her phone before June could read the message.

'I know you don't want to hear this, but I really think Poppy might have been the one to take my bike,' she said, as everyone tucked into their food.

Kimmy almost dropped her fork. 'You can't be serious? I thought you were over all that!'

'Please, I'm begging you. Won't you all at least consider that it might have been her?'

She looked from one face to the next but not one of them would give her so much as a nod.

'Fine,' she said, getting up from the table. She stormed off to her room and slammed the door behind her.

A moment later, there was a knock at the door.

June opened it a crack.

Tamsin peered in, her eyes gentle and caring.

'I don't know who took your bike, but I'm certain it wasn't Poppy.'

'You don't know that.'

'I know Poppy. I've spent time with her. I know she's a bit off the wall sometimes but she wouldn't do something like that, believe me. You need to change the record, June. People are starting to say you're paranoid.'

TWENTY-FIVE

JUNE

One Year Ago

'Dinner's ready!' June yelled to her housemates.

She had worked for hours in the kitchen, preparing a delicious Sunday dinner and the kitchen was filled with the aroma of garlic and herbs.

Tamsin appeared first and helped carry everything through to the dining room. June followed, her arms laden with dishes of steaming food. Her eyes narrowed as she noticed that Flick was hunched over her phone.

'I thought we agreed to no phones at the table?' she said.

Flick hastily put her phone down and June set down the dishes. Tamsin sighed and pulled her own phone out of her pocket, silencing it. Then Kimmy's phone beeped and June's temper threatened to bubble over.

She took a bowl from the side cabinet and placed her phone in it. Then she walked around the table, collecting each housemate's phone. There was a bit of eye-rolling but she had gone to a lot of trouble with the cooking so in the end they all gave in.

June took the bowl out to the living room and left it there for the duration of the meal.

She returned to the dining room and put on her vintage record player. The calming notes of a violin filled the room as she served their meal, artfully arranging a generous portion of pork tenderloin and creamy mashed potatoes on each plate.

When they had finished their main course, she returned to the kitchen, humming along to the music as she heated up some dark chocolate. Her housemates exclaimed with delight when they saw her bubbling chocolate fondue.

She laid out an assortment of fruits and they all talked at once as they dunked strawberries, grapes and bananas into the sea of molten chocolate. She thought she had chopped too much fruit but they devoured the lot.

'Best dessert ever!' Kimmy proclaimed.

'I'm fit to burst,' Tamsin said, patting her stomach.

June smiled with satisfaction. She would personally have preferred a delicate white chocolate mousse but she had had a feeling this would be a hit.

Tamsin and Kimmy cleared the table, whilst June retreated to the living room for a well-earned rest. She closed her eyes and must have drifted off for a few minutes when she was awoken by a loud shriek from Tamsin.

She had just pulled her phone out of the bowl and was staring at it in dismay.

'I have eleven missed calls. Wait, there's a voice message.'

June swallowed as Tamsin played it back on loud speaker. A woman's voice filled the room.

'Tamsin, this is Gladys, your dad's neighbour. I found him collapsed in the garden. You need to get to the hospital, love. Quick as you can.'

Tamsin gasped. Fingers shaking, she rang Gladys back. Tears slid down her cheeks as she listened. June couldn't make out what was being said, but the woman sounded hysterical.

Kimmy stood in the doorway. 'Come on. I'll drive you.'

'We've all been drinking.'

'I'm okay. I only had one glass.'

'Thank you.'

June rose to her feet. 'I'm coming too.'

They both stared at her for a moment, but neither objected.

'Should we pack a bag?' Kimmy asked.

Tamsin shook her head. 'There's no time.'

They let Flick know where they were going and raced out to Kimmy's Volkswagen.

They barely spoke a word as the car sped through the night, racing from Clapham to Pontypridd in record time. When they arrived at the hospital, Tamsin jumped out and ran to the entrance, where a grey-haired woman in a thick blue coat enveloped her in a warm embrace. June ran after her while Kimmy parked the car.

Gladys pulled back and gazed at Tamsin, her eyes full of regret. 'I'm sorry, my lovely. I'm afraid he passed a few minutes ago.'

'No!' Tamsin let out a wail that shook her whole body. She sobbed into Gladys's arms. Through teary eyes, she looked up and said, 'Did he ask for me?'

'He was pretty much out of it the whole time but when I told him you were on your way he seemed to relax a little. I'm sure he understood.'

They headed inside, where a doctor greeted Tamsin, his white coat illuminated in the darkness.

'He went peacefully. He wasn't in any pain. You can see him now if you'd like?'

Tamsin nodded, and June took a step to follow but Kimmy placed a hand on her shoulder.

'No, let her go alone,' she murmured.

June sank into a chair, her legs feeling like lead. She let out a deep breath. Her heart raced in her chest as she looked down at her hands. Kimmy stood beside her and gazed out of the window at the car park. She didn't say anything, but June knew instinctively what she was thinking. If only Tamsin had had her phone when Gladys called. If it weren't for June, she would have made it.

TWENTY-SIX

JUNE

June listened to an audiobook as she diced carrots for the evening's stew. She was deep in thought, completely wrapped up in the story when she heard the kettle sputter to life. She whipped round and saw Poppy leaning against the countertop, watching, as steamy tendrils flowed from the kettle's spout like a genie freed from its lamp.

June managed a polite half smile and Poppy gave her a slight nod. Her shoulders tightened and she paused her audiobook, unable to concentrate. She didn't like anyone interrupting when she was cooking, it made her lose her flow. Poppy's presence was especially unwelcome. Was it her imagination or was the kitchen unbearably hot all of a sudden?

This was how it was between them these days, sharing space but saying nothing. It wasn't a comfortable silence, like the ones she often shared with other members of the household. It felt loaded.

She finished chopping and left the stew on the stove to cook. She sat down in the living room, watching TV and checking the pot every so often, to make sure it didn't boil over.

An hour later, the stew was ready and she scooped it into

five deep earthenware bowls. The aroma was heady and thick with herbs, just the way she liked it.

She called the rest of her housemates to the table, even making the trip down to the basement to bang on Poppy's door.

'Dinner!'

The housemates all sat around the table, grumbling loudly about the weather – they had hoped for a sunny day, but it was cold and windy, ruining their plans for a barbecue.

Poppy stuck her spoon in her bowl and swirled the stew around. 'Does this have mushrooms in it?'

June lifted an eyebrow. 'Just a handful. You can pick them out if you want.'

Poppy shook her head so vigorously that a strand of blonde hair came loose from the bun on top of her head. 'No, the last time I did that I swallowed one by accident and then I had mushroom burps all day.'

'Too much information!' Flick called out.

Poppy snickered. 'Just telling it like it is. Don't worry about me, I'll get myself something else.'

She rose from the table, a whirlwind of motion as she dug through the cupboard for an alternative. June watched as she decided on a tin of spaghetti. She opened and closed the drawer, looking for the opener. There was a short pause, and then the microwave hummed, filling the room with a deep thrumming sound. A high-pitched beep cut through the air announcing Poppy's food was ready.

Kimmy clapped her hands together, her eyes wide and sparkling. 'I booked the hen week,' she said, looking round the table. 'We're going to be spending a week in Mykonos!'

Excitement rippled through the group like a gust of wind. June couldn't remember when the hen night had become a hen weekend, and then a hen week.

Her own suggestion had been a day spa but she'd been outvoted.

'How much is all this going to cost?' she asked.

After all, it was only a few months ago that they'd been struggling to pay the bills. She didn't want to risk her housemates spiralling into debt.

'I've paid for the villa,' Kimmy said. 'You just need to find the money for your flights.'

Poppy smiled as she carried her bowl back to the table. 'I'm broke but Kimmy's kindly offered to lend me the money for my ticket,' she said.

June darted a horrified look at Kimmy. 'Are you sure you can afford that?'

Kimmy waved her concerns away. 'Ralph can,' she said. 'He'll help me out if necessary. He wants to make sure I have an unforgettable hen week.'

'What a guy,' Flick muttered.

June shot her a look but the conversation had already moved on. They chatted about all the things they could do in Mykonos, from dancing in the clubs to soaking up the sun on the beach. June had her own ideas. She envisioned herself pedalling along the scenic coastal roads and discovering hidden coves.

'When's Ralph having his stag?' she asked.

'Same week. He's going to Ibiza.'

'I'd better get saving,' Flick said. 'Going to need some beer money.'

Poppy picked up a fork full of spaghetti hoops.

'Ow! Hot!'

She blew on it before placing another forkful in her mouth. June watched with a mixture of horror and curiosity.

'Talking of spending money, I've taken up busking,' Tamsin said.

June frowned. 'Where?'

'Down by the tube station. It's going quite well. I made fifty quid last night.'

'Nice one!' Kimmy said.

Flick nodded in agreement but June frowned. 'Are you doing it all by yourself?'

'Just me and my guitar. I'm playing all my own material. It's a great opportunity to try it out live.'

The prospect made June uneasy. Though she admired Tamsin's enthusiasm, the thought of her being alone out there concerned her.

'Don't you need a permit for that?'

Tamsin gave a careless shrug. 'No one's complained.'

'But is it safe?'

'You're such a worrywart, June,' Poppy said with a smirk. 'It's like living with my own grandma.'

The comment stung. June didn't think she was making a fuss. The area around the tube station could be dangerous at night, especially when people had been drinking. It unnerved her.

Poppy slurped her spaghetti hoops noisily.

'I don't know how you can eat that stuff,' June said, shaking her head.

'Uh oh, food police,' Flick said.

Poppy shrugged. 'It reminds me of my mum—she used to make it for me all the time.'

June didn't have the same association. In her childhood home, there had been no special concessions for anyone at the dinner table. You ate what was put in front of you.

Tamsin finished first. She was already in the kitchen, loading the dishwasher.

'Did everyone bring their washing in from the garden?' Flick asked. 'I think it's starting to rain.'

June grabbed a basket and dashed outside to rescue her washing. She could hear her neighbour in the next garden, whistling to himself as he smoked a cigarette. He didn't seem the least bit bothered about the rain.

She gathered all her clothes and brought them inside. She

carried them to her room, folded them all neatly and put them away so they wouldn't crease. When she came out, she saw Kimmy kneeling on the floor in front of the bathroom. She took a step towards her. 'Are you okay?'

'I've just been sick.'

'Oh, poor you,' June said. She glanced across at Flick who was curled up on the sofa, her pale skin glistening with sweat.

'You don't look so hot either,' she said. Flick shook her head.

June brought them both sick bowls then she went to the linen cupboard and grabbed blankets for them.

'I think I heard Tamsin,' Kimmy said.

June went upstairs to Tamsin's attic bedroom and knocked. 'Tamsin, are you...?'

She heard a moan from inside and threw open the door.

A wave of putrid odours washed over her, and she gagged at the sight of congealed vomit on the bedspread. Tamsin lay in a foetal position on the floor. There was a pile of vomit next to her and more in her hair.

'Oh, Tamsin! Let's get you into the shower.'

Tamsin was so weak, she could barely walk.

June took her arm and led her down the stairs. Step by step, they descended slowly until they reached the bathroom.

She guided her to the shower and helped her undress. Tamsin leaned heavily against her for support. Then she turned on the water and hosed her down with it. Tamsin was so jittery, she didn't dare let go of her in case she fell. Once she was clean, June wrapped a warm towel around her shivering body and handed her a dressing gown. Then she helped her down the stairs to her own room so she could get some rest while June cleaned up.

She cleaned quickly, fighting the urge to vomit herself. She wasn't sure if she was also falling ill, or if the smell was getting to her. Once Tamsin's sheets were in the washing machine, she went to check on Flick and Kimmy. The air reeked of sickness.

She heard the sound of Poppy clumping up the stairs from the basement.

'We're all ill!' Flick called out.

Poppy took one look at them and backed away.

'Thanks for your help!' June yelled at her retreating back.

'I'm sorry, I'm not good with sick people. If I come up there I'll be vomiting too.'

June took a deep breath and headed for her own room, where she found Tamsin rocking gently, moaning in pain.

'I want my dad,' she whispered.

Tears sprang to June's eyes. She hugged her housemate gently and wished she could take her pain away. While she was comforting Tamsin, her own stomach gurgled and she rubbed it gently, willing the nausea away.

Tamsin seemed to be getting sleepy, so she left her and sat on the stairs to call the out-of-hours surgery. She was put on hold for several minutes. Through the wall she could hear Flick in the bathroom, retching over the toilet. Each wet heave echoed off the walls, drowning out all other sound.

Eventually, she was put through and she listed her housemates' symptoms.

'Vomiting, diarrhoea, fever and stomach pains. It all came on this evening. We were all fine before.'

'Did you all eat anything unusual?'

'No, we just had a beef stew.'

'Hmm...sounds like gastroenteritis,' the doctor said. 'Make sure everyone drinks plenty of water and try to get some rest.'

'Isn't there anything we can take?'

'These things usually run their course, but please phone again if anyone gets worse.'

'Okay, thank you.'

She leaned forward and buried her head in her lap. She couldn't fight it much longer, the nausea was getting worse.

· · ·

Kimmy and Tamsin slept, but Flick and June were both sick several times in the night. Poppy only came upstairs to use the toilet and get herself a drink. June studied her carefully. She still had colour in her cheeks and she wasn't shivering like the rest of the household.

'Are you okay?' she asked her.

'As long as I don't breathe in your germs,' Poppy said. She went to the fridge and pulled out a can of Irn-Bru.

Flick groaned from the sofa. 'Don't you worry, you'll be getting it next.'

'I bloody hope not,' Poppy said, retreating back down to her room. A moment later, her music started but June was too weak to ask her to turn it down.

Poppy never did get the bug. The rest of the household all felt rough for three days, after which they were all weak and pale, but no longer heaving up their insides. For all that time, no one but Poppy went out, and no visitors were allowed into their home. Kimmy pined for Ralph and June found herself constantly thinking of Dan. They texted back and forth, exchanging little jokes and snippets.

'I miss you,' Dan told her during a video call.

'I miss you too.'

'When can I see you?'

'Soon. I just need to make sure I've shaken this thing.'

She watched as he reached for something off screen and popped it into his mouth.

'What are you eating?'

He held a slice of cake up to the camera.

'Kelvin's been baking,' he said, panning in on a tray of white cakes with colourful sprinkles.

'You're making me hungry.'

'That's a good sign, isn't it?'

'I suppose.'

'As soon as you're well enough, I'm going to take you to this amazing patisserie I've just found in Abbeville. They make the most delicious millefeuille.'

Her mind began to wander as he described his favourite pastries. Her energy was depleted, and she could feel her eyes drooping.

'Okay, I can see you need your rest. I'm going to let you go now. Speak the same time tomorrow?'

'Yes please, and thanks for calling. It was really good to hear your voice.'

'Does anyone want to go for a walk?' Tamsin asked once June had hung up. 'I'm getting cabin fever. I really need some fresh air.'

'Yeah, sounds good,' said June, stretching out her arms. She didn't want to sleep through yet another day.

'I'll come,' Flick said.

Kimmy nodded. 'What about Poppy?'

'She only just went to bed,' June said.

'Okay, we'll leave her.'

Kimmy and Flick put on their coats and the four of them staggered out into the sunlight.

'I feel like we've just survived a zombie apocalypse,' said Flick, as they walked slowly up the road.

They walked over to the common, too tired to do anything but sit on a bench and watch other people jog by. It felt good to be outside. The fresh air warmed June's face.

'Hey, isn't that Ralph?' Flick said, pointing at a figure in the distance.

'No!' Kimmy laughed. 'That's his brother.'

They all craned to see, but he had jogged away out of view.

'You didn't mention he had a brother,' Flick said. 'That'll make the wedding more interesting. Is he single?'

Kimmy covered her eyes. 'Please don't hit on him! That would be so awkward.'

Flick grinned. 'We might end up married. We could be sisters-in-law!'

They all cracked up.

'How's everything going with the wedding?' June asked. 'Do you feel like it's all coming together?'

'Mostly,' Kimmy said.

'I think you're doing the right thing, keeping it small. The last wedding I went to felt like a circus. I mean, what's the point in inviting a bunch of people you barely know?'

Kimmy nodded. 'That's exactly what Ralph says. We don't want to look back at the pictures and find we can't name half the guests. It's just going to be our nearest and dearest.'

Tamsin yawned as they headed back home. 'I'm going to take a bath when we get in,' she said. 'And then maybe a nap.'

June nodded. Her phone buzzed in her pocket. It was Marilyn.

'Just checking how you are,' she said.

'Getting better,' June told her.

'That's good. You take as much time as you need. But you will be back in Monday, won't you?'

June smiled. 'I'll be back in as soon as I'm not contagious,' she promised. She actually missed work, except for the meetings. She was happy to have a break from those. She ended the call and caught up with her housemates.

Their front path was looking overgrown, she noticed as they approached. Maybe she would get her gardening gloves and do a little weeding. Tamsin froze just in front of the flower beds. June thought she was looking at the flowers too but a strangled sound escaped her throat, then she was on the ground, limbs twitching and jerking as if electricity was surging through her body.

TWENTY-SEVEN

JUNE

Kimmy frantically dialled 999 as June dropped to her knees beside Tamsin. Flick's voice quivered with fear. 'What's happening?'

'She's having a seizure,' Kimmy said.

June's heart raced as she tried to reassure Tamsin.

'It's okay. The ambulance is on its way. Can you hear me, Tamsin? Can you look at me?'

But Tamsin only stared forward, unseeing, her mouth moving in a silent struggle to form words.

'I'm right here,' June said, placing her scarf under Tamsin's head. It was frightening, seeing her friend lose control of her body.

Tamsin's movements gradually slowed but now she looked startled, her eyes darting about as if she didn't know what had happened. Saliva dribbled from the corner of her mouth. June fumbled in her pocket for a tissue to wipe it with.

The faint wailing of a siren filled the air. The sound grew louder as the bright yellow ambulance turned into their street. June waved her arms and it came to a sudden stop in front of the house. Two paramedics dressed in green quickly hopped out. They walked over with purposeful strides, speaking in calming tones as they moved to Tamsin's side.

'Hello, love. Can you hear me? What's your name?'

'It's Tamsin Davies,' June said, when Tamsin didn't answer.

At that moment, Poppy flew out of the door and into the garden, her eyes wide. 'What the hell's going on?' she shouted, panic threading through her voice. 'What's happened to Tamsin?'

She looked to June for an answer, but June just stood there with her lips pressed together. This wasn't the time for Poppy's drama.

'Has anything like this ever happened before?' the paramedic asked.

Kimmy and Flick shook their heads.

'No,' June said. 'She's not epileptic or anything like that. No health conditions, but we're all recovering from gastroenteritis.'

'All except me,' Poppy said.

A second paramedic was looking at June. 'Had you eaten anything unusual before the gastroenteritis?'

June shook her head, her jaw tightening. 'No, we just had a home-made stew. I made it myself. All fresh ingredients.'

'You used field mushrooms, didn't you?' Poppy piped up.

Her words dangled between them, heavy with accusation. June felt her pits grow sweaty as she struggled to meet Poppy's gaze.

The paramedic seemed unfazed, his focus solely on finding out what had caused the sudden illness. 'Where did the mushrooms come from?' he asked.

June cleared her throat and shifted her weight from her left foot to her right. 'I... I pick my own from the woods. I know what I'm doing. I've been foraging since I was a kid,' she said, horrified by the implication that she may have poisoned everyone.

'Well, it would be helpful if you could get a sample of the ones you used, just in case.'

June swallowed hard and nodded her head. 'Will do, but I'm pretty sure it wasn't the mushrooms.'

She turned her attention back to Tamsin. A dull flush of pink had returned to her cheeks, and her eyes were beginning to regain their focus. She kept opening and closing her fingers, as if trying to process what had just happened.

'Tamsin, we'd like to take you into hospital,' the paramedic said.

June looked at Tamsin. It was hard to tell if she'd heard.

'I'll come with her if that's okay,' Kimmy said.

'Alright then. We can just about squeeze you in.'

June watched in a daze as they got Tamsin ready. She couldn't stand seeing her so unwell, but it couldn't be the mushrooms, could it? She had picked the same ones as always. She was so careful. There was no way she would put her housemates in danger. She reached out to squeeze Tamsin's hand and let her get into the ambulance, Kimmy close behind.

As soon as the ambulance left, she spun round to look at Poppy. Her face was illuminated by the flash of red from the vehicle's tail lights. Poppy opened her mouth to say something but June didn't want to hear it.

'Get out of my way,' she barked.

She barrelled past and ran inside to her room, where she collapsed onto the bed and buried her head in the pillows.

A couple of hours later, Kimmy called from the hospital.

'She's been okay but they're keeping her in overnight to run tests. Can you pack a bag for her? And don't forget to get a sample of the mushrooms. I'll pop home and collect it.'

'Yes, of course.'

'Great, thanks.'

She went upstairs to Tamsin's room, and immediately thought of their time as roommates at St Winifred's. Whilst June had thrived in the safe, structured environment, Tamsin had suffered horribly from homesickness. She had often woken in the night, covered in sweat and tears. Sometimes, she had crawled into June's bunk, and they'd both lain there, waiting for morning. June had always been the one to look after Tamsin. She couldn't bear the idea of her stew making her so sick. She knew it wasn't true. There was no way she'd pick the wrong mushrooms. No way.

She opened a drawer and found a pair of pyjamas and some clean socks and underwear for Tamsin. Then she picked up one of the cuddly dragons and placed it in the bag too. She packed Tamsin a washbag from the bathroom and set it all on the dining room table. Then she slipped on her coat and shoes and headed back to the woods to pick another batch of mushrooms.

She found some in her usual spot, down by the hedge. She picked a handful and examined them carefully before placing them in a zip-up bag. They were edible mushrooms, she was sure of it. Whatever had caused their illness, the mushrooms could not be to blame.

She lay in her bed that night, the moonlight flickering across her face, and thought back to the evening they'd fallen ill. She could still smell the earthy aroma as she washed then chopped the mushrooms and threw them into the pot. She had prepared them exactly the same way she always did, before she'd left the stew cooking on the stove. She clutched the pillow tightly. Poppy had been hanging around the kitchen while she'd been cooking. And then she'd left the room for a while and gone into the living room while she waited. What if Poppy had slipped in something extra? She had refused to eat even a spoonful of the stew. Was she really so set against mushrooms, or was it because she'd added something toxic?

In the morning, June spoke to Dan on the phone.

'You should go to the police,' he urged. 'If your housemate tried to poison you, you should report it.'

'I've got no proof,' she said. 'We finished all the stew and I'm the one who cooked it. If anyone's going to get the blame, it's me.'

'But you're adamant you didn't pick any bad mushrooms?'

'I know I didn't.'

'I wish I could do something to help you,' he said. 'I feel so useless.'

'Don't say that. It means the world to me, having you to talk to. Sometimes I feel as if this whole house is against me.'

'Well, I'm here to help you fight your corner.'

'Thanks. I appreciate it.'

'So when can I see you again?'

She hesitated. 'I'm not sure. I need to make sure we're rid of this... whatever it is first. I don't want to make you ill.'

'I'm willing to risk it.'

'All the same, I really don't need that on my conscience, and to be honest, I still feel like I've been hit by a lorry.'

'Alright then, you let me know when you're ready. I love you, June.'

She almost dropped the phone. 'Do you?'

'That wasn't quite the response I was hoping for.'

'No! I'm sorry, no one's ever said that to me before.'

'Well, I mean it, June, I love you. And maybe one day, when you're ready, you'll say it back to me.'

Stunned, she said goodbye and stared at the wall. Was it love? It might be. She certainly had a warm feeling in her chest.

She wandered into the kitchen. There was a pink Post-it note on the fridge.

Gone to collect Tamsin from the hospital, back soon, Kimmy x

June smiled. That sounded promising.

She was thirsty. She poured herself a tall glass of orange juice then wandered into the living room. Where was everyone? She glanced at the clock. Poppy should be at work and Flick was probably asleep.

She wasn't quite sure what led her down the stairs to the basement, but it felt like there was a little voice, calling to her, daring her to take a look.

'Poppy?' she called out, just in case her housemate was in there.

There was no reply. She pushed the door open and found the usual chaotic mess of clothes strewn across the floor, empty drink cans piled on the desk and bookshelves overflowing with cosmetics.

If she was right and Poppy had poisoned them all, then she might have bought the poison off the internet. And if that was true, then there might be evidence: an empty container or something. It was worth a look.

Her eyes swept over the mess, trying to pick out anything that could be of use. Under the bed was the obvious place to start, but all she found was a heap of dirty clothes. She delved through the bin, but there was nothing of consequence in there, just a bunch of empty crisp packets.

Where would she keep something private? The locker beside the bed felt like a good bet. She rummaged carefully, moving aside loose photos, postcards and sweet wrappers. Then, tucked between an old, crumpled envelope and a button, she found what looked like a library card. She pulled it out and examined it. Sure enough, it had 'June Worth' embossed on it.

Her blood boiled. Why would she have this? Angrily, she slipped it into her pocket and continued her search.

She moved quickly, rummaging through each of the drawers in turn. She was almost ready to give up when she caught sight of a gleaming gold rectangle tucked inside an ornamental bowl. She grabbed it and held it up to the light. It was her student union badge. The raised letters spelt out her university's name, surrounded by delicate swirls of gold paint. It was just a cheap bit of metal they'd given out in freshers' week. She hadn't seen it in weeks and now she knew why; Poppy had taken it.

She frowned, trying to make sense of these discoveries. These things were not valuable. They were of little consequence to anyone but June. Just like her bike.

TWENTY-EIGHT

CREEP

He heads towards the common. I follow his route on the running app until I see him, face set in concentration, earphones blocking out all noise. I fall into step behind him. It's exciting, the prospect that he might spot me, but he's far too self-absorbed. He never once thinks to turn and check. He lopes ahead of me, his breath forming a fog in the chill morning air. His feet strike the ground with military precision, pounding out an even rhythm. The trees blur as I struggle to keep up, sweat dampening my shirt, lungs burning with exertion. He rounds a corner and darts into the woods, and for a second, I think he must have seen me. But no – he is far too focused on his run. We jog around the common, leaving our mark in the dewy grass, until he veers left towards a small pond. My side aches from my attempt at keeping up with him, so I slow down as he continues on his way. Through the trees, I watch him grow smaller until, finally, he's gone.

TWENTY-NINE

JUNE

June heard Kimmy and Tamsin's voices approaching the house and she hurried up the stairs to greet them. Tamsin's hair looked lank and her steps were slow. June could see that exhaustion had taken over her body.

'Welcome home,' she said, reaching out to hug her. 'You're looking better.'

'I'm fine now,' Tamsin said with a weak smile. 'Just a bit tired. They told me to get plenty of rest.'

She sat on the sofa. Kimmy tucked a blanket around her shoulders and made her a cup of tea.

'Did you get the test results through yet?' June asked.

Tamsin shook her head. 'Not yet. Hopefully today or tomorrow.'

June brought her laptop out to the living room and opened up her work email. Her eyes widened as she saw how many meetings she had missed but she was resolute that she would stay off for the rest of the week. She'd barely taken any time off since she'd started her job so she felt entitled.

Kimmy put on one of Tamsin's favourite films.

'Aren't you going to watch with us?' Tamsin asked.

'No, I thought I'd head into work for a few hours. I feel bad being off for so long as it is.'

June sat up straight. 'Your boss can't blame you for getting ill,' she objected.

'He doesn't, but there's no one else to run the shop in my absence.'

'Okay, don't work too hard.'

'I won't. I'm just going to do a couple of hours, then I'm meeting Ralph for lunch. We need to decide where we're going on our honeymoon.'

'Have fun. I'll stay here with Tamsin.'

Tamsin leaned back against the cushions and soon she was snoring softly. June rubbed her eyes. She was also feeling a little sleepy. She dozed for a while until she heard Poppy come home, and all at once, she was wide awake.

Poppy glided into the kitchen. June followed, feeling a mixture of curiosity and anxiety. She slapped the library card down on the table, followed by the university badge.

'I found these in your room.'

Poppy lifted her eyebrows. 'What were you doing in my room?'

'Looking for my stuff.'

'What made you think it would be there?'

June shrugged. 'Just a hunch.'

'Based on what?' Poppy leaned forward and looked at the items on the table. 'It looks like I've picked up your library card by mistake. Did you leave it in the kitchen? I must have thought it was mine.'

'You don't even have a library card.'

'Don't I? How would you know? As for the badge, that's mine.'

June felt a spark of excitement. 'No it's not. It has the name of my university on it.'

'That was *my* university,' Poppy said evenly.

'You went to Guildford?'

'Yup.'

June was floored. It appeared Poppy had an answer for everything.

'You really shouldn't go through her stuff though,' Flick said from the doorway. 'I wouldn't like it. If you want to get something from someone's room you should ask first, and probably wait till they're home.'

June ground her heels into the floor. Flick didn't get it.

She looked at Poppy. 'If you went to my uni, how come I never saw you?'

'It's a big uni.'

She peered closer. 'Did we... did we know each other?'

'I doubt it. I studied history and social policy. You took English lit.'

June's mouth twisted. There was something venomous about the way Poppy said those words. Her heart was pounding and she felt like if she stayed in the kitchen a moment longer, she was going to explode. She walked out with as much dignity as she could muster and headed to her room. She pulled out her phone. She might not remember Poppy, but maybe Grace would.

THIRTY

JUNE

June heaved her bulging duffel bag onto the crowded train and squeezed into a seat. It was busy today and the carriage reeked of sweat. She took out her book and threw herself into it, desperate to escape the thoughts swirling around in her head. She had no recollection of meeting Poppy before, and yet Poppy seemed to hate her. There had to be some connection.

She was coming into Guildford station when she got Tamsin's message.

June, my tests came back. There were trace amounts of a poisonous mushroom. However, they agree that the mushrooms you sent into the hospital were completely fine to eat. The doctor has suggested that you somehow picked one of a different kind and it got thrown into the mix. Please know that I don't blame you. Just thought you would want to know. Love Tam.

June stared at the message in horror. Tears welled in her eyes. Mushroom poisoning could be deadly. She could have killed them all.

No, she didn't believe that. She never touched anything

remotely dubious. She was more certain than ever that Poppy was behind the poisonings. But why?

She stood up and elbowed her way through a swarm of commuters to reach the overhead luggage rack. She helped an elderly woman free her suitcase before reaching for her own bag. She'd already spotted Grace on the platform. Tall and broad-shouldered, Grace's hair hung like a curtain of gold down her back. June rushed forward to hug her old friend. Grace seemed surprised by the tightness of her embrace.

They pulled apart and walked out of the station. June couldn't help but notice how quiet Guildford seemed when compared to the hustle and bustle of London.

The house they had shared was just round the corner. June must have taken this route hundreds of times before. Everything looked familiar, yet different. A couple of the shops had changed, houses had been renovated. There was scaffolding up on the house next door.

'I did "no mow May",' Grace said, waving her hand at the overgrown garden. 'And somehow it extended into "no mow summer". The neighbours haven't complained yet and the wildlife is loving it.' June nodded, admiring the wildflowers that had sprung up in the long grass. If Dan were here, he'd have his camera out, snapping pictures of the bees. She tried not to look at the rosebush as Grace unlocked the door. They stepped inside. The house still smelt the same. She kicked off her shoes. Some of her old posters still hung on the wall outside the living room. The inspirational quotes filled her with a mix of nostalgia and embarrassment. What had once seemed inspiring now seemed a little hollow and pretentious.

'My housemate is away for the weekend, so you can sleep in your old room,' Grace told her.

'Really?'

She pushed open the door and peered inside, delighted by the familiar sight of her old daisy-print curtains. She dumped her bag on the bed and took in her surroundings – the yellow walls had faded with age and the pinboard that had once held her schedule was now covered with postcards. The faint whiff of sandalwood candles reminded her that someone else lived here now. She hoped Grace's new roommate enjoyed the view over the River Wey as much as she had.

'I'll put the kettle on, shall I?' Grace called. 'Or would you prefer a glass of wine?'

'Wine please,' June replied, her voice lingering in the stillness of the room. She found her slippers and stepped into the living room, where she collapsed onto the old familiar sofa, amused to see that Grace still had the same coffee table with the uneven legs.

'You're looking a little tense,' Grace said as they clinked glasses. 'Your face is pasty and your alignment is all out of whack.'

'Yeah, well...'

She gave Grace the low-down on her problems with Poppy and her old housemate listened, eyes wide.

'Do you remember her at all?' she asked, showing her a picture on her phone.

Grace had a good long look. 'I can't say I do. Do you know what course she was on?'

'History with social policy.'

'Ah, well. Not my department.'

'Nor mine.'

June lifted her wine glass, then slowly set it back on the table. She took a deep breath, reflecting on how futile her plan was. Her uni years were long behind her now, and what was more, she was sick of worrying about Poppy all the time. Maybe she should concentrate on enjoying her weekend with Grace.

'I could really use some distraction,' she said. 'How about a game of chess?'

Grace smiled, and stood up to retrieve the board from the

shelves next to the fireplace. June felt a wave of nostalgia wash over her as she remembered how often they used to play. But as she set up her pieces, she realised she was probably a little rusty since none of her current housemates played. She was not the least bit surprised when Grace beat her. Grace always had been as sharp as a tack.

'Do you want to play again?' Grace asked.

'Actually, I was thinking we drink the rest of this wine and then head over to the student union. What are the debate club arguing about this week?'

'The debate club's been disbanded,' Grace said with regret. 'The Dungeons and Dragons crowd has taken their slot.'

'Oh... Okay, well... Are there any bands?'

'There might be. Let's go and find out, shall we?'

As June strolled around her alma mater, the feeling of nostalgia quickly washed over her. She stopped in front of the university library, admiring its angular architecture. She had spent many a happy day in there.

'Hey, I've got an idea. How about we go to the Top Banana?' she suggested. 'I would love one of their ice cream sundaes.'

'The Top Banana is no more. It closed down a couple of years ago.'

'Is that right? What a shame! Remember their giant Viennese whirls?'

'I liked their apple strudels,' Grace said wistfully.

'Oh, those were heaven on a plate! Are you sure it closed?'

Grace laughed. 'We can walk that way, if you want? I'll show you.'

They headed across the campus, past the old travel agent and what had once been the bank. It seemed a shame that all these old businesses had closed down and no one had taken over the premises.

'Steady,' Grace called as they took the steep steps where June had once tripped and sprained her ankle.

The Top Banana café was still there but the walls were papered with old adverts. There were posters for the Friday night disco, the archery club and a rally to legalise drugs.

They walked until they heard music in the distance. They followed the sound to a little patch of lawn where a group of musicians were playing. A small crowd was swaying along with the music and sipping beers they'd bought at a nearby stall.

June bought the beers and they sat down on the lawn.

'Do you ever think about leaving?' she asked.

Grace shook her head. She had found work in the administration building, transitioning naturally from student to staff.

'It feels like home,' she admitted. 'That's a bit sad, isn't it?'

'I don't think so,' June said. She could completely understand the desire for an uncomplicated life.

As they sat there listening to the music, Grace pointed out a man with thinning hair on top.

'There's Richard,' she said.

June blinked in surprise. Richard had been Grace's on-off boyfriend. They'd spent a lot of time with him, back in the day. They were all cut from the same mould: hard working and studious.

They had looked down on the party people, the women who wasted their time shopping for disposable fashion and dancing till all hours, and the men who had chugged yards of ale and chanted tuneless rugby songs. It was a self-defence mechanism, she supposed. Being brainy had been their identity, their superpower. At school they'd simply been nerds. At uni, they were in their element.

'What does he do now?' she asked, watching him disappear into the crowd.

'He's a lecturer.'

June blinked. 'You mean, he works here?'

'He did, until a couple of years ago. He transferred to Portsmouth but he still lives around here, I believe.'

In their time, Richard had been president of the student union. He hadn't been especially popular. He had a habit of speaking a little too bluntly. Regardless, he was the hero of the hour when it came to thwarting the faculty's attempts to close down the on-campus bars.

Grace yawned widely. 'I think I'm ready to head back soon.'

June looked at her in surprise. For once, she could quite happily have stayed, listening to the music all night. They finished their beers and rose to their feet, leaving by the south exit so June could get a look at the old bike sheds. There were more old posters plastered on the walls.

'Hey, I've found one of Richard's campaign posters,' she called to Grace.

Grace leaned over to take a look. Richard had a slogan written across him. 'The only man for the job.'

June didn't care much for the slogan, but Grace was looking at it fondly. 'Didn't he look young?'

It wasn't a particularly flattering portrait. He had a moustache back then and the posters were printed in black and white, making him look vaguely like Hitler.

A shadow fell over them, and a deep voice interrupted her thoughts.

'You know, I can sign that for you if you like.'

THIRTY-ONE

JUNE

June swung round. 'Richard! You made me jump!'

He smiled broadly. She was glad to see he'd lost the moustache.

'What brings you back to Guildford?' he asked.

'Just visiting Grace, and reminiscing.'

'Well perhaps you'd both like to come and do some reminiscing round at my place? I've got an excellent bottle of Chianti.'

June was about to make her excuses, when it occurred to her that Richard might be just the person to ask about Poppy. She wasn't sure if his photographic memory was limited to facts about train timetables and computer games, or if it extended to people.

'That would be very nice,' she said, with a smile.

It was only after she'd accepted that she noticed the hostile look that flashed across Grace's face, but she couldn't back out now. She would just have to make it up to Grace later.

The three of them left the grounds together, June walking in the middle, flanked by Grace and Richard on either side. As they walked, Richard quizzed her about her new life in London. He was especially keen to hear where she was living.

'I can't imagine doing a houseshare,' he said. 'I get on my own nerves, if I'm honest.'

June laughed, but Grace remained deadly silent.

Richard's street was well-lit and lined with neatly kept houses, but something felt off. It was as if a dark cloud of dread had descended. Grace's breathing became shallow and her grip on her handbag tightened as they walked up the path.

'Are you alright?' June murmured.

Grace gritted her teeth. 'I'd rather visit the dentist.'

'Sorry. We won't stay long.'

She gazed up at the house, and realised that this must have been Grace's second home at one time. She didn't know what had caused her break-up with Richard, but she suspected he had met someone new since Grace had clearly not moved on.

Richard unlocked the heavy front door and gestured for them to enter. The living room was decorated with antique furniture. A square table had been positioned in the middle of the room, with a bottle of wine and glasses waiting for them, as if he'd anticipated having guests. On the wall, she noticed a display of criss-crossed swords and hunting trophies.

She tried not to laugh. The whole set-up was a bit weird, but then Richard had always been an old man in a younger man's body.

He opened the wine and poured it with aplomb.

'To old friends,' he said, handing them each a glass. They clinked glasses politely, and she and Grace sat down on the sofa.

Richard rattled on about nothing in particular. He started on one topic, then veered off wildly on another, not really caring if he carried his audience with him. The whole time he was talking, he kept his gaze trained on June, and barely glanced at poor Grace, who stared firmly at the wall.

'I was wondering if you remember my new housemate,' she

cut in, before he could start yet another tedious anecdote. 'Her name is Poppy Kendrick. She claims she studied history at Guildford. Do you remember her, by any chance?'

Before he could say anything, she pulled out her phone and showed him a photo.

She waited with bated breath as he examined it.

'You want to get the target of your photo right in the centre,' he noted. 'You need to shoot from eye level, that way, you get a better picture.'

'She doesn't care about the quality of the freaking picture,' Grace exploded. 'Do you remember Poppy or not?'

Richard blinked and scratched his head. 'Yes, I think I do remember a Poppy. Short blonde girl. Loud voice.'

'That's her!' June confirmed. 'What do you remember about her?'

He thought for a moment. 'There was something wrong with her, wasn't there?'

She leaned forward. 'What do you mean?'

'Didn't she do a midnight flit? Left a few months before she'd completed her course.'

'Did she?'

Richard thought hard. 'Yes, I seem to remember something about that. There was some rumour about her running off to Mexico. It was all a bit odd.'

June nodded. 'She did spend a year in Mexico, but I've no idea why she left. All I know is that she seems to have it in for me, and I really need to know why.'

Richard frowned. 'Well, I wish I could help you but that's all I can recall.'

She set down her glass. 'Well, thank you anyway. At least I've got something more to go on.'

She rose from her seat. Grace immediately jumped to her feet.

Richard looked disappointed. 'Oh, don't go just yet, there's plenty more wine where that came from.'

'Thank you, but I've got an early start in the morning. It was nice seeing you again.'

'Likewise.'

He closed the distance between them, leaned in and kissed her cheekbone. His lips felt cold and wet against her skin but she managed not to shudder.

She turned to Grace and saw that she looked wistful, as if she too had questions that he had not yet answered. She waited, but neither of them seemed willing to talk to the other.

'At least let me call you a taxi,' Richard said. 'It's a bit late for you ladies to be walking back in the dark.'

'Nonsense, we'll be fine,' Grace said abruptly. She strode towards the door and June gave an embarrassed wave as she followed.

They walked out into the silent night, their shadows merging in the darkness. Neither of them spoke as they headed along the deserted street, but June's mind was buzzing. What could have caused Poppy to leave so abruptly, and in her final year at that? She was aware that some students couldn't handle the pressure of exams, but she had a feeling the answer was something more personal. She glanced at Grace, but her friend's face was closed, a little sad even.

'Are you alright?' she asked.

'Yes. Yes, of course.'

'You still care about him, don't you?'

Grace gave her a stern look.

'Alright, I'll mind my own business.'

They kept walking, their footsteps the only sound on the dark, deserted street. June's neck prickled as if someone was watching them. She glanced behind her, but all she saw were receding pools of light from the street lamps. A chill ran up her spine, and she quickened her pace, rushing towards Grace's house.

Grace jogged along to keep up with her. 'Hey, what's the rush?'

'I really need the loo,' she lied. She was probably overreacting, but the events of the past few days had put her on edge, and she couldn't shake the feeling that she was in danger.

Tamsin had done her hair and make-up when June returned home to Clapham. That seemed like a good sign. She sat in the living room with her guitar in her lap, strumming idly as she watched TV. June greeted her with a hug.

'How are you doing? You're looking more like yourself.'

Tamsin nodded. 'I managed to eat a Pop Tart this morning, so I must be on the mend.'

'Just let me know if you want any real food. I bought a sourdough loaf on my way home. What are you watching, anyway?'

'It's a Brazilian soap opera Poppy got us into. It's totally addictive. Why don't you come and join us?'

'Maybe later,' June said. 'I'm going to get a bit of work done so it's not too horrendous when I go back on Monday!'

'Suit yourself!'

June headed for her bedroom and switched on her laptop. Her inbox was jammed with emails. She began going through them, quickly junking the ones that didn't matter. She stopped at an email address she didn't recognise. For a moment, she thought it was one of the men from DatingLocal. She still received messages from them now and then, although she hadn't had one in a while. Then she realised it was from Richard.

Dear June,

It was lovely to see you, quite the surprise! After you left yesterday, I finished the rest of that bottle of Chianti and had a listen to some Gilbert and Sullivan. Do you remember how we used to listen to their operettas? Anyway, I spoke to an old colleague in the history department at the university and he told me that Poppy Kendrick was about to be suspended when she left. It seems she cheated on her coursework. The university was trialling some new plagiarism software at that time and it caught a few people out. In Poppy's case, she had handed in an essay which was almost identical to one that had been submitted the year before. When the university informed her of their suspicions, she left before they could investigate properly. I think that speaks to her guilt, don't you?

Your old friend,

Richard,

PS – You have my number. If you come back this way again, do feel free to pop in. My door is always open.

June stared at the email, her stomach churning. Her hands shook as she slowly closed the laptop, and a deep chill spread through her body.

She picked up her phone. Grace took a few rings to answer.

'Grace, Richard's remembered something. Poppy was in trouble with the university for plagiarising her coursework. Don't you get it? It must have been down to us.'

THIRTY-TWO

JUNE

'Are you talking about The Inky Quill?' Grace said.

'Yes.'

'But no one knew that was us.'

'I know.'

The Inky Quill was their essay mill. It was a small, secretive operation. No one was supposed to know who was behind it. The only way to contact them was by email. Grace and June had placed tiny ads in the library, on noticeboards around campus and slipped handouts between pages of textbooks. Their business gave desperate students the help they needed to get through university and had kept Grace and June in beer money for their entire university careers.

They sold model essays for £100 a pop. More, if they needed the essays in a hurry. As they were both excellent students, it was no trouble for them to write example essays on a variety of subjects. In theory, those essays were only intended to be model answers. But they both knew that people handed them in as their own work. This must have been what Poppy did. Unfortunately, on this occasion, one of them must have written an essay that was too similar to one of their previous efforts, and then Poppy had tried to pass it off as her own. So, when it was run through the plagiarism checker, it had been flagged. Poppy should never have cheated. But the reason she had been caught? That was down to them. They had not given her what she'd asked for. Her essay was not sufficiently unique.

'There's no way Poppy could have traced that back to us,' Grace said. 'We didn't tell people who we were. It was all done in secret.'

'She must have found out somehow. And now she wants revenge.'

June hung up the phone and typed in the address for The Inky Quill's email account. She hadn't logged in in years, but her ancient laptop had retained the password. She had half expected it to have been deactivated but she was pleased to see that it had remained intact.

The inbox opened and a long list of emails greeted her. She didn't recall the business being this busy. Some of them were dated only last week. In disbelief, she scanned further down and saw that someone had already replied to some of the enquiries. How was this possible?

She slumped back in her chair, her mind racing. She thought Grace had shut down their business when they graduated. After all, Grace had taken a job with the university administration. But these emails told a different story. The Inky Quill was very much alive and running – Grace had even raised the prices. She must be raking it in.

June was in no position to judge, given that she had once been a partner in this business, but she was a little surprised at Grace. The thing that really got her was that she hadn't said anything when she'd mentioned The Inky Quill just then. Was Grace embarrassed by what she was doing or did she have something else to hide?

She searched further back through the emails, and there it was: an old message from Poppy complaining that she wasn't given a unique product. June clicked on Grace's reply, unable to contain her surprise as she read it.

Dear Poppy,

I take full responsibility for the below-par essay you were given. I am deeply sorry for the inconvenience this has caused and wish to make it up to you in any way possible. As a representative of The Inky Quill, I cannot express how seriously we take our commitment to excellence and strive to provide products that meet our highest standards. We will of course refund your purchase. Please accept my sincerest apologies,

Vanessa

June stared at the message. There was no Vanessa. It had just been the two of them. Grace must have made that name up to make herself more personable whilst concealing her identity. She thought her reply was very reasonable, but she was puzzled as to why Grace hadn't mentioned this at the time. If their essay had got Poppy into trouble, that was a pretty big deal.

Poppy had replied:

I have had to drop out of university. My life is ruined. I would like the name of the employee that wrote my essay. Otherwise I will go to the papers and expose your business.

There was another email from Grace.

Dear Poppy,

Your essay was written by June W, who is no longer
employed by this organisation. I hope your future holds the
success and joy that you deserve,

Kind Regards,

Vanessa

June nearly fell off her chair. Grace had outed her! Okay,
she hadn't given her full last name but she was the only June in
her year. Why would she do that? She could have given a false
name. Why risk ruining June's reputation?

She thought hard, but she was fairly certain that she and
Grace had never even had a conversation about this. It was true
that June had left the business around that time to concentrate
on her final year exams, but what would Grace possibly gain
from giving out June's name in this way? Poppy could still have
gone through with her threat to go to the papers. It was one hell
of a risk, one that could have got them both thrown out of uni.
And a really crappy thing to do to a friend. She thought she
knew Grace. It seemed she didn't.

She held her breath as she descended the stairs to the basement.
She stopped just outside Poppy's door and rapped on it three
times. A few moments later, Poppy opened up, a scowl fixed on
her face. June fiddled with the hem of her shirt.

'Can I come in a minute? I want to talk to you.'

Poppy looked at her with suspicion.

'As long as you're not going to go through my stuff again.'

June gritted her teeth and followed her inside. She tried not
to wince at the state of the walls. The blue paint had started to
flake off, revealing patches of aubergine and yellow underneath.

'Look. I didn't come down here to argue with you. I wanted to apologise.'

Poppy did a double take.

'I'm the reason you had to leave uni, aren't I?'

'You wrote my essay.'

June nodded.

'You have nothing to apologise for,' Poppy said stiffly. 'It wasn't like you did it on purpose.'

'I am sorry it got you in so much trouble.'

'You're right. I was upset, but you know what? It was a long time ago. I'm over it.'

June bit her lip. Somehow, she didn't believe her.

'It wasn't entirely my fault, you know. You could have just... not cheated.' June puffed out her cheeks.

Poppy stared at her, her large blue eyes unblinking.

She stared back. 'Tell me the truth. Did you poison the stew to get back at me?'

Poppy looked appalled. 'No, of course not! That was all you, June. Man, you've got a nerve.'

'Then why were you the only one who didn't eat it?'

'I told you. I hate mushrooms and I'm sick of you putting them in everything.'

June leaned closer. 'Did you steal my bike?'

'Don't be ridiculous. Look, I admit I messed with you. I... set up a dating profile in your name and a couple of other silly things but they were just pranks, right? I don't go round poisoning people or stealing their bikes.'

June looked her in the eye and she didn't flinch. But then, Poppy could be very convincing when she wanted to be.

'Truce?' Poppy said, offering her hand.

June took it. 'Truce,' she agreed.

She still didn't trust Poppy as far as she could throw her.

. . .

June wrestled with the decision about whether or not to confront Grace. She was desperate for explanations. But also apprehensive about what Grace might have to say. The decision was taken out of her hands a little while later when Grace rang her.

'Why did you do it?' June asked. 'I've just read back through the old emails. I know you told Poppy about me. I also know that you're still running the business.'

Grace was silent for a moment. 'I've always regretted giving out your name,' she finally said.

'So why did you?'

'I told myself I was just protecting the business. I wanted to keep it going. The money was too good to give up. I knew that you would end up moving on to London and getting a proper job but I didn't want to leave. I wanted to carry on with things just the way they were.'

'You didn't have to give my real name.'

'No, well I suppose I also wanted to get my own back.'

'For what?'

'I know you slept with Richard.'

June almost dropped her phone.

THIRTY-THREE

JUNE

Neither of them spoke for over a minute. She knew Grace was still on the other end of the line because she could hear her breathing. She could picture the grief and pain in her eyes. Grace must hate her. The least she could do was explain.

'You went home for Christmas and I was left on my own. I suppose I was feeling a bit sorry for myself, so when Richard asked me to go down the pub with him, I agreed. I thought we'd just have a drink and a chat like we always did. He talked about you the whole time. It was obvious he was missing you. I was feeling a bit sorry for myself too. A bit lonely. So I suppose one thing led to another and we ended up back at our place. It never would have happened if we'd been sober. And for what it's worth, you weren't even going out with him at the time. You told me you wouldn't get back with him if he was the last man on earth.'

'Then why didn't you tell me?'

'I suppose I... I just wanted to pretend it had never happened. I didn't even like him that way. It was a gigantic mistake.'

'Richard didn't think it was a mistake.'

'What?'

'When we got back together after that Christmas break, things just weren't the same. Then one night, we got into an argument, and he told me. He said it had been weighing on his conscience.'

'Oh, Grace, I'm so sorry.'

'I needed time to process it. I didn't see him for a couple of weeks. I didn't see much of you, either, because I didn't trust myself not to say something I'd regret. I threw myself into my studies, and I wrote a lot of essays for the business. I needed something to keep me busy. And then I got that email from Poppy, demanding to know who had landed her in trouble.'

June pursed her lips and sat back in her chair, fighting the urge to interrupt.

'I was so angry, I couldn't stop myself. I wrote back to her and said it was you. It wasn't even true. It was one of my essays. One I wrote a little too late at night, with a big glass of whisky. I didn't usually write the social policy stuff so I used one of your essays as a guide, and I suppose I must have copied it more closely than I intended. It was me who screwed up, not you.'

'But you said it was me?'

'I immediately regretted that. I even tried to recall the email, but it was too late. The damage was done. After that I was bracing myself, waiting to see if there was going to be any fall-out. But Poppy seemed satisfied with my answer. I didn't hear from her again. I thought she'd left us alone.'

'Grace, I'm so sorry. If I could take it back, I would.'

Grace sighed heavily. 'He was the love of my life, but sadly, I think you're the love of his.'

THIRTY-FOUR

POPPY

Five Years Earlier

Poppy looked hopefully at June, her long blonde hair falling over one shoulder.

'I really need help with my social policy essay,' she said. 'Is there any way you can fit me in next week?'

'Let me check what I've got on.'

Poppy waited politely as June pulled out her phone and checked her schedule.

She had been struggling with her social policy module all semester and she was glad she had finally decided to get herself a tutor. She had only been coming to June for a couple of weeks but she clearly had a knack of breaking down the work into easily understood segments. She even seemed to enjoy it.

'I can do Tuesday at nine thirty.'

Poppy frowned. 'My social policy lecture is at nine thirty.'

'Well that's the only period I've got free next week.'

Poppy hesitated. 'Maybe I should just go to the lecture.'

June's face twisted slightly. 'Who have you got?'

'Dell McDonald.'

June pulled a face. 'My friend had him last year. Couldn't understand a word he said.'

'He has a strong accent,' Poppy agreed.

June slipped her hands into the pockets of her dungarees. 'Look, it's completely up to you, but I reckon you'd get more out of a session with me than you would get out of McDonald. We can go over everything you need. I can talk you through it and help you plan your essay, point you towards some good references. Then you'll be all set. Once you know what you're doing, the actual essay writing doesn't take long.'

Poppy laughed. 'Maybe not for you. It takes me forever.'

'Well it doesn't have to.'

She weighed up her options. 'Alright then, I'll go for the Tuesday slot. Where should we meet?'

'In the library. Grab yourself a table near the social policy books and I'll come and find you.'

Poppy felt a knot in her stomach as she made her way across the campus on Tuesday morning. She glanced up at the large lecture theatre, watching as her peers moved inside, ready to learn. Gnawing on her lip, she turned away and kept walking until she arrived at the library.

The airy room was quiet, although there were a few students already at work, tapping away at laptops or poring over books. She found herself a table and surveyed the rows of bookshelves that towered up towards the ceiling. The spines of the social policy books caught her eye, and she began selecting volumes that looked relevant to her topic.

She sighed, overwhelmed by the number of books spread out around her. The essay topic was dry and dull, and she couldn't seem to wrap her head around it. Five minutes had passed since the time that June said she would meet her here, and a nervous tension filled her stomach as she checked her phone.

The phone was on silent, but the screen lit up with an incoming call, so she placed it against her ear. A slight crackle echoed down the line and June coughed. Poppy glanced self-consciously around the library, aware that other students were studying.

'Hello?'

'Sorry, Poppy, I'm going to have to cancel. I think I'm coming down with the flu and I'd hate to pass it on to you.'

'Oh dear!' Poppy tried to sound sympathetic but all she could think about was her coursework. She'd skipped her lecture to come here and now she wasn't even getting a tutorial.

'Can you fit me in later in the week?' she asked hopefully. 'I really do need some help. I've tried to make a start on my own but I'm not getting very far.'

There was a pause. June coughed again. 'I don't think I can fit you in till next week,' she said.

Poppy gripped the phone tighter. 'Next week is too late. My essay is due in on Monday. I really need your help, June.'

'You could talk to McDonald.'

'We both know how that would go. Do you know any other private tutors?'

'No, but there is The Inky Quill. Have you heard of them?'

'No?'

'It's an essay writing service. They write example essays. You'd get an essay completely tailored to you. It might make a good starting point.'

'Yes! That sounds brilliant.'

'Alright, I can text you their email address and you can contact them. I'd better get back to bed.'

Poppy nodded. 'Thank you for your help.'

A moment later, her phone beeped with The Inky Quill's email address.

She crafted a quick email and waited. A little later, she got a reply.

'Yes, we'd be happy to write you a model essay. Our essays are bespoke and crafted to the highest standards.'

She panned down and found a bunch of testimonials from happy customers. She read through them quickly. They seemed impressive. Too good to be true, she wondered. A feeling of unease settled inside her as she clicked out of the site and opened a search engine. Nothing showed up for The Inky Quill, but June had recommended the service, so it ought to be legit.

She replied, giving them the details of what she needed. Five minutes later, she received a personalised quote. She baulked at the amount. They wanted £100 for an essay; £150 if she needed it this week. Her stomach churned. That was a lot of money and she was already up to her ears in debt.

She thought it over as she stepped out of the library, squinting against the bright sunlight. She navigated her way between groups of students who were sprawled out on the grass and headed across campus for her shift at the Top Banana.

As she walked into the café, she was surrounded by chatter and the clinking of silverware against glass dishes. The summer heat had everyone clamouring for ice creams and cool drinks.

Mr Lin, the owner, spotted her and rushed over. His forehead glistened with sweat.

'Poppy, thank goodness you're here. The dishwasher's broken down. I need help in the kitchen urgently.'

Poppy offered a tight smile. She liked Mr Lin; he was always kind. She followed him into the kitchen and scrubbed the dishes with a determined vigour, her hands turning soft soap into suds as Mr Lin bustled around the kitchen, making up the orders. Once she'd cleared the backlog, she stepped out into the sun-soaked lawn to take her break.

Inhaling the fresh air, she watched a group of students relaxing in the sun, seemingly without a care in the world.

She pulled out her phone and read over the last message from The Inky Quill one last time before placing an order.

The estimated delivery date was set for Friday – that gave her just enough time to read through it and construct her own version of the work. It would be a little tight, but she ought to manage.

As she turned to head back inside, she saw June running across the grass, her hair flying behind her in the breeze. Her face was lit up with laughter as she chased after the frisbee an athletic man had flung into the air. His broad shoulders filled out his navy polo shirt, and his neat crew cut showed off his chiselled features. He smiled at June each time she caught the frisbee, and she reciprocated with an even brighter smile. Poppy shook her head in disbelief, but June didn't even see her.

The essay arrived in Poppy's inbox Friday lunchtime. She had to read it a couple of times to understand it, making notes on the essay's structure and trying to figure out how she was going to write her own essay. She had lectures all afternoon, but she intended to get stuck in straight after dinner.

In the end, she fell asleep on the sofa. The next thing she knew, her roommate was shaking her awake, telling her to go to bed.

'I'm supposed to be writing my essay,' she moaned.

'For goodness' sake, it's Friday night. Get a life.'

On Saturday, Poppy worked all day at the Top Banana, then she headed to the library. Thankfully they stayed open late. She really needed to get cracking if she was going to write 3,000 words before Monday.

She wrote her introduction, then waded through the first section, but she knew she was regurgitating the model essay answer. She found herself referring to it again and again as she moved on.

'The library is closing in ten minutes.'

She looked up, startled. How could that be? She wasn't even halfway done.

She gathered up her books and headed home, exhausted. She would finish the essay in the morning.

But the further she dug into it, the more she found herself repeating lines from the model essay. She knew she was supposed to be putting her own personal spin on it but she didn't really have one. She didn't have a good grasp of the material to start with.

On Monday, she read through her essay again and wanted to scream. It was terrible. A poor copy of the model essay. That was when it hit her. Why didn't she just hand in the model essay? It had been written especially for her. Perhaps that's why it was so expensive, because the writers at The Inky Quill fully expected people to hand in the essays as their own work. Why else would they charge so much? She felt like an idiot. But she really had tried to do the work herself. She printed it off, along with a cover sheet with her name and course number on it.

Then she walked down to the pigeonholes and handed it in.

Instantly she felt like a huge weight had been lifted from her shoulders.

She headed for the student union, looking to celebrate with a beer. She'd barely seen her friends all week and was looking forward to a night of drinking and socialising. This was the part of university she excelled at. As she entered the building, she spotted June, sitting by herself at one of the little tables.

She marched up to her, ready to give her a piece of her mind. 'You're looking better,' she said pointedly.

June smiled and seemed to miss her sarcasm. 'Oh yes, much better thanks. Did you get your essay done?'

Poppy nodded tightly.

'Here you go, babe.'

June turned and accepted a foamy pint of beer from the

same lad she had been with earlier in the week. She seemed to forget Poppy was there as he pulled her into his arms.

'Get a room,' Poppy muttered, walking off in disgust.

The lad glanced back at her and his handsome eyes twinkled. She recalled a friend pointing him out to her in the food hall one day.

That was his name.

Ralph.

THIRTY-FIVE

JUNE

One Month From Now

June held Dan's hand as they sat across from each other at a cosy Italian restaurant. The smell of bubbling sauce and melted cheese wafted through the air, and the candlelight cast a cosy glow over the room.

'Given all the trouble you've had with Poppy, do you ever think about moving out?' Dan asked. 'Maybe it's time to get a place of your own?'

June twirled her fork through the thick layers of ricotta cheese and marinara sauce.

'Living alone is pricey, besides, I like company. Things have been a bit easier now I know the truth about her. At least I know where she's coming from.'

His eyebrows narrowed. 'You're very forgiving, considering she tried to poison you all.'

'I don't know for sure if that was Poppy. I tell you what, though. It's put me off cooking anything else for the house. We've been living on jacket potatoes and ready-made pizzas these last few weeks, not that anyone's complained.'

'Well, I still don't like the thought of you living with her.'

June shifted in her seat. 'Let's talk about something nice, shall we? I don't want to think about Poppy tonight. Let's concentrate on this delicious food.'

As she raised her wine glass to take a sip, her gaze drifted across the room to the table in the corner. That was when she spotted Ralph, his arm draped casually over the back of his companion's chair as he whispered something in her ear. The woman threw back her head and laughed, a radiance illuminating her face. June felt a wave of nausea as she watched them.

'That's Ralph,' she said urgently to Dan.

'Who?'

'Kimmy's fiancé.'

Dan swivelled his head to watch them.

'Could she be a friend?' June asked, looking at the woman he was with.

'I don't think so.'

'His sister maybe?'

They both watched for a few more minutes, then Ralph leaned forward and pressed his lips against the woman's.

'They're a very close family,' Dan said.

June was too angry to raise a smile. Her fingers dug into the skin of her palms as she fought to contain her rage. How dare he do this to Kimmy? And he was so brazen about it. Like her feelings didn't even matter.

She started to rise from her seat, but Dan's hand shot out and clasped her wrist.

'June, this is Kimmy's fight. Let her decide what she wants to do.'

She hesitated for a moment, then settled back down in her chair.

'Shall I call her? If she comes now, she could catch him red-handed.'

'I wouldn't. She needs to process this in private, and then decide how she wants to handle it.'

'I'm going to take a photo of them,' June said. 'Just in case she doesn't believe me.'

'She'll believe you. She might not want to, but she will.'

'Do you mind if I don't invite you in?' she asked when Dan walked her to her door. 'It was a lovely dinner, but seeing Ralph spoiled the mood for me.'

He took her hands. 'I completely understand. We can do this another time. Good luck with Kimmy.'

A wave of warmth rolled over her. 'Thank you.'

She rose up on her toes and got so lost in their kiss that she almost forgot what she was doing.

Finally, he pulled back. 'If I'm going, I'd better go.'

She nodded. 'I'll let you know how it goes with Kimmy.'

She opened the door and went inside, placing her keys on the hook.

Her housemates were all in the living room, wearing vivid fuchsia T-shirts, emblazoned with word 'Team Bride' across the backs, and a nickname on the front.

Kimmy's said 'Bridezilla', Poppy's said 'The Loud One'.

June took her shirt and puzzled over the caption: 'The Quiet One'.

'I'm not quiet,' she objected.

'You are compared to Poppy,' Kimmy said.

'Go on, try it on,' Poppy urged. 'We'll take a selfie in these at the airport on the way out, and then another later when we're all wrecked.'

June held the shirt in her hand, uncertain what to do. She couldn't tell Kimmy here, in front of everybody.

'Try it on,' Kimmy urged.

She wriggled into it and the rest of them applauded. She

swallowed hard, looking around at their excited faces. She was going to have to tell Kimmy. She couldn't let her go on thinking everything was fine.

They were talking about the hen week now.

'If something happened, would we be able to get our money back?' she asked. 'You know, like if Kimmy broke her leg or something?'

'No, it's fully paid up,' Kimmy said. 'The final payment went out last week.'

June clenched her teeth together. 'Good.'

She went off to her room and sat with her head in her hands for a few minutes. Then she rang Dan.

'How did she take it?' he asked.

'I tried but I couldn't tell her. She's so excited about the hen week. She's already paid in full and it's non-refundable.'

'Maybe you should just enjoy the holiday then,' he said. 'Give Kimmy a last hoorah before you break the bad news. When you get back, you can sit her down and tell her the truth.'

She nodded. Kimmy did deserve a great holiday, even if that meant that June would have to hold on to her awful secret for the whole time they were away.

She said goodbye to Dan and lay back against her pillow. The selfish, inconsiderate part of her was happy. Because she'd just realised what this meant. She wouldn't have to endure another unknown housemate. Kimmy would be staying.

THIRTY-SIX

JUNE

June's phone buzzed in her pocket, and the sound grated on her nerves. She picked it up, then frowned at her mother's name flashing on the screen. Irritation coiled in her chest as she rejected the call. Her phone rang again and she silenced it without answering.

She was being irrational, she knew, because today was Thursday, and it wasn't even the end of the month. Once again, she'd called on the wrong day. Was she doing it deliberately, to annoy her? She did her best to get on with her life, but by Saturday afternoon, her guilt was like a parasite, clawing at her insides. She fumbled for her phone and held her breath as it rang.

'Hi Mum. Sorry I missed your call.'

'That's okay,' her mother said with a sigh. 'I'm glad you called. I... I've been thinking about things lately, and I was wondering if you'd like to come for Christmas this year?'

'Christmas?' June laughed. 'Mum, it's August. Why are you talking about Christmas?'

'Because you haven't been home in over a year, and I have to say, I miss you.'

'Do you?'

'Will you stop saying things like that? Of course I miss you. I'm your mother.'

June searched her mind but failed to come up with the correct response to this. It always fascinated her whenever people talked to their mothers on the phone with such ease, as if they were talking to one of their friends. Her family had never been like that. As a child, she had worked hard to keep them out of her life, so that she could actually have one. And now she was an adult, things just seemed to carry on with the same dynamic.

'Do you... do you have any plans for Christmas?'

'I haven't even begun to think about it,' June said.

'So will you come?'

'I'll think about it.'

Which they both knew was shorthand for no.

Her mother sighed. 'I suppose I'll have to come and see you then. It just isn't so easy, with me being in this chair. We'll have to stay at a hotel or something.'

June felt her shoulders tense.

Why was she doing this? Her visits were so awkward. She doubted her mother got any more out of them than she did.

June let her mother weigh up the implications of coming to visit. If she let her talk long enough, she'd probably talk herself out of it. Predictably, her monologue moved on and soon she was telling June about her tedious weekly visit to the supermarket. There was really very little June could add to a conversation about the price of carrots. She hadn't even noticed they'd gone up.

'Right, well I suppose I'd better let you go now,' her mother said, winding up the call.

'Yes, it's been nice talking,' June said, playing her part. She waited for her mother to say goodbye, but instead, she said something she couldn't quite hear.

'Sorry, what was that?'

'I said, I'm sorry I sent you away.'

June blinked. 'What are you talking about?'

Her mum hiccupped. 'We never should have sent you off to boarding school. You were just a little girl...'

The confession was so unexpected that June wondered if she'd heard right.

'Don't worry about it, Mum. I loved St Winifred's.'

'I know you did. But what I'm trying to say is that I should never have sent you away so young. You were at that rebellious, troublesome age, and I had to focus on my recovery.'

'I get it. You were angry and didn't want to deal with me.'

'Yes,' her mother acknowledged.

June was shocked to hear her admit it. She'd never known her mum to be so honest.

'I know a lot of time has passed. You've built a life for yourself and I'm very proud of all you've achieved.'

Her words were like spears against a shield. She didn't need her mother now. She'd needed her sixteen years ago. Still, since her mum was making an effort, maybe she should too.

'I know the accident was my fault. I'm the one who shoved you, without thinking about the consequences, but it really was unintentional and you and Dad treated me like I did it on purpose.'

'I'm sorry, June.'

'I'm sorry too, but to answer your earlier question, no, I don't think I can make it home for Christmas.'

'How about Boxing Day?'

'No!' She hadn't meant to be so harsh, but the thought of visiting her parents had become unbearable.

'I'm sorry, Mum, I don't want to promise something I won't be able to do. I've got a lot on now. A lot of commitments at work and with... my housemates.'

For a moment there, she had almost slipped up and

mentioned Dan. That was the last thing she wanted to do. She would never hear the end of it.

Her mum seemed to pick up on it, like a sixth sense. 'Are you seeing someone?'

She gritted her teeth and rolled back her head. She really, really didn't want to be having this conversation.

'It's early days. Too soon to be talking about it.'

'You can talk to me about anything. I'm your mum.'

June cringed. Didn't she get it? That was precisely why she couldn't talk to her. Nothing about their family was normal. Even mentioning Dan's name could ruin the delicate balance of their fledgling relationship. Heaven forbid she should want to meet him. Heaven forbid she would have to tell him the whole shameful story. She could picture his face, shocked, yet sympathetic. She'd just been a kid, he could hardly hold it against her. But he would look at her differently, the way they all did once they knew.

'June? Are you still there?'

'Yes, Mum, I'm just tired. Can we talk about this another time?'

'If that's what you want, darling.'

Darling? She hadn't been her mother's darling in years, maybe never. She said goodbye and switched off her phone. She stared blankly at her bookcase, wondering for the billionth time what her life would be like if she hadn't made that big mistake.

THIRTY-SEVEN

POPPY

Three Months Earlier

Poppy's eyes widened as she read Flick's text:

> *Sorry to be the bearer of bad news but I'm afraid June wants*
> *you out of the house. She's kind of backed us all into a corner.*
> *Look, I know this sounds nuts, but she's got it into her head*
> *that you don't like her. Perhaps you could have a word with*
> *her, get her back onside?*

Instantly, she regretted all the games she'd been playing. It was one thing to mess with June, another to end up on the streets. She couldn't afford a different room. She couldn't even afford the removal van. She slapped her palm against her forehead. Stupid, stupid Poppy. Why couldn't she have been more subtle about her revenge? Why did she have to make it so obvious to June that she was messing with her?

She avoided June for as long as she could, but if June was determined to throw her out, then at some point, she was going to have to face up to it. She considered begging, but she didn't know if she could stomach that. She still hated June, still wanted her to pay for messing up her university career.

She liked the other housemates. Maybe there was a way to win them round? An idea formed in her head. What if she staged an accident of some sort, so that June would get the blame?

She had watched enough football to know how to dive. The trick was to make it look worse than it was. What if she stood at the top of the stairs and deliberately rolled down a couple of steps? She should be fine if she was careful, and she could make out that June had shoved her. That was bound to win her some sympathy from the others.

She was in the kitchen when June arrived home. She heard her stomp down the stairs and bang on her bedroom door. She was tempted to avoid her again, but maybe she should just get it over with.

She put down her snack and headed towards her bedroom. There was a triumphant look on June's face as she caught her in the hallway. She barely even looked at Poppy as she launched into her speech.

'I'm sorry but it's not working out. I'm going to have to ask you to leave the house. Of course, you can stay while you find a new place and I will be happy to help you—'

Poppy swallowed hard and let out a piercing scream that echoed through the house. June looked up in surprise, and Poppy took a step back, misjudged it and overbalanced. She grabbed desperately at the banister but missed. Her body hit each step with a painful thump until she landed on her back at the bottom.

She stared up at June, and June stared back down, both equally startled. Poppy tried to inhale but all the breath had been knocked out of her and it took her a moment to get it back.

She remained where she was as the others came running in to help but, by now, she had become aware of a sickening pain in her arm. Flick drew nearer and gasped at the sight. Poppy turned her head and saw what she was gawping at. Her arm was all bent out of shape. The pain grew stronger as she attempted to move. She couldn't believe she'd done this. She'd pulled some crazy stunts in her life but this was on another level.

THIRTY-EIGHT

CREEP

I get up early for my morning jog, changing into my running gear and filling my water bottle before I leave the house. I check the running app, pleased to see he's leaving his house too. It's so much easier when he's consistent. Sometimes, he decides to go for a random jog right in the middle of the day. It isn't always convenient to join him them. After all, I do have a job.

I run along the pavement, getting into my stride. I see him up ahead. He's wearing his lightweight raincoat, with the hood pulled up over his ears.

I fall into step behind him, and allow my eyes to stray around the common. It's quiet this morning, not too many people up just yet. He begins a long lap around the pond and I head for the bushes. I wait there, unsure precisely how long it will be until he appears. Sometimes he veers off and heads in a different direction entirely, but today he seems to be keeping the course.

I unzip my backpack, pull out the brick and wait.

THIRTY-NINE

JUNE

June was engrossed in Marilyn's weekly bulletin when she heard a soft but insistent knock. Gulnara stood just outside her office door.

June waved her inside. 'Do you want a biscuit? I have some good ones.'

Gulnara shook her head and shifted her weight. 'No thanks, I'm just off to lunch but I wanted to let you know I saw your profile on another dating site. Shall I email you the link?'

June groaned and rolled her eyes. 'Yes please! And thank you for letting me know.'

Gulnara pulled out her phone and sent it to her before dashing off again.

June clicked on the link, and there was her profile – complete with the same picture Poppy had taken of her that night on Clapham Common. She scrolled further down. Yes, it was the same bio as the one Poppy had posted on the other dating sites. Presumably, this had been up there all along but she and Gulnara had somehow missed it.

She looked for a help link so she could notify the site's admin that she wanted it taken down. As she did, something caught her eye on the left-hand side of the page. It was a strip of men's profiles, and at the top was a picture of Dan.

She clicked to enlarge it. He was laughing and hugging an adorable hedgehog close to his chest. Underneath was a short but heartfelt description of himself. Much as she wanted to believe Poppy had done this, those words, and that picture, could only have come from him.

She swallowed hard. Dan had never mentioned using dating sites before. In fact, she distinctly recalled him making fun of them.

Hands shaking, she hammered out a text, then deleted it. This was too big to talk about over messenger. She needed to see him face to face. She needed to know why he'd lied.

They met in a corner café tucked away on a side street. Dan had a gift for finding these places. He took her to a different one every time. He was wearing his faded blue shirt and he smelt of detergent and cologne. She breathed him in, trying to keep her mind steady.

He kissed her lightly on the cheek and pulled out a chair for her. They both sat down, their knees brushing against each other's.

'How was work?' he asked.

June couldn't answer. 'I saw your profile on a dating site,' she said in a tight voice. 'What's going on?'

His arms dropped to his sides and his shoulders slumped.

'Tell me the truth, Dan, I can't stand being lied to.'

He swallowed hard. 'Okay, I did make a profile. It was months ago and I wasn't having any success meeting anyone in real life.'

'So why did you tell me you never used those sites?'

'I never have. Nothing came out of it. I didn't go on any

dates or anything. I didn't like the vibe. Until I saw your picture.'

June squeezed her eyes tight. 'Go on.'

'I saw your picture, and I read your profile. I saw that you liked cycling and good food. I could tell you were my type of person. You were so natural and so... different to all the others. And the thing is, I thought I recognised you from my morning commute. So instead of getting in touch, I kept my eyes open. And there you were, just outside Sainsbury's. I went over and made up that thing about the chain. I hadn't planned it, it just came out of my mouth. I know I should have told you, but I wanted a good origin story. I thought, if this works out, if we get together, I don't want to have met online. I want this to be real. Please, please don't hate me.'

June's eyebrows knitted together. She slowly shook her head, pressing her lips into a thin line of disbelief.

'I'm struggling to get my head round this. You lied to me. Even if it was with good intentions. It doesn't feel right. I feel like I don't know who you are anymore.'

She rose quickly, and in a single, fluid motion, grabbed her bag and flung it over her shoulder.

Dan's eyes pleaded with her. 'Don't go.'

'I need to go home and think about this.'

'Will you call me?'

'I'm off to Mykonos on Saturday. I think we'll just leave it until I come back.'

He swallowed. 'What time are you leaving? I'll come and see you off.'

'No, Dan. Let me sort things out in my head. I'll call you when I'm ready.'

'June...'

She stood up abruptly, stepping around the barista who was sweeping the floor. As she walked down the street, she took one last glance back at Dan, at his soulful brown eyes, and his thick, wavy brown hair. Then she swung a leg over her bike and pedalled away.

June took a sip of her tea and folded the T-shirt twice, then rolled it into a tight bundle. She placed it in her suitcase and patted it down, checking there was still enough room for the souvenirs she would inevitably buy. Satisfied, she zipped it up and headed upstairs to check on her housemates.

She stopped in front of Kimmy's door to find a large blue suitcase overflowing with clothes and other items. The zipper was half-open, revealing hastily packed belongings that appeared to have been crammed into the already bulging case.

'Make sure you leave a bit of room in case you want to bring anything back with you.'

Kimmy waved her away. 'Oh, it'll be fine.'

A throbbing beat emanated from Flick's room. A quick glance through the half-closed door revealed Flick and Poppy dancing, their limbs a blur as they twisted and spun. There was a suitcase open on the bed with a few shirts in it. It looked as if they'd got distracted halfway through.

She headed up the next flight of stairs to Tamsin's attic bedroom. Tamsin was busy painting her nails.

'Are you packed?'

'I'll do it later,' Tamsin said.

'How much later?'

'Don't worry. It's all under control.'

Honestly, they were all supposed to be getting up at six. They had a taxi booked to take them to the airport.

Shaking her head, June trudged back down the stairs. She was sure that if Kimmy's bulky suitcase was anything to go by, they were going to be well over the weight limit for their baggage, and she didn't want any nasty surprises at check-in. She marched into the bathroom and dragged out the creaky green scales. Placing them on the tiled floor, she yelled up the stairs: 'Don't forget to weigh your bags!'

'Oh, someone's getting stressed!' Poppy said loudly.

June ignored her and returned to her room. She sat down on the bed and pulled out her phone. She badly wanted to text Dan, but she was still hurt by what he'd done. Instead, she forced herself to set it down and reached for her guidebook.

She had been looking forward to Mykonos when Kimmy first mentioned it, but now she was feeling nervous. Every time Kimmy mentioned Ralph or her wedding plans, the knot tightened in her stomach. How could she possibly enjoy herself knowing that she would have to break Kimmy's heart on the return?

She yawned widely. It was still early but she decided to get ready for bed. She stood in the bathroom cleaning her teeth, listening to the steady hum of her electric toothbrush when she heard someone behind her. She whipped around. Her housemate had a weary expression with furrowed brows and dark rings under her eyes.

'June, I need you to come and look at something,' she said in a low voice.

June blinked twice. 'What is it?'

'You need to come now. It's urgent.'

FORTY

POPPY

'Everybody wake up!' Poppy yelled. She couldn't resist banging loudly on June's door as she walked past. Some habits were hard to break.

It was a sure bet that June was already up. She was probably standing by the front door, looking at her watch. Their taxi was due in half an hour to take them to the airport. June would be counting every minute.

The house was quiet. She spent a few minutes getting ready then climbed up the stairs. Tamsin opened the door to her attic room and looked down, yawning.

'I'm awake,' she called.

'Me too,' Flick said.

Poppy banged on Kimmy's door. There was no response. She went inside and found Kimmy face down on the bed.

'Wake up!' she said, opening the curtains. Light streamed in but Kimmy didn't stir. Poppy reached for the light switch and shook her gently.

'Kimmy?'

Kimmy murmured something, but her eyes remain closed.

'Kimmy!' she said louder, clapping her hands. 'You need to wake up! We're going to Mykonos!'

Kimmy did not respond. Poppy went and banged on Flick's door.

'Help me wake Kimmy!'

Flick scurried out of her room and headed towards the bathroom. She emerged moments later holding a jug of cold water. She headed into Kimmy's room and sprinkled a few drops over her head.

A startled shriek followed as Kimmy jolted awake, still groggy but now fully upright in bed, sending droplets of water across the sheets. Her expression was unmistakably annoyed, until Poppy said, 'Mykonos!'

At that, Kimmy perked up. 'Mykonos!' she echoed.

Flick picked up the jug and deposited it safely back in the bathroom.

Poppy headed back to her room to apply her make-up and style her hair.

A little later she heard Kimmy. 'The taxi's five minutes away! Everybody downstairs! This is not a drill!'

There was an excited panic as the housemates flapped about. Suitcases were hauled downstairs, and feet thundered as everyone charged about. Poppy emerged from her room to find Tamsin sitting on the bottom stair, lacing her shoes.

Flick headed down the stairs with a grim look on her face.

'I've just had a text from June. She's on her way to Kent. Apparently, she got a call in the night to say her mum's been taken seriously ill.'

A shadow passed across Tamsin's face. Poppy guessed she was thinking of her own father. Kimmy had told her how Tamsin had missed being there when he died.

'Poor June. That's awful.'

They all looked at Kimmy, who was checking her phone. 'I've got a text too.'

Her eyes moved quickly as she digested the message. 'She says we should go ahead without her. Send her lots of pictures and we'll see her when we come back.' She swallowed and looked up at them. 'What are we going to do? Do you think we should cancel?'

'We can't cancel. This is your hen do,' Poppy said, barely repressing a smile. 'I mean, this sucks for June, it really does, but there's no reason why the rest of us shouldn't go. It's not like we can do much to help.'

'I could go after her,' Kimmy said hesitantly. She didn't want to, Poppy could tell. She was looking for reassurance.

She shot a quick glance around the room, taking in the subtle shift in body language as her housemates digested the news that June would not be joining them. She watched as tension left their frames and shoulders softened. She let out a long breath. It seemed they all felt a sense of relief at not having to deal with June's insistence on eating proper food and following the rules. Fond as they clearly were of her, everyone needed a break once in a while.

'Let's get her something nice,' Tamsin said. 'What do you think she'd like?'

'Knowing her, she'd like a boring book about Mykonos,' Poppy said.

'She really would,' Flick said with a smile. 'And maybe a tea towel.'

Kimmy's face clouded over again. She looked uncertain, indecisive.

'It's too late to cancel,' Flick said firmly.

'Yeah, come on, Kimmy,' Poppy said. She was damned if she was going to let June's bad luck spoil their fun. It was just bad timing, that was all. It couldn't be helped.

As if on cue, a car beeped its horn on the street below. Flick ran to the window.

'The taxi's here,' she confirmed. A moment later, the doorbell rang and everyone sprang into action. Poppy sprinted to the door while the others raced around, zipping up bags and double-checking that windows were locked.

'Everyone got their passports?' Tamsin yelled, as she checked the back door.

'Chargers!' Flick added, swiping hers from the wall outlet.

Poppy paused for a moment, and cast her gaze around the kitchen and then the living room. She had a gnawing feeling in her stomach, as though she was missing something, but she had no idea what. There was an atmosphere of frenzied excitement as they burst outside, Flick and Tamsin were singing as Kimmy locked the door behind them.

The taxi driver had the boot open ready for their luggage. He helped them stow their bags, then they all piled into the car, with long-legged Flick bagging the front seat. It was only as the taxi pulled away that it occurred to Poppy that the taxi company had only sent them a normal sized car. If June had been there, they wouldn't have all fitted. She might have lingered on that thought, but everyone was chattering loudly, excited for the holiday to begin.

FORTY-ONE

POPPY

Poppy pressed her forehead against the window and inhaled sharply as the plane descended. The horizon was dotted with whitewashed buildings, and the sun was a blazing ball in the bright blue sky. As they touched down on the runway, she was practically vibrating with anticipation. The plane sat on the tarmac for several minutes and everyone was getting restless. Flick stood up and sat down again. Tamsin wriggled about, then pulled out her phone and started taking selfies.

'I can't wait to get a drink,' said Kimmy, stretching her hands above her head.

'I just want to jump into the pool,' Poppy said.

When they made it out of the airport, they crammed into the back of a taxi. The driver spoke rapid Greek into his Bluetooth headset as they weaved through the increasingly narrow streets.

The holiday villa was nestled among olive trees, a low building constructed from pale white stone that glowed in the late afternoon light. The Aegean sea shimmered beyond, just a few feet from the terrace, and Poppy could hear the waves crashing on the shore.

Kimmy pulled a wad of notes from her pocket and paid for the taxi. The sun beat down on them as they offloaded their bags. Flick located a small grey lockbox with their keys in it.

'Kimmy, what's the code?'

Kimmy stepped up, squinting in the sun as she punched it in. It didn't open.

Poppy's stomach twisted, and she shifted from one foot to the other. The taxi was already reversing out of the driveway. She yelled to the driver to wait but he took no notice.

'Do it again. Perhaps you made a mistake.'

'I didn't,' Kimmy insisted.

She punched it in again with the same result.

'Here, let me try,' Tamsin held out her palm for Kimmy's phone. She peered at the instructions then clicked her tongue.

'You missed out the zero at the beginning.'

She punched in the correct code and to everyone's relief, the lock clicked open. Tamsin grabbed the keys and hurried to the door. They slotted smoothly into the lock, and she pushed it open. Everyone cheered as they got their first peek of the holiday house.

Poppy stepped inside, instantly drawn to the living room with its airy white curtains and wooden floors. She peered down the hallway, where two small bedrooms were tucked away, then glanced into the bathroom and kitchen – both of which were charmingly decorated with whitewashed walls and terracotta tiles.

Kimmy and Flick had claimed the front bedroom, so she dragged her bags into the second one. She surveyed the room. The beds were lined up against the walls, covered with plain white duvets. A desk was wedged in between them, along with an old wicker chair and a copy of the bible.

'Which bed do you want?' Tamsin asked.

'I don't mind,' Poppy said, her brow furrowed.

Tamsin set her suitcase down on one of the beds, and pulled out a bright red swimsuit. She stopped and looked at Poppy. 'Something wrong?'

'No. Well... it's just... where was June supposed to sleep?'

Tamsin glanced around. 'I suppose the sofa in the living room flips out into another bed.'

They changed into their swimsuits, eager to get down to the pool. As they stepped onto the veranda, Poppy saw that the pool was already crowded with tourists seeking relief from the heat.

'All the sun loungers are taken,' Flick complained.

'Never mind, let's get a drink,' Kimmy said.

They found seats at a small wooden table near the bar and ordered bright blue Mati cocktails.

Poppy pulled the drink towards her lips and took a long sip. The fruity flavour danced on her tongue.

Flick pointed across the road to an old-fashioned café. 'That café serves fish and chips,' she said. 'Maybe we could go there a bit later.'

Poppy smiled. 'I can just imagine what June would say!'

'Hey, talking of June, let's get a photo for her,' Tamsin said. She waved to the waiter and he obligingly took their photo.

'Everybody say cheese!'

'Make sure you get the fish and chip sign in the background,' Flick said. 'June's going to be screaming at her phone!'

Kimmy's shoulders sagged. 'Let's not talk about June. I feel guilty enough as it is.'

Tamsin threw an arm around her. 'It's not your fault her mum got ill. Let's try to enjoy ourselves. This is your hen do, after all.'

They became creatures of habit, rising just in time to claim the last four sunbeds, lounging on the beach or by the pool.

Lunch was always at the same beach café, with bright umbrellas shading the tables. After the first couple of days of chips, they branched out and tried local dishes like souvlaki, dolmades and freshly caught fish, accompanied by a carafe of white wine from local vineyards.

Afterwards, they swam and sunbathed until nightfall, with the occasional game of table tennis or volleyball if they were in the mood.

As the sky grew dark, they would find a lively bar where they'd drink frozen ouzo blended with watermelon and mint and dance until morning.

Only on the last day, Poppy realised with a jolt that they hadn't seen much of the island, so she convinced the others to join an afternoon tour.

The sun beat down on them as they hiked along stone pathways until they reached Chora's iconic windmills.

'Satisfied?' Flick said, after they'd posed for dozens of photos.

Poppy nodded and fanned her straw hat in front of her face.

They headed back to the villa to get dressed up for one more night of dancing.

They stayed out later than usual, continuing the party on the beach with another group of holidaymakers. Gradually, the others drifted back to their villas until they were the last people left on the beach. Poppy yawned and sat down on a big rock at the edge of the water. She dug her toes into the cool sand. Kimmy dropped down beside her, shivering slightly as a gentle breeze blew. Together, they watched as a pale pink streak rose from the darkness. Delicate wisps of orange smeared the sky, creating a vivid wash of colour in the clouds.

'June would have loved this,' Kimmy murmured.

'June would have gone to bed,' Poppy said.

Somewhere behind her, Flick snorted.

'We'd better head back,' Tamsin said, slipping her feet into her flip-flops.

Poppy nodded. She stood and gave Kimmy her hand to help her up. The four of them walked back to the villa for the last time.

'How has it gone so fast?' Kimmy asked with regret.

'I don't know, but it's been amazing,' Poppy said. 'Best holiday ever!'

Back in London, the taxi inched its way through the traffic-clogged street. Poppy shifted in her seat, careful not to wake Tamsin, who was dozing beside her. The bus in front of them had ground to a halt, so Poppy's eyes were drawn to the common.

The grass verge was bustling with police, and along one edge of the parkland a barricade of yellow caution tape had been strung up.

'They found a body in the water,' the taxi driver said.

'Oh, how awful,' Flick said from the front seat.

Kimmy hugged her arms over her chest and a tingle crept down Poppy's spine. She wished the bus would get moving again. She was suddenly desperate to get home.

When the taxi pulled up outside their house, they all clambered out, dragging their suitcases up the path. Kimmy was the last to get out, her sunburned skin almost matching the Team Bride T-shirts they were all wearing. They dumped their bags in the hall and collapsed onto the sofas like sloths.

'Hey, wait!' Poppy said, jumping up. She retrieved her selfie stick from her bag. After a few clicks and turns, she positioned it perfectly to capture the four of them, squeezing herself into the frame at the last minute.

'Has anyone heard from June?' Tamsin asked as they held the pose.

'Not for a few days,' Kimmy admitted.

'Well what's the latest? Is her mum any better?'

'I don't know. She hasn't returned any of my calls. I assume she's still in hospital.'

'I hope she's okay.'

Since no one felt like cooking, Tamsin pulled out her phone and ordered a takeaway from their favourite Chinese restaurant. They lounged around, waiting for the food to arrive. Poppy couldn't help thinking that if June was here, she would probably insist they all took their bags to their rooms. As it was, they were piled all over the place, blocking the hallways. The sand from their flip-flops spilling onto the floor.

The food arrived quickly and they all gathered around the table to eat.

Poppy sniffed appreciatively, the sweet aroma of curry and garlic wafting up her nose. Steamy prawns and fried rice sat on the table, along with chicken, dumplings and spring rolls. It all looked delicious, but Poppy was vigilant for mushrooms, raking through each dish to ensure there were none.

They had just started eating when the doorbell rang again.

'Maybe it's June!' Tamsin said.

Poppy jumped up to open it. Dan stood on the doorstep, his curly hair dishevelled. Stubble dotted his jawline, emphasising the tiredness in his eyes. He looked disappointed to see her.

'Can I speak to June?' he asked.

Kimmy stepped in front of Poppy. 'She doesn't want to see you.'

Dan tried to look past her into the hallway.

'She's not even here,' Poppy said. She glanced at Kimmy in confusion. Did Dan not know about June's mum?

Kimmy didn't bother to tell him.

'Can you tell her I called round?' he asked, looking desperate. 'I really need to see her.'

Poppy's heart went out to him. 'Yes, of course we will,' she said gently, but Kimmy was already shutting the door.

'June's made it quite clear she doesn't want to see you, thank you.'

Poppy stared at her. 'Don't you think June should be the one to decide that?'

Kimmy rubbed her arm. 'June's vulnerable right now. Her emotions will be all over the place. Trust me, Poppy, I've known her longer than you have. She needs to focus on her family right now.'

Poppy returned to the table but found her appetite had diminished. Something was nagging at her, causing her stomach to churn. She felt unsettled. She just couldn't quite say why.

Once everyone had finished, she helped clear the table and dumped all the empty containers in the bin. The others sat in the living room, fiddling with their phones, or in Tamsin's case, painting her toenails.

Poppy finished clearing up, shoving the plates in the dishwasher any old how and slamming it shut. She pulled her phone out of her pocket and texted June.

Just thought you'd want to know, Dan popped round to see you. He seems really desperate to talk.

Immediately, she heard a phone ping in the living room. A moment later, she got a reply.

Thanks for letting me know, but I can't deal with him right now.

Kimmy wandered into the kitchen and flicked on the kettle.

Poppy glanced down at her phone.

OK. Totally your decision.

She glanced at the living room, her heart in her mouth, and clicked send.

And for the second time, she heard the ping.

FORTY-TWO

POPPY

Poppy inhaled deeply. She stuffed her phone into her pocket and walked into the living room.

'Did I leave my phone in here?'

'Is that yours on the window?' Tamsin asked.

'No, that's mine,' Flick said.

There was another phone on the coffee table next to Tamsin's. It was bright pink, clearly Kimmy's.

'Okay, I probably left it in my room,' Poppy said, doing her best to sound unconcerned.

But as she headed towards the basement, she paused in front of June's room, her hand resting on the door handle. She glanced quickly behind her to make sure no one was watching, and in she went.

The first thing that struck her, as always, was June's tidiness. The bed was perfectly made, the pillows plumped just so, and she could make out the faint smell of citrus cleaning solution. She knelt down and peered underneath the bed. There was nothing but boxes of dusty old books stored there. She stood and walked over to the window, drawing back the curtains to let the light stream in. She wasn't entirely sure what she was looking for. She just sensed that something wasn't right.

She cast a critical eye over June's desk, taking in the neat stack of library books, a slim laptop and keyboard, and a set of pens lined up in rainbow order. She opened one of the drawers and peered inside. Everything was just as she would expect. She closed it and tried the one below, but it contained nothing but more books. As she stepped away from the desk, she saw that there was something on the chair: June's handbag.

Curiously, she picked it up. Obviously, June might have other handbags, but Poppy had never seen her with anything other than this one. She delved inside. There in the front pocket was June's passport, and in the back pocket, her wallet. She pulled it out and looked through it. There were two credit cards inside. A ten-pound note. A library card and a Nectar card. She felt a gnarled, twisting sensation in her stomach. Something was off here.

She left the bag where it was and walked quickly out of the room, bumping into Tamsin in the corridor.

'What are you doing?' Tamsin asked.

'I was looking for my curling tongs.'

Tamsin laughed. 'I highly doubt June has them.'

'I distinctly remember lending them to her,' Poppy lied. 'Perhaps she's taken them with her?'

Tamsin tilted her head but said nothing.

'Anyway, I'm tired,' Poppy said. 'I think I'll have an early night.'

'Yeah, me too.' Tamsin let out a yawn.

Poppy slipped past her and took the stairs to her bedroom. Once inside, she leaned against the door, her heart thumping out of her chest. It wasn't right. Something wasn't right.

She changed into the oversized T-shirt she liked to sleep in and settled into bed. It was an uneasy night. She tossed and turned, thoughts swirling around in her head. Perhaps she should go to the police? They could go to June's parents' house and check that June was okay. No, she was being ridiculous, letting her imagination run away with her. There had to be a simple explanation for all this.

She wasn't quite asleep when she heard the creak in the darkness. The sound of the front door softly opening and shutting. She lay awake, trying to work out what was happening. Who would be going out at this time? What on earth could they be up to?

Somehow, she drifted off to sleep but she woke up on Sunday morning with an even greater feeling of unease.

Her housemates were already up when she wandered upstairs.

Kimmy was on the phone to the caterers, arguing about something to do with the wedding cake.

'No, I said no fruit cake. We want chocolate cake, covered in fondant. Three layers.'

She shook her head in exasperation and listened for a moment before hanging up the phone.

Flick stepped forward, a steely expression on her face. 'That's enough, Kimmy. It's time for you to stop playing around and admit the truth.'

Kimmy's eyes widened in shock, and for a moment, Poppy thought she might cry.

She looked from Flick to Kimmy, trying to figure out what was going on.

Flick sighed. 'There isn't going to be a wedding, is there?'

'What do you mean?' Poppy asked. 'Did something happen?'

Kimmy went pale. Tears rolled down her cheeks.

'There never was a wedding,' Flick said, her voice low and accusing. 'He didn't ask you to marry him, did he, Kimmy?'

Kimmy sank down onto a stool and shook her head, tears streaming down her face.

Poppy gasped. 'What happened?'

Kimmy took a few deep breaths and blew her nose.

'He broke up with me. I couldn't handle it. I loved him so much, I wanted to get married so badly.'

'So, you lied,' Flick said, her expression softening. 'You paid for the holiday and the bridesmaid dresses yourself. How on earth could you afford that?'

'I... I put it all on my credit card. And when I couldn't afford the repayments, I took out another one. And another.'

Flick gestured towards the ring on Kimmy's finger.

'You bought that too, didn't you?'

Kimmy nodded, her chin quivering.

Poppy looked at Flick. 'How did you know?'

'Well, first off, Kimmy said he proposed with a flash mob at Marble Arch. I looked online because I wanted to find a recording of it but there was nothing up there. Not a picture, not a video, not even a comment. I couldn't understand that. Someone would have filmed it. And then we saw Ralph jogging in the park, but Kimmy said it was his brother. She had a weird look on her face when she said that and it made me wonder. He looked exactly like Ralph and he ran right by us without so much as a wave. The more I thought about it, the more I realised it didn't add up. And then there were no invitations, just the save the date card stuck on the fridge. So, I just rang the venue and enquired about the day the wedding was supposed to be. They told me they're going to be holding a Hindu festival that day. No weddings.'

Kimmy's tears streamed down her cheeks as a heavy silence filled the room.

'That's why you deleted your Instagram,' Poppy realised. She had thought that was odd at the time. 'Because you were linked to Ralph.'

'He changed his status to single. I felt angry and humiliated.'

'Damn, Kimmy. You should have said something. You must have spent so much money...'

'It doesn't matter,' Kimmy said. 'Don't you see? None of it matters. If I don't have Ralph, I don't have anything.'

Flick wrapped her arms around her. 'That's not true. You have us!'

Poppy backed away and headed down to her room, trying to understand what the hell was going on. It seemed Kimmy was a very convincing liar. Everyone but Flick had been suckered in. What else had she lied about?

Someone had gone out in the night. Was that Kimmy too? What was she up to? Poppy was getting a really bad feeling. Everyone thought June had gone home, but how could she, without her bag? Without her wallet?

Maybe she'd taken her bike. She loved that bike. She remembered how upset she had been when she stole it. She felt bad about that now. She ran her hand along the back of her head, feeling the beads of sweat gathering at her hairline. She slipped on her flip-flops and stepped out into the garden, trying to recall the codes for the shed.

June had done a thorough job of reinforcing it. The new locks glinted under the sun's rays. The code for the old one had been 2512, meaning the twenty-fifth of the twelfth, because everyone loved Christmas. As for the new one... Poppy thought for a moment. That was right. It was the date of Kimmy's supposed wedding. She punched in 2809 and heard a click as the second padlock opened.

She grasped the door handle and pulled it open. She was assaulted by a pungent odour of cleaning products. She squinted into the dim light. There were dents on the walls and empty paint cans strewn across the floor. She looked up to see June's bike still hanging from its hook, but something felt off about it. Her stomach churned as she caught another scent hidden beneath the overpowering chemical stench. It smelt as though something had died in there.

FORTY-THREE

JUNE

Eight Days Earlier

They'd left her. They'd really left her.

Even now, she wondered if it was all a cruel joke. A tiny, wishful part of her still thought they were going to drive around the corner, then come back for her. Maybe they would reveal that she was on some hidden camera programme? Or perhaps they'd gone to the police station to report her missing.

But the ropes digging into her wrists were real, and so was the fear and betrayal churning in her stomach. Tears stung her eyes as she wondered how they could do this to her. If they got on that plane, she could be stuck here until next Saturday – a full week with no food or drink and nowhere to relieve herself. They had treated her worse than an animal; how was she supposed to survive? She slowly sank to the floor, exhaustion and hopelessness settling in her bones.

Time ticked by. She didn't know precisely how much. She had no way to quantify it. She felt naked without her watch and phone. There was nothing to do but explore the contents of the shed, and the results were not encouraging. She searched as thoroughly as she could without her hands to help her, but she was fairly certain there was nothing whatsoever to eat or drink. And not a knife or a pair of scissors to be found anywhere. Her own suitcase stood in the corner. How she wished she had packed it full of food and water, but she knew there would be nothing in there except clean clothes and toiletries. Cold fear crept into her bones as she thought about what was in store for her. How long could a person survive without water?

Meanwhile, a relentless pressure was building inside her like a balloon ready to burst. Her legs trembled and she broke out into a cold sweat. Unable to contain it any longer, a warm trickle raced down her inner thighs and pooled around her feet. She shivered, cold now and unable to take off her trousers.

A memory drifted into her mind. She'd been five years old and she'd wet herself on the playground at school. She had been mortified, but Kimmy had had her back. June had hid behind the slide while Kimmy brought her a clean uniform from the lost property. It was massive on her. It had probably belonged to one of the year threes, but June was grateful to have something clean to put on. There were no spare socks or underwear so she had had to wear her PE shorts. She and Kimmy had linked hands. Even at five, they had felt like family. There was no way June would tell her mum what had happened, but Kimmy understood.

A fat black fly circled the pool of urine, its wings beating a distorted rhythm against the still air. It seemed to follow her every move, buzzing in her ears and making her feel like crawling out of her own skin.

She had to assume it was Poppy who had done this to her. But how did she hope to get away with it? When June got out she would go straight to the police. Unless she didn't get out. Then she would die here, all alone in this shed.

Fuelled with fury, she tried again, yelling and screaming

and throwing herself against the door, but all she did was get hurt. No matter how loud she yelled, no one came.

She sank down onto the floor to rest for a few minutes, then she tackled her suitcase, pulling on the zipper with her teeth. Once she had it open, she stuck her head inside, surveying the contents, but as she feared it was mainly clothes. There weren't even any books. She'd planned to read on her phone to save space.

She fought against the bindings, her wrists and legs aching from the tight ropes. The coarse fibres scraped against her skin and beads of sweat formed on her forehead. After several attempts to free herself, hope began to slip away. She shifted her weight, pressing her back firmly against the wall, and tried once more. She rocked back and forth with all of her strength, feeling the jagged edges of an old nail brushing her skin every time she made contact. Hours passed until finally, a strand snapped. She felt a momentary exhilaration, but it wasn't enough to free her, and she was becoming exhausted.

The light was beginning to fade and her eyes were growing tired. She shifted her weight, desperately trying to get comfortable. She positioned a pile of clothes on the floor beneath her but there were still hard edges, and the cold night air seeped in from outside. She wrinkled her nose at the pungent scent from her urine soaked clothes. Her stomach gave an uneasy lurch. What she wouldn't do for a nice hot bowl of tomato soup right now...

She heard faint rustling noises. Her pulse quickened as she tried to determine if the sound was coming from an animal or if it was her mind playing tricks on her. Then she heard a distinct snuffling noise that she hoped was just a hedgehog. What she feared the most was that rats and mice would come in during the night, drawn to her foul body odour. The stale mix of sweat and urine would surely attract them.

Struggling against the tight knots, her wrists and ankles

refused to let go. She felt the unforgiving coldness of the wooden floor pressing into her skin. Taking a deep breath, she pushed herself back up and hopped over to a stack of flattened cardboard boxes left behind from when Poppy had moved into the house. Clenching each one between her teeth, she dragged them across the floor until they formed a makeshift bed. She rearranged her clothes on top, lay down again and tried to get comfortable. She imagined being tucked up in her own bed, safe beneath soft cotton sheets and her cosy duvet. Her body ached from the stiffness of the floor, but she eventually dozed off, succumbing to exhaustion.

Heavy raindrops pounded against the roof. She was woken by a droplet running down her neck and sat up, suddenly alert. Her body ached and her head spun as she pushed herself to standing, but she stood with her mouth open, desperate to catch as many drops as she could.

After a while, the rain stopped and it gradually became light. Her stomach growled from hunger and she was so thirsty she would have drunk puddle water. She ran her tongue along the edges of her teeth, hoping to rub away the sour flavour that permeated her mouth. But no matter how much she licked, the unpleasant taste remained.

She sat in silence for a while, unable to process why this was happening to her. She already needed to urinate again, and her trousers and socks were still damp from the day before. Hot, angry tears rolled down her face, and she tried to catch them with her tongue. She had never known such deep, terrible desperation. Poppy must hate her more than she could possibly have imagined.

She heard a faint melody and realised it was coming from her next-door neighbour's garden. He was out there, whistling.

'Help!' she shouted as loud as her lungs would let her, and she threw her body against the shed door, making as much noise as possible. After a while, the whistling stopped. Desperate, she kept pounding and screaming until her throat was raw, but there was no response. The neighbour must have gone back inside.

Hours passed and no one came to check on her, confirming her suspicion that this was Poppy's doing. Did her friends wonder at all about her sudden disappearance, or did they blindly accept whatever lie they'd been told?

Marilyn would notice, she realised. She had only taken one week of holiday for the trip to Mykonos. When she failed to turn up on Monday morning, Marilyn would ring her and, when she didn't hear back, she would probably contact the police. But Monday was a long way off. There was a significant chance she wouldn't last that long.

Dan was her best chance. But he probably believed she'd gone off on holiday. She regretted her last words to him. She had been so harsh, telling him she'd speak to him when she got back. What he'd done seemed so minor now. But it was too late to fix it. He would take her lack of communication to mean she was still angry, and by the time he realised there was something wrong, it would be too late.

Even her mother wouldn't suspect. This coming Sunday was the last one of the month, but she doubted she was going to ring. And if she did, she'd simply think June was ignoring her. How could she expect her family to care when she was constantly pushing them away?

She didn't remember the last time she'd spoken to her father. Her mother occasionally put him on the line when the two of them ran out of things to say. He was an even worse communicator than she was. Their phone conversations consisted of nothing but discussions about the weather, or the results of the rugby. He was a dull man with dull pursuits. She hadn't thought about him in ages, but now she had an inexplicable urge to hear his voice. To have him ruminate on the chance of his team winning the championships this year, or even to talk about the plants he had growing in his greenhouse.

Plagued by regret, she checked through her suitcase again and this time she found something she'd missed: there were four little sugar sachets tucked into the inside pocket. She shook them out onto the floor. It was going to be a job to open them, but she needed the energy.

She didn't eat them all in one go. Instead, she sucked on two. The sweet granules stuck in her throat but she knew she needed the energy boost, so she forced them down. She kept the other two for the following day. By then, her head spun every time she stood up. Her cheeks felt warm and her heart raced. She was exhausted from the effort of trying to break free.

Her days were filled with monotony, pain and despair. She thrashed and moaned, squirming against the ropes in a vain attempt to loosen them, but she never succeeded in gaining more than a few millimetres of breathing room and she suffered many agonising spasms, when she would writhe around on the floor, unable to ease her binds.

When it all became too much, she began to withdraw into herself, living in a corner of her mind filled with fragments from her past. She found herself thinking of things she had long forgotten, like a camping holiday she'd been on with her parents, before her mother's accident. It had been a happy time. One she hadn't thought about in years. Then she'd recalled the whirlwind romance she'd had with Ralph at university. How quickly she'd fallen for him, and how she'd pined for him when he'd moved on to someone else. Perhaps that was why she'd encouraged Richard's advances, even though she knew he belonged with Grace.

On her third morning trapped in the shed, as she picked

herself up off the floor, she spotted a jagged shard of glass shining in the sunlight. She leaned forward and clamped her lips around it before cautiously rising back up. Now what?

She lay down and curled her body into position, pulling her feet up towards her mouth, and held the jagged piece of glass between her teeth. Slowly, painfully, she rubbed against her constraints. She could only manage a few of minutes of this before she needed to take a break because her stomach ached so much but she did not give up. It took a great deal of work and concentration, but she worked against the ropes until they began to fray.

As soon as she realised it was working, she dropped the glass and had to twist around and pick it up again, cutting her lip as she did so. She licked the blood with her dry tongue, desperate now for any kind of moisture, and then tried again, until she managed to position it between her teeth once more.

She sawed and sawed at the rope, her stomach spasming from holding the uncomfortable position. But bit by bit, her ankle constraints were coming loose. She kept at it, filing them down until finally, they snapped.

'Yes!'

Mentally, she pummelled the air, wishing she could reach out and massage her sore ankles.

Getting her hands free was going to be trickier. She couldn't reach to cut the ropes with the glass. She had been working her wrists against the small nail poking out of the wall, but she hadn't made much progress. Yet, now she had got her feet free, she was more certain it could be done.

She renewed her efforts, rubbing her wrists furiously against the nail. The rope dug deeper and deeper into her skin until she cried out in pain, but she kept going, pulling and straining at the ropes with all her might, her muscles burning from exertion until she finally felt the ropes fray.

Once they loosened, her job became easier. She worked her

hands up and down, desperate to be rid of them. She felt something snap like an elastic band and realised that she could move much more than before. She ground the ropes harder against the nail until, at last, they were off.

FORTY-FOUR

JUNE

A wave of shock rushed through her body as she realised she was free. Her hands were an icy shade of purple and a tingling sensation raced up and down her arms when she wiggled them. Great red welts encircled her wrists where the ropes had dug into her skin. She clenched her fists in an effort to stem the pins and needles radiating through her fingers.

Without waiting for the circulation to return to her hands, she turned towards the door. Her body shook badly as she tried to work the knob. Of course, it was locked. Padlocked from the outside. Probably bolted too. She recalled with regret the lengths she had gone to to secure the shed after her bike was stolen. Even the window seemed impenetrable. She had hammered thick sheets of plywood on either side. It was going to be tough to break through. Tears of frustration slid down her nose, knowing she had built her own prison.

She searched the shed again, hoping to find a tool that could help her open the door. She remembered there used to be a saw on the top shelf, but someone had been thorough in clearing out all useful items – the hammer, screwdriver and even the scissors were all gone.

She curled her fingers into a fist and pounded her knuckles against the hardwood door, again and again, wincing as blood spilled from her skin. Then she picked up Flick's scooter and hurled it. A faint crack appeared and she let out a victorious cry before launching a second attack with renewed energy. After dozens of attempts, she gave up, exhausted.

She stripped off her dirty clothes and changed into clean ones from her suitcase. The sensation of fresh, dry clothes against her skin was a joy. She found her brush and raked it through her filthy tangled hair, wincing as she found a large bump on the back of her head. Then she sprayed a little deodorant, enjoying the pleasant scent of lily of the valley.

Next, she fumbled around the shed, sorting through everything again, in case there was something she'd missed. She stopped when she spied a familiar shape wedged behind a can of engine oil. She brushed away the dirt and grime. It was a tin of spaghetti hoops.

Her mouth salivated. She looked all along the length of the shelf but there was no tin opener. And yet she knew this had been placed here deliberately. To taunt her. She hurled it onto the hard floor. The tin bounced off the ground with a metallic clang, but stubbornly refused to split open.

After several attempts, the metal was dented and scored but still stubbornly clung to its lid. Summoning all her strength, she put one foot against the wall for leverage, grasped the tin tightly, and squeezed with every ounce of energy she had. She imagined herself as Popeye from the old cartoons. She worked her muscles and growled like an animal. Finally, it opened with a satisfying pop.

Her hand trembled as it slid into the cool metal can of spaghetti hoops. She winced at the sharp edges, but her hunger overpowered all other sensations and she tipped back the tin to her lips. With each slurp, she greedily sucked down more spaghetti, barely pausing to swallow the slimy strands before taking another mouthful. She gulped it down, forcing herself to stop while there was still half a tin left. Her stomach ached with fullness, but her throat still begged for more.

She lay down, feeling the heavy languor of a full belly. Her stomach let out a loud gurgle and seized in painful spasms. A fly circled around the open tin, buzzing insistently. She slapped it away and covered it with a T-shirt.

She tried to relax once more but there was no avoiding the fact that she needed to go. She positioned herself above a strip of cardboard and closed her eyes. She felt immense relief as the hard knot in her stomach finally released. The smell of waste spread quickly, but she was thankful to at least have something to wipe with. The foul smell lingered so she sprayed deodorant and swatted at the increasing number of flies that buzzed around her.

She had intended to save the rest of the spaghetti for the following day, but later she was hungry again, and she couldn't resist taking down the tin and peering into it. The sauce had formed a slimy film, and the hoops were limp and oily. But in that moment, she had never seen anything so delicious. She had to have just a little taste. She gulped down a mouthful, and another, and within minutes, it was all gone.

The meal gave her a temporary reprieve, but with nothing more to eat or drink, she became increasingly low. The days passed in a blur of hunger and weakness. She slept more often than not, barely able to move. She used the spaghetti tin to catch rainwater from the roof, but it was never more than a mouthful. Then there was a moment of great excitement when she discovered some water in a rusty old watering can. She poured it out into her spaghetti tin and saw that it was murky and speckled with dirt but it was water, so she drank it, stirring in what was left of the sugar packets to mask the taste.

She knew she must be seriously dehydrated. Her attempts to escape became feeble and uncoordinated until they ceased entirely. Her mind drifted from her body and she knew without a doubt that she was dying.

June's head lolled to one side, her senses awakening at the sound of voices out on the street. She forced herself to sit upright, leaning on the wall for support. With a jolt, she realised those were her housemates outside. It sounded like they'd just arrived home. She was shocked to realise it had only been a week since they'd left. It felt like months. Her body was betraying her. She could no longer stand. No longer needed to. The urge to urinate had long left her and there was little reason for her to get up anymore.

If her housemates were home, that meant this was almost over. At some point Poppy would come and check on her. What would she do when she found her still stubbornly clinging to life?

Would she leave her here until her body gave up the fight, or would she finish her off? Poppy had never been violent towards her before. Not outwardly, anyway. She had always been secretive, and underhand. All the same, locking her up like this seemed pretty drastic. June needed to be prepared for anything.

She really ought to find a weapon. She reached for the

shard of glass and stashed it in her pocket just in case but she doubted she'd have the strength to use it. So she lay there and she waited, her eyes straining to make out shapes in the dying light.

Sometime later, another voice drifted in from outside, deep and familiar.

'Can I speak to June?'

Dan. It was Dan!

June's breath caught and her heart thudded as she listened.

'She's not even here,' came a different voice, Poppy's.

'Can you tell her I called round? I really need to see her.'

A spark of energy surged through her veins and she lunged forward.

'Dan!' she yelled hoarsely into the night air. 'Dan!'

The shed walls shook as she thumped her feet against them. She paused to see if he'd heard her but the street had descended back into silence.

'I'm in the shed!' she yelled. Her voice was frustratingly weak. 'Dan! Help me! I need you. I'm sorry!'

She thought she heard someone coming into the garden.

'Help!' she yelled, her heart beating faster. She stopped and listened. There it was, a small creaking sound. It sounded like the garden gate.

She thudded her feet against the wood, then stopped again. The gate was still creaking, as if it were swinging loose in the wind. She waited, and waited, but there were no footsteps on the path. No more voices carrying up the garden.

Dan was gone.

Her vision blurred and tiny pinpricks of light swirled in her pupils. Her head felt hot, and she was half convinced there was a bomb ticking in the base of her skull. The sounds of the city became distant as the underlying nausea gnawed at her stomach, leaving it feeling empty and bruised on the inside. Even her bones seemed clumsy, heavy with fatigue that made her limbs tremble.

When she heard the metallic click of the locks, she almost discarded it, until she heard Kimmy's voice, sweet and familiar.

'June?'

Her weary body somehow reacted. She blinked into the darkness. That was definitely Kimmy.

'Kimmy!'

She felt too weak to say anything else. Soon Kimmy's arms were around her. She sank back with relief that she was being rescued. Kimmy's body was warm against hers as she helped her to her feet, then out of the shed and into the garden. All around her, she heard the sounds of life, from the faint hum of traffic to the rustle of the trees. The night sky was peppered with twinkling stars and the moon shone down like a spotlight.

Kimmy half carried her through the overgrown garden, stumbling into the narrow alleyway. She had left her car parked close by and ushered her inside. June lay down on the back seat and felt the warmth seep into her bones. She relaxed, knowing she was safe now. Kimmy would take her to the hospital. She sighed in exhaustion and closed her eyes. She heard the click of the doors being locked and then Kimmy started the engine. As the car began to move, she was startled by a bolt of memory.

A week ago, she had been brushing her teeth when Kimmy knocked on the bathroom door.

'June, I need you to come and look at something.' She'd said it in a low voice, as if she didn't want any of the other housemates to hear.

Intrigued, June had spat out her toothpaste. 'What is it?'

'You need to come now. It's urgent.' Kimmy had said.

June had put down her toothbrush and wiped her mouth. She had slipped on her shoes and followed Kimmy outside. She had thought perhaps Kimmy had discovered evidence of Ralph's infidelity and wanted to talk about it in private. Maybe she wanted to sit in the car for a heart to heart, so they wouldn't be disturbed by the other housemates. Or perhaps she had discovered something about Poppy. Something that would prove June had been right all along. Of course, it could be something else completely. The garden came alive at night. There might be something out there.

As they had entered the garden, Kimmy had shone her phone over the grass and June's eyes had followed the beam, expecting to see a fox or badger. A hedgehog perhaps, but to her confusion, Kimmy had led her towards the shed. She had unlocked it and switched on the outside light before leading June inside.

'I really need to talk to you,' she had said. June had detected a slight wobble in her voice.

'Is everything alright? Is it Ralph?'

It had suddenly occurred to her that she hadn't actually seen Ralph and Kimmy together in weeks. She sensed a change in Kimmy's demeanour. She was never usually this quiet.

'I know,' Kimmy had said.

'About what?' June had said carefully, not wanting to put her foot in it.

'I know you slept with Ralph.'

'What?' June had forced out a laugh.

'You were together back at uni. Poppy saw the two of you together.'

June had inhaled deeply. 'She... she did?' She blew out some air. 'Well, it's true, I did go out with him for about a month. But that was years ago, Kimmy. It hardly matters now.'

'Then why did you keep it a secret?'

June had closed her eyes. 'I didn't realise at first. It didn't click, until you brought him home the first time. He completely blanked me. I don't think he remembers me at all.'

It was painful to admit this, even to herself. But Ralph was a good-looking man, and charming with it. He'd probably had a lot of girlfriends before he met Kimmy.

'Why didn't you tell me?'

June had shrugged. 'Partly, I was embarrassed, but also I thought you might be upset and it seemed so pointless to say anything when he doesn't even remember me.'

'Of course he remembers you.'

They had sat in silence for a few minutes. June wished she knew what Kimmy was thinking.

'Anyway, I don't have to worry about Ralph anymore,' Kimmy had said with a smile.

'What do you mean? I thought you loved him.'

'I do love him. If I didn't, I would have just let him walk away, that day at the funfair. Do you know what he said to me? He actually said, "You need someone who will love you like you deserve to be loved".'

'That's bullshit,' June had commiserated. But her mind was whirring. He'd broken up with her at the funfair? That was months ago, way before she had seen him out with another woman. Before they'd even got engaged.

'I used a brick,' Kimmy had clarified. 'He's in his own little world when he's jogging. He didn't even see me coming. One quick knock to the head and he was out cold. It was just like the first time I saw him, when I found him fast asleep on the grass. Except this time, he had blood trickling from his ear.'

June had blinked. Obviously, Kimmy was joking. They'd known each other for ever. She wouldn't hurt a soul. She had rubbed her eyes. They were getting droopy, and her head had nodded as she struggled to stay alert. She had wished Kimmy would skip ahead to the punchline. Unless she was having some sort of psychotic break? Kimmy was still talking, almost to herself as much as to June.

'After that it was no bother to just roll him into the pond. Problem dealt with.' June had felt a chill run down her back.

Kimmy's expression was so solemn. As if she had believed what she was saying. As if she had really killed Ralph.

She had thought for a minute, choosing her words carefully. 'If you like I could come to the police station with you? Is that what you want? To confess?'

'The police!' Kimmy had burst out laughing. 'Do you really think I'd be telling you all this if I was going to let you talk to the police?'

'I... don't get it. This isn't funny.'

'It isn't supposed to be.'

June had looked curiously at Kimmy's face. Her eyes had seemed shiny in the dim light. There was something cruel in those eyes she had never noticed before. Something that made her want to run and hide. That was when she had been struck by an epiphany. 'You tried to poison us all, didn't you? You put those mushrooms in the stew.'

In fact, now that she thought about it, it made sense. Kimmy was the only housemate, besides her, who knew how to forage. They had done so together years ago, guided by Kimmy's grandmother.

Kimmy didn't deny it.

'But why? You could have killed us all.'

'Not me. I didn't eat any of the mushrooms,' Kimmy had said. 'I hid them in my napkin. It was only the three of you that ate them, and I didn't really want to kill everyone, only you. I just thought it would be less suspicious if you all ate the stew.'

June had rested her head in her lap. 'Why would you do that? What have I ever done to you?'

Kimmy had let out a bitter laugh. 'What haven't you done? If it wasn't for you, Ralph and I would still be together. He was totally committed to me until he set eyes on you again. Then it started to unravel, week by week, thread by thread. That's what you wanted, isn't it? That's why you showed up when we were in the pub together, and why you went out and got a new boyfriend. You wanted to make him jealous. Well, it worked.'

'I... I wouldn't do that.'

'Wouldn't you? You did the same thing to your friend Grace, didn't you? You told me all about it. She was supposed to be your best friend at uni. But you slept with her boyfriend behind her back.'

'They weren't together at the time. They'd broken up.'

'But you knew she was still in love with him, so that's just as bad, isn't it?'

June couldn't answer.

Kimmy's lip had trembled as she'd reached behind her, grabbing Flick's old cricket bat.

'If you could do it to her,' she had whispered, her voice shaking, 'then you could do it to me.'

Their eyes had locked and June wasn't sure what had come first: the searing pain in the back of her head, or the sickening sound of the bat connecting with her flesh. She had dropped to the ground, the world fading around her as she had gasped for breath. The last sensation she was aware of was the weight of Kimmy's shoe pressing down on the back of her neck, grinding her face into the dirt.

FORTY-SIX

KIMMY

Two Months Earlier

Kimmy waited for Ralph outside the tube station. Her breath caught in her throat as she saw him emerge. He was wearing the green shirt she'd bought him. It looked even better than she had imagined, making him stand out, godlike among the throng.

She had always spotted him before he spotted her. It had been like that since the very beginning of their relationship, when she used to trail him round the park, looking for the perfect opening to introduce herself. She had truly been concerned when she found him fast asleep the morning they got together. Concerned and more than a little angry, when she'd discovered he'd just had too much to drink.

He was looking in her direction now, his eyes lingering on her scarf, but he said nothing as he walked towards her and their fingers entwined. Her fingertips lingered in his palm and he gripped her hand lightly, a nervous energy lingering between them as they walked up Clapham High Street.

She clung to him, feeling a swell of pride as they arrived at the fair. The lights from the rides illuminated his face, emphasising his strong jawline and bright blue eyes. She had taken care with her own outfit, choosing the green scarf to match him, and she'd had her hair blown out at the hairdressers so she felt great, knowing everybody thought they made the perfect couple.

She hoped tonight would be the night Ralph proposed. She had been dropping hints for a while, mentioning that her younger cousin had recently got engaged. She had even pointed out a suitable ring in the window of the jewellers.

'Don't you want to wait for your friends?' he asked her. 'I think I saw them queuing to get in.'

Kimmy shook her head. Why was he always trying to involve her friends? She wanted to be with him, and only him.

'I can't wait to go on the rides,' she said.

'Alright then.'

He cast a glance back over his shoulder, then allowed her to propel him forward. She forced a smile but her stomach was in knots. As much as she wanted to have faith in him, she sensed he was pulling away from her. Their conversation had all but dried up, and he had barely responded to her messages throughout the week. She hoped that she was imagining it, but she knew she wouldn't be able to relax until she got that ring on her finger. Then she would know he was truly hers.

They walked around the fair, trying out various stalls and rides. Ralph looked excited as they headed for the rollercoaster. This one had always been his favourite. She held on tight as the ride started. The wind whipped through her hair as they soared around sharp turns and over steep inclines. When the ride finally came to a stop, Ralph hopped out and offered her his hand. She took it eagerly, admiring the way his skin glistened with sweat.

She gave him a coy smile. 'You know, all my housemates are here tonight.'

'Yeah?'

'So we could have the house to ourselves if we want...' She watched his face, searching for a smile that never came. Instead, his jaw tightened and his eyebrows drew closer together. Stupid Kimmy. They'd been having fun. Now she'd gone and ruined it. 'You want to go on the rollercoaster again?' she said quickly.

'No, it's not that.' His voice was flat and he couldn't look at her.

She moved closer and tugged at his hand.

'What about the waltzer?'

'Kimmy...'

He sighed and shook his head. Kimmy inhaled. She knew what was coming before he even said it.

He shifted his feet, unwilling to meet her gaze. His voice cracked and all but disappeared as he said, 'Kimmy, I can't do this anymore. You need someone who will love you like you deserve to be loved.'

Kimmy felt as though her heart was being squeezed. 'Don't do this. I love you. Whatever it is, we can work through it...'

He shuffled his feet uncomfortably. 'I just can't. You're too intense, Kimmy. Like the way you keep asking me what I'm wearing so you can match.'

She fingered her new green scarf. 'I'll stop.'

'It's not just the clothes. You want too much from me. I'm not looking for forever. I just wanted a little fun.'

His gaze shifted over to where her friends stood. Was he looking at all of them, or just at June?

Her heart thudded as he walked away. She wanted to run after him, to grab him and keep him from leaving, but her throat closed up. All she could do was stare at his departing back, clenching her fists so hard that her nails dug into her palms. Since the day she had first laid eyes on him, she'd felt like he was a piece of her. For him to leave left her broken, incomplete. And confounded. It didn't seem possible.

Tears burned in her eyes but she would not allow them to

fall. With a shaky breath, she dragged her feet across the grass, feeling as though the bottom had dropped out of her world. Her hands shook like she'd just touched an electric fence, so she stuck them deep in her pockets.

When she finally made it over to her friends, she focused on June, the one person who had promised to always be there for her. But June failed to register the despair in her eyes. The conversation was light and breezy, and Kimmy was barely aware of what they were saying. Then a good-looking man walked over to join them. Instantly, June's body language shifted as she gazed up into his eyes.

Dan had thick, wavy hair and gentle eyes. Kimmy watched as he interlaced his fingers with June's and it felt like a punch to the gut. Why did everyone want June? She wasn't even conventionally pretty – there was just something about her that everyone was drawn to.

She made an excuse and turned as if she was planning to go back to Ralph. Instead, she snuck behind a stall and waited a bit before following at a distance. Her body shook with anger. She had no idea what she was going to do, just that she had to do something to ease her pain.

They all went on the dodgems and she watched, furious to see June having so much fun. She saw Poppy trying to ram her with her car. Poppy didn't like June either. Kimmy had wondered about that. Having Poppy around had reminded her of June's true nature. She couldn't forget the way she plotted to get Poppy thrown out of the house, and then when Poppy had stood up to her, she'd shoved her down the stairs. If anyone else had done something like that the police would have been called but June somehow got away with it. She always did. She pretended to be everyone's friend but really she was just out for herself.

After the dodgems, June and Dan stopped in front of the haunted house and decided to go inside. Kimmy had been in there earlier. It had been very dark. She pulled off her bright green scarf and tucked it in her pocket, then she followed them inside, using her phone to guide her. At first, Dan and June stayed together but then Dan got distracted by a glowing pumpkin and June wandered off, into one of the dark tunnels.

Kimmy crept silently behind her, her black hoodie blending into the darkness. She felt a thrill of power surge through her body as she crept up behind her unsuspecting target. Light from the entrance barely illuminated them, and Kimmy's heart pounded with anticipation as she snaked her arms around June's neck and held it for a moment, in a vice-like grip. It was just a few seconds, but it was enough to give June the fright of her life. As soon as she let go, June sprinted off down the passageway while Kimmy stayed in the shadows. It was an incredible feeling. Finally, she was in control.

She crouched in the shadows of the narrow tunnel, hugging the gritty walls. She listened as her breathing echoed through the darkness. Then she rose up on her toes and traced over the cool stone walls with her fingers, peering into every crevice, belatedly searching for any sign of surveillance.

She stayed there for some time, fear and sweat mixing on her skin. Every now and then the distant chatter of voices drifted towards her, but thankfully no one came close. Cautiously, she moved forward, bracing herself for an encounter with the search party that was surely on its way. If they asked why she was here, she'd say she'd got lost.

When she emerged from the darkness, no one paid her any attention. She spotted Flick and Tamsin across the field. Her stomach tightened as she made her way over to them.

'Ralph and I are heading back now,' she said.

'Oh, okay,' Tamsin said with casual indifference.

She had often wondered if Tamsin even liked her. She had been so possessive of June when they were children. She hadn't liked that Kimmy had such a connection with her.

'Where is Ralph?' Flick asked, always a little sharper than she seemed.

Kimmy forced a smile. 'He went ahead with his friends. I'm just going to catch him up.'

She wasn't quite sure Flick swallowed this explanation, but if she was suspicious, she kept it to herself.

'Okay, take care,' Tamsin said, waving her away.

She trudged out of the fairground, dragging her feet along the pavement as she headed towards home. As she reached Queen Anne's Crescent, she saw that the lights were on and she unlocked the door to the sound of June's laughter. It felt like a knife, cutting her heart in two. She saw the open bottle of wine on the kitchen counter and Dan's coat hanging neatly on a hook. Then the laughter turned to ecstatic moaning and it was all she could do to cover her ears and pelt up the stairs to her room.

She fumbled with her phone, mindlessly scrolling through Instagram as tears welled in her eyes. She looked back through all her recent photos, every one of them featuring Ralph. There were pictures of the two of them in front of an open fire at Christmas, snaps of them on holiday in Dorset, one of them laughing and sweaty after taking part in a charity fun run. She couldn't understand it. They had been so happy. How could he not want her anymore? She went to his profile and her mouth dropped open. He had already changed his relationship status to 'single'. The pain of rejection seared through her chest once more and humiliation took hold. Immediately, she deactivated her account.

She spent the night alone in her room, reading and rereading every text message he'd ever sent her until she knew them all by heart. In the morning, she wandered down to the antique market and found a stall that sold costume jewellery. She delved through a box of rings until she found one that looked quite realistic. The diamond wasn't genuine but the ring was pretty. It should be good enough to fool her friends.

On her way back, she checked Ralph's run-mapping app. He was heading towards the common, on his daily jog. She followed his route until she spotted him, face set in concentration, earphones blocking out all noise. She fell into step behind him. He never once thought to turn and look. They made a big loop of the common, past the bandstand and through the woods. She began to slow as they neared the pond. She was getting a stitch. She gulped down a lungful of air and then took off after him again, keeping him in her sights. She was tempted to follow him all the way back to his flat, but she held back, letting him slip away. He'd be back tomorrow. And so would she.

FORTY-SEVEN

KIMMY

Now

Kimmy clutched her mug of coffee. She had her laptop open in front of her. They were showing footage from Clapham Common on the news. Residents gathered around the camera crew, a little overeager to voice their shock and grief at what had occurred. A man with a large golden retriever reported how he'd discovered the body, floating on the edges of the pond, with limbs like dead seaweed.

'Chester here was the one who spotted it,' he said. 'I would have walked right past, but once he got a whiff, he wouldn't let up. He kept tugging on the lead until I let him investigate and...' His voice trailed off as a grimace of disgust crossed his face. He took a moment to compose himself. 'Sorry, you can't unsee that. As soon as I realised it was human remains, I ran to get help. I didn't have my phone on me so I had to go over the road to the shop and I got them to call it in.'

Kimmy took a sip of her coffee. The words wrapped around her like a cold blanket, but she could not tear herself away from the screen. When the report ended, she flicked through the other news channels, looking for more updates. It was annoying how consistent they all were, as if working from the same script. The police had yet to identify the body but it wasn't rocket science. The real question was how long it would take them to link it to her.

Her knees quivered beneath her. She wasn't ashamed of her actions. She had done what was necessary, but she couldn't ignore the weight of guilt that pressed down on her chest. Her heart cracked with sorrow for a life lost, no matter how justified it had been. Even though there was no other choice, it still left an indelible mark on her soul.

Tamsin knocked on her door and she quickly changed the channel.

'You okay?' Kimmy asked, seeing the serious expression on her face.

'Yes, listen. I've just seen a post on the community board. Did you know Ralph's gone missing? Apparently, no one's seen him in over a week.'

'Really?' She widened her eyes and drew in a deep breath. 'I wonder if he's taken himself off for a few days? He used to do that sometimes. He suffers from terrible bouts of depression.'

'Does he? I didn't know that.'

'Yes, well he puts on a brave face, but deep down he's a very troubled soul. I hope he's okay.'

Tamsin lingered. 'Can you think of anywhere he might have gone? His family are frantic.'

Kimmy nodded. 'I can think of a few places. I'm surprised the police haven't reached out to me. I mean, I know him better than anyone.'

Tamsin looked down at her slippers. 'Perhaps they don't know you're his... you used to be together.'

Kimmy straightened her shoulders and slowly nodded her head. 'Well, wherever he's got to, I'm sure he'll turn up soon.'

She turned back to her coffee. Her body was so out of whack lately, she couldn't tell whether she was tired or not.

Her phone buzzed. She glanced down at the screen.

'Ugh, sorry, Tamsin, I have to take this.'

Tamsin nodded and left the room. Kimmy closed the door behind her.

'Hello?' she answered anxiously.

'Hi, this is Jim from Clapham Security. Sorry to bother you, but we got an alert that the alarm has gone off at your shop. Do you want us to check it out?'

Her heart leapt into her throat but she managed to force out a strained laugh.

'No! That's just my... just my fiancé, he must have forgotten the code.' Her voice quivered slightly as she said it.

'Alright then, you have a good evening, madam.'

'You too. Thank you for letting me know.'

She frowned. Where were her keys? She grabbed her bag and pulled out the whole bunch. Her house keys were there, front and back. But no shop keys. Someone had taken them.

FORTY-EIGHT

JUNE

One Day Earlier

June hoisted herself up so that she could see out of the car window. Street lamps flickered, casting eerie shadows on the pavement. A few people were still milling around despite the lateness of the hour. As they drove past the common, she saw, to her shock, a flurry of yellow police tape stretched between two trees, and a large white tent that must have been put up for forensics.

Ralph, she thought with a start. *Oh my god, she really did it.*

Fear curdled in her stomach. She watched Kimmy's eyes in the mirror. Saw her head turn a little, felt the car slow to a crawl. Then she too was peering out of the window, as if seeing it all for the first time.

'They haven't even identified him yet,' Kimmy said proudly. 'His flatmate has only just got around to reporting him missing. Men are so unobservant, don't you think? I bet if one of our housemates went missing, the others would be all over it.'

June swallowed painfully. Something bumped against her foot and she looked down to see what it was. A bottle of water.

She couldn't believe it. She bent down to retrieve it, her head swimming as her fingers closed around it. It took all her strength to get the cap off. She drank as quickly and quietly as she could, getting as much down her face as she did into her mouth. She wasn't sure if Kimmy was aware of what she was doing, or if she was simply too captivated by the crime scene she had created.

They turned the corner, past a row of shops. They were all closed now, but June had an idea where Kimmy was taking her. Sure enough, she pulled up outside The Paper Pantry. They sat in the car for a moment, waiting for the electric shutters to slowly inch their way up.

Kimmy climbed out of the car and came round to open the door for her.

'Get out.'

'What are we doing here?' June asked uneasily, letting the plastic bottle fall from her hand.

'Jesus, your breath stinks. Didn't I tell you to get out?'

Before June could object, Kimmy yanked her out of the car and dragged her towards the shop.

June spotted a woman walking down the street, her eyes focused on the ground in front of her.

'Help!' she yelled. But her voice was weedy and pathetic. The woman kept on walking. June wasn't sure if she'd heard her, or if she just chose to look the other way.

Kimmy opened the door and shoved her inside. June went flying, sprawling onto the floor. Kimmy locked the door behind her and switched on the lights.

'Get up!' she barked.

'I'm so thirsty. Can I just have a glass of water?' She looked longingly towards the bathroom, where she knew there must be a sink. Her throat was parched, despite the water she'd drunk in the car.

Kimmy ignored her and hauled her to her feet, shoving her towards the back of the room.

'You can't keep me in here forever.'

'Why not? No one comes in here, anyway.'

'My body is dying. There will be gases and foul smells.'

'Sorry about that. My preference would have been to shove you in the pond with Ralph, but the police are kind of cramping my style. Doesn't matter. They're going to knock this place down soon anyway. Did I tell you that? In the space of a few months, I've lost my fiancé and my job.'

'He was never your fiancé.'

'And that, June, is why people don't like you. Never mind, it doesn't matter. You'll be dead soon. You look like a freak already. Your eyes have started turning yellow. You always liked that colour, didn't you? Once your kidneys give up, I'll just heap some stuff on top of you and leave you to get buried in the rubble.'

'That won't work,' June said. 'They'd still find my remains, and they would trace it back to you.'

Kimmy's eyes glinted, and her lips twisted into a cruel smile. 'See if I care. Nothing really matters now anyway.'

She shoved June into the store cupboard and slammed the door shut with a bang that reverberated around the shop. Trapped in the small, airless room, June struggled against the door, as Kimmy locked it from the outside.

'Kimmy, don't do this!' she yelled to her oldest friend. 'I never wanted to take Ralph from you. It's not my fault he ended it.'

There was silence, and she hoped Kimmy was considering what she was saying.

She tried again. 'Let me out, Kimmy. I'm not going to tell anyone. I just want my life back. Please, I'll do anything.'

There was a sound. Footsteps walking across the shop. Was Kimmy listening to her? She couldn't tell. 'Please, Kimmy!' she yelled again. 'Please, if our friendship ever meant anything to you.'

As Kimmy's footsteps receded, the lights flickered and went out, plunging June into darkness. The sound of clanking security shutters echoed through the silent space, filling her with dread.

The darkness was intense and all-encompassing, and a heavy silence settled on her like a suffocating cloak. The store-room was not as damp and dingy as the shed – but she was still far from free.

When daylight came, her eyes adjusted sufficiently to make out shapes all around her. There were shelves above her. She looked up and saw rows of shiny staplers, paper clips and other stationery supplies. She found hole punches, masking tape and jars of pens. But there was nothing to eat or drink, and no way to signal to the outside world where she was.

If her housemates had arrived home yesterday, it must now be Sunday. Kimmy didn't usually work Sundays. There would be no customers, no one coming in. No one to hear her cries. She sank to the floor, bitter and frustrated.

She took the shard of glass out of her pocket and examined it. Who was she kidding? She couldn't defend herself with this. Her movements were too slow, too weak. And for all she knew, Kimmy might have weapons of her own.

The shard felt cold against her fingertips, and she looked at it more closely, dread coiling in her stomach. She rolled up the sleeve of her shirt to reveal the faint 'K' on her arm. It had almost faded away entirely. She dragged the shard over the mark, leaving a soft scratch.

Then she held it over her left wrist, tracing it lightly over her veins. She pressed harder, flinching as the cut deepened. She squeezed her eyes shut and tears streamed down her face. The smell of cold, coppery blood filled the air, and her hand started to shake. She was scared but determined that this would be the end of it all.

She stopped dead as she heard a low hum of electricity. She listened intently to the rattling of keys, and then the lights came on, illuminating the room.

'Hello?' she shouted. 'Help me! I'm locked in the store cupboard.'

Please, please, please don't be Kimmy.

No one answered. She held her breath and prayed silently that it was the police. Or the shop owner.

There was the sound of footsteps as someone crossed the shop floor.

'Hello! Please help me!' she yelled again.

The shuffling and jingling of keys grew louder as the door to the storeroom creaked open.

FORTY-NINE

JUNE

Now

Squinting into the light, she saw Poppy's face framed in the doorway, eyes wide with surprise. 'Poppy!'

Joy pulsed through June's body; it was almost too much to take in. She'd never been so happy to see anyone in her life. She staggered forward to embrace her housemate.

'How did you... how did you know?'

Poppy shook her head. 'Kimmy's been behaving really weirdly. I think she's been texting people from your phone. I thought I was being paranoid, but then I found your handbag in your room and I heard her slip out last night, so my mind started jumping to all sorts of mad conclusions. I wondered if she had done something to you. Then I thought if I were her, where would I hide you, and the shop seemed like the obvious place. I never expected you to actually be here but we can talk about all that later. We need to get the hell out of here.'

June felt a moment of uncertainty. *Could this be part of some cruel joke?* She searched Poppy's eyes for a hint of deception, but only found the same shock that she felt mirrored in them. Despite the improbability of Poppy being the one to save her, she had to trust her now. Her legs were far too wobbly to make it out of there alone.

Poppy slid an arm around her waist. 'My god, what did she do to you?'

'Leave that for later,' June said. 'Please, let's go!'

She struggled to keep her balance as she shuffled through the store. Her limbs felt like jelly and every few steps she had to grab onto a product display for support.

As she glanced up at the CCTV monitor, a thought struck her.

'What about the alarm? How come it didn't go off when you arrived?'

Poppy shrugged. 'Maybe she didn't set it.'

'Unless it's one of those silent alarms?'

They both looked at the door.

'Come on!'

They quickened their pace. June's vision blurred as she staggered through the shop, but she kept pushing forward. If it weren't for Poppy, she would have been down on her hands and knees by the time she reached the door. Weak as she was, nothing was going to stop her getting out.

She chose to live.

The fresh air hit her and she inhaled deeply. She promised herself she would never take her freedom for granted, ever again. Now if she could just get a drink and a large plate of fish and chips, she would be deliriously happy. She looked around. The street was deserted. Was it always this quiet on a Sunday?

'I'll ring the police,' said Poppy. 'But let's get somewhere safe first. I'm scared she's going to realise the keys are gone and come looking for us.'

'You know what, it'll be faster to get an Uber,' June said.

Poppy pulled out her phone. She fiddled with it for a

minute while June leaned against a lamp post. Even the simple act of breathing felt like an effort.

'I don't think I can walk much further. Can you have it pick us up here?'

'I think across the road would be safer.'

'I don't suppose you've got anything to drink?'

'Afraid not but the garage should be open. We can ask the driver to stop there on the way.'

'I hope you've got some cash on you?'

'Don't worry, I'll put it on your tab.' A moment later Poppy said, 'Uber's on its way.' She slipped her phone into her pocket, and had started to cross the road when a pink Volkswagen came careering down the road. The car lurched to the right, and June realised before it happened that it was about to ride up onto the pavement.

She screamed, but it came out as barely more than a whisper. In one fluid motion, she leapt to the side, narrowly avoiding being hit. She looked up just in time to see Kimmy slam the car into the wall. There was an ear-splitting crunch of metal crushing against glass and Poppy was sent flying backwards, through the shop window.

June scrambled to her feet and staggered inside. Poppy lay motionless on the floor, glass fragments glinting around her.

She took a step towards her, but there was no time to help. She heard the car door open and shut. Kimmy was coming for her. She ducked behind a display case and listened, trying to figure out what Kimmy was up to. Slowly, she peered out and saw that Kimmy had blood dripping from a wound on her temple. Her left hand rested on her hip but, in her right hand, she held June's favourite fillet knife – the one she used for gutting fish. She hovered over Poppy, staring down at her with interest.

'I thought you, of all people, understood.'

Poppy didn't answer. She didn't move at all. June couldn't even tell if she was still breathing.

Kimmy raised her right foot, holding the pointed heel above Poppy's face. June stifled a scream. Thankfully, Kimmy lowered her foot again, smirking to herself.

'I don't know what you were thinking, letting her out like that. After everything she's done to you. Some people are just gluttons for punishment.'

June glanced at the window. Someone must have seen or heard the crash. She just had to hold on until help came. She glanced all around her, searching desperately for a weapon. She searched her pockets frantically for the shard, but it was nowhere to be found. Her whole body shook at the sound of Kimmy's heels.

Kimmy rounded the corner, and now, there was no getting away from her. Her face spread into a wide, toothy grin, eyes glinting with anticipation, and her eye movements seemed increasingly rapid, as if she was struggling to focus.

June grabbed the fire extinguisher from the wall. 'Stay back!' she croaked. She drew a ragged breath as she wrapped her finger around the trigger. But Kimmy still came at her, leaving her with no choice but to fire, unleashing a stream of foam.

Kimmy coughed and spluttered, the white foam covering her face and hair like a grotesque mask. The stink of chemicals wafted between them, as she wiped her face with one hand. The other remained clenched in a deadly grip. She didn't drop the knife as June had hoped. She'd only succeeded in making her angrier.

As Kimmy raised the knife, June flung her body against a shelf full of desk lamps and picture frames, sending them cascading down onto Kimmy. Kimmy released her grip and the knife hit the ground with a metallic clang. They both lunged for it but June managed to seize the handle. Kimmy grabbed at her arm, determined to take it back and June knew that she had only seconds to act. She locked eyes with her best friend, her housemate, her blood sister, then she drove the knife deep into the soft flesh of her abdomen, slicing through her like butter. Kimmy let out a strangled gasp as the blade dug deeper, and a gurgling sound escaped her lips as hot blood spilled in waves on the tiled floor. She fought down to the last, thrashing about wildly, each movement bringing fresh spurts of blood from her gaping wound.

June edged away from the carnage. She gritted her teeth and lifted her chin, dragging her feet forward, inch by inch, until she reached her other housemate. Poppy looked just as if she were sleeping, the shards of glass twinkling around her like stars. June laid one hand on her neck, feeling for a pulse, and with the other, she pulled the phone from her pocket and dialled 999.

'I need an ambulance,' she told the call handler. 'I think... I think my housemates are both dead.'

FIFTY

JUNE

One Month Later

June led Daria up to the attic room on the top floor.

'This is Tamsin's room,' she said. 'Top of the house.'

'Wow, she's really into dragons,' Daria said.

June smiled. 'Yes, you could say that.'

She let Daria have a quick look, then hurried her down the stairs.

'This is Flick's room.' She opened the door a crack to check if it was untidy. It was.

'This is one of the rooms we have for rent,' she said, moving on to Kimmy's old room. Kimmy's pink duvet was still on the bed, her clothes in the wardrobe. They would have to chuck all that out soon if her family didn't claim it.

Daria looked impressed. 'Nice,' she said. 'I like the picture on the wall.'

June glanced up at Kimmy and Ralph's portrait. Now that was an oversight. She really should take that down. No one was going to be comfortable with a picture of a killer and her victim on their bedroom wall. Fortunately, Daria didn't seem to have twigged who Kimmy was despite the extensive coverage the case had received. She probably didn't watch the news.

They headed downstairs and June opened the door to her own room.

'This is Poppy's room,' she said.

Poppy would need the ground-floor room when she came out of hospital. She was making good progress, but she still had a long road ahead of her.

'And finally, downstairs we have the other room for rent,' she finished. She led Daria down the steps and threw open the door.

'Oh, it's really cosy,' Daria said, her eyes lighting up.

June was pleased. She and Tamsin had done a bit of cleaning while Poppy was in hospital. The walls were now a tasteful baby blue.

'I think I like this room best,' Daria said. She walked over to the window and peered outside.

'Well have a think about it,' June said. 'But first, let me show you the garden.'

They headed outside. Inevitably, Daria's gaze landed on what used to be the shed. Charred planks of wood and embers were scattered across a large patch of singed grass. She spun around to face June, her brow furrowed questioningly.

'What happened here?'

June's jaw clenched. Flick and Tamsin had salvaged what they wanted from the shed, then June had unleashed the full force of her rage, smashing it to bits with a sledgehammer.

'You're supposed to be resting,' Tamsin had said with concern. She had tried to take the hammer, but June had refused to let go.

'This is my therapy,' she had argued, and she had kept hacking away at it until the shed was reduced to a pile of wood. Then she'd built a huge bonfire.

The man next door had got quite worried. He didn't say

anything to them directly but she heard him talking loudly and purposely to his partner, clearly hoping June would hear.

'There's so much smoke, it's blowing all over the washing... that fire will spread to our garden if they're not careful. It's totally irresponsible.'

June had chosen not to acknowledge him. It was astonishing how hard it could be to hear people in the neighbouring garden.

Now she turned to Daria. 'We're getting a new lockbox for our bikes and the girls were talking about putting in a hot tub.'

Her eyes sparkled. 'Oh, that sounds amazing!'

They headed back inside and she finished showing her the kitchen and the living room.

'It's a great house,' Daria said, unable to contain her enthusiasm. 'So where are you heading off to, if you don't mind my asking?'

Now it was June's turn to smile. 'Actually, I'm moving in with my boyfriend.'

'Oh, right! So, you're staying local?'

June nodded. 'He has a place on the other side of Clapham.'

In actual fact, she had only been to Dan's house once or twice. They had always met in town or at her place. When she finally got round to visiting him, she was pleasantly surprised to find that he was almost as neat and tidy as she was. That had sealed the deal as far as she was concerned. There was no way she could live with a slob.

'What about Kelvin?' she had asked, thinking of Dan's flatmate.

'I own the flat, so I'll just give him notice,' Dan had said. 'He's a good guy. He'll understand.'

'You could tell him we have rooms to rent in this house,' June had suggested.

'Thanks, but I don't think he'd want to live with a bunch of women. He's more of a man's man, if you know what I mean.'

June had shrugged. 'Well, that's up to him.'

In the meantime, the doctor had signed her off for a few more weeks, and she intended to spend some of it visiting her parents. She wasn't foolish enough to stay with them for the duration. She'd found a low budget bed and breakfast just up the road from their place that ought to suffice. But she was determined to sit down and have some real conversations with them, even if it made them all feel a bit uncomfortable. It was about time they all grew up.

She showed Daria out, checking first that she had all her details. She was the last one for today, so now all June had to do was to take the first load of her stuff round to Dan's. She wasn't officially moving in until next month, but Dan had suggested she start bringing some of her stuff over.

She arrived at the flat before Dan came home from his photography gig. He was photographing a wedding that was being held in a butterfly enclosure. She couldn't help thinking how much Kimmy would have loved that. It was strange, having to separate Kimmy, the friend she'd grown up with, from Kimmy, the woman who had nearly killed her. She wondered if there would ever come a time when they weren't competing for space in her brain.

Her new key was a bit stiff in the lock, but she twisted it a few times and got it to work. She walked inside and set her suitcase down in the hallway. She decided to take another look around before she sat down to relax. She peered into Dan's room. Their room, she corrected herself. He had a nice big bed. She opened the wardrobe and found there were just one or two items hanging there, leaving plenty of space for her things. He had nice hangers too. Padded ones that would help keep the wrinkles out of her clothes.

She peered into Kelvin's room opposite. The spare room, she corrected herself, looking at the stark white walls. Dan had already started to use the space. A computer hummed on the desk, surrounded by stacks of photo equipment and boxes of slides.

She opened the wardrobe and saw that he had filled it with his jackets, trousers and shoes. Probably so she could make use of the wardrobe in his room. Their room, she corrected herself again. It felt strange to think of this place as theirs. It was going to take some getting used to.

She headed into the utility room and spotted a picture of a cute dog on the wall. Not one of Dan's pictures, but a postcard he must have just liked the look of. Then her stomach rumbled, and she headed urgently for the kitchen, automatically filling a glass with water, before searching the fridge for something to eat. She located crackers and cheese and ate them quickly, without really noticing the taste. She tapped her fingers on the table, waiting for the calm to return. Perhaps a cup of tea, she decided, flicking on the kettle. She opened the cupboard and searched through his mismatched collection of mugs. She couldn't decide between the one with the fox and the one with the badger, so she pushed them both aside and searched the row behind it. She found one with an owl on which was definitely a contender, until she saw another one hidden behind it. She pulled it out and stared at it for a moment. It was one of those bespoke picture mugs. This one featured Dan and an unknown woman, their faces encircled in a large lilac heart. She turned it round. There was an inscription on the back.

Happy birthday, love Kelsey x

Not Kelvin. Kelsey.

She set it down and sank into one of the kitchen chairs. Dan had been single as long as she had. So, who the hell was on this mug?

A LETTER FROM LORNA

Dear reader,

As you turn the final page of *The Perfect Housemate*, I want to thank you for reading. I hope you enjoyed June's story. The choice June and her friends made to invite Poppy into their home was quite brave, and perhaps a little ill-advised, considering that they barely knew her. After all, they already had a houseshare that worked, where everyone seemed to like each other and get along. But I don't think any of them could have anticipated quite how badly it would all go wrong.

If this book resonated with you, I'd be immensely grateful if you could leave a short review. Reviews serve as invaluable encouragement for readers who may be considering reading my work for the first time.

To stay informed about new books as soon as they're released, simply visit the link below to join my email list. I won't bombard you with emails or share your address with any third party – I promise!

www.bookouture.com/lorna-dounaeva

If you ever want to catch up with me online, you can get in touch through social media or my website. Thank you once again for reading, and I hope to see you again soon!

Lorna

KEEP IN TOUCH WITH LORNA

www.lornadounaeva.com

facebook.com/LornaDounaevaAuthor

x.com/LornaDounaeva

instagram.com/lorna_dounaeva

goodreads.com/lornadounaeva

PUBLISHING TEAM

Turning a manuscript into a book requires the efforts of many people. The publishing team at Bookouture would like to acknowledge everyone who contributed to this publication.

Audio
Alba Proko
Sinead O'Connor
Melissa Tran

Commercial
Lauren Morrissette
Jil Thielen
Imogen Allport

Data and analysis
Mark Alder
Mohamed Bussuri

Cover design
Aaron Munday

Editorial
Billi-Dee Jones
Nadia Michael

Printed in Great Britain
by Amazon